John Goldsmith was born in 1947 and educated at Winchester and the University of Aix-Marseille. He has published four novels, most recently the best-selling *Bullion*.

His non-fiction includes *Voyage In The Beagle*, an account of his own adventures aboard a square-rigger in South America. He has contributed to many TV series – *The Protectors*, *Space 1999*, *The New Avengers*, *The Professionals*, *Return of the Saint* – and has written documentaries: *Mrs Livingstone, I Presume*, *A Secret Place*. His latest editorial commission is the *Journals* of Stephen Spender. He is married, with one son, and lives in Hampstead. He is currently Chairman of the Writers' Guild of Great Britain.

D1439914

John Goldsmith

Return to Treasure Island

Pan Original
Pan Books London and Sydney

First published 1985 by Pan Books Ltd
Cavaye Place, London SW10 9PG
9 8 7 6 5 4 3 2 1
© Primetime Television Ltd, John Goldsmith,
Television Reporters International Ltd 1985
ISBN 0 330 29160 2
Photoset by Parker Typesetting Service, Leicester
Printed and bound in Great Britain by
Cox & Wyman Ltd, Reading

For
Robert Baker

With gratitude and affection

And

In memoriam
Ivor Dean

Part I
The Treasure Map

Chapter I
I Renew An Old Acquaintance

I came down from Oxford University in the early spring of 17—. Ten years had passed since the adventure of Treasure Island, which story I have told elsewhere*; I was rising twenty-two and looking forward to a venture proposed to me by Squire Trelawney – a sea-voyage to the West Indies, where he had sunk some of his share of Captain Flint's gold in a Jamaica plantation.

All but the final arrangements having been agreed by letter between me and the Squire, I bade farewell to the meadows and spires of Oxford, took post to Bristol, thence by the new turnpike to the Royal George – where I kept a horse at livery – and so, on horseback, along the old familiar coast road to the Admiral Benbow inn.

Night had fallen before I quit the Royal George, a black, wild night with a storm threatening. The good people at the inn begged me to stay until morning, but I was eager to press on to the piping supper and Prodigal's welcome that awaited me at my mother's house. Besides, the air of my native West Country, strong and heady like wine, and full of the tang of the salt sea and the open moor, had blown away all the fatigues of my journey and put me in a fever to be home.

The storm broke before I had been on the road a half

*Treasure Island.

hour, one of those shrieking spring storms that seem to boil up out of the sea, with lashing rain and thunderclaps and blue lightning, as if to remind a man that he is not yet done with winter. All along the coast the gales drove the white-backed waves against the cliffs, where they exploded with a roar like a broadside.

That was a tempest brewed in Hell, and I could have believed, as the country folk do, that the Devil himself was riding out. What I made certain was that there were devils in human form abroad and at their work: as I passed by Kitt's Hole I spied the flash of a lantern down in the cove and guessed that the smugglers were seizing the advantage of the storm, which would keep the revenue officers snug to their quarters. Having no desire for an encounter with those gentlemen, I pressed on harder.

Twenty minutes later I breasted Black Hill and reined in a moment, expecting to see the yellow shine of candles in the windows of the Admiral Benbow below.

But there was no light to be seen.

I dashed the rain from my eyes and looked again. In the same instant a terrific bolt of lightning lit up the sky like noon, throwing up the roof and gables of the inn in stark relief and showing me the windows, blind and empty, as if the house was deserted. Fearing that some harm had befallen my mother, I forthwith primed and loaded a pistol under my riding-cloak and loosened my sword in its scabbard. Then I fairly dug in and went hell-for-leather for the inn.

The old signboard of Admiral Benbow was swinging and squeaking and cracking like a sail aback as I jumped down from my saddle and tried the door, which to my increasing alarm, I found to be unbolted. Drawing my pistol, I stepped through into the little hallway, and closed the door behind me. It was pitch dark inside, and what with the wind howling round the house and rattling the slates, and the groaning of the timbers, I could fancy myself below decks in a ship that laboured in a foul sea. I was groping for the lamp that hung by the stair when I heard a sound that brought me up all standing and, I swear, caused the hairs on the nape of my neck to rise.

'Pieces of eight! Pieces of eight! Pieces of eight!'

It was the shrill voice, rasping like a file on iron, of Long John Silver's parrot, Captain Flint, a voice I had not heard these ten years, except in my nightmares. Here was a nightmare come to reality, and Silver himself, inconceivable though it seemed, within the house! For a moment, I confess I stood trembling from crown to heel, like a petrified boy. Then I gave a great start and let out a cry as the parlour door gaped suddenly open and light flooded into the hallway.

It was only by God's mercy that I did not instantly loose off my pistol and thereby make an end of Squire Trelawney, for it was he, not Silver, who loomed in the doorway, a candlestick in his hand.

'Steady, Hawkins!' booms the Squire and then, seeing me, I suppose, so utterly dumbfounded, breaks into his hearty laugh.

'Mrs Hawkins! Doctor! Smollett! Look here! You'd think the boy had seen a ghost!'

And there were Dr Livesey and Captain Smollett crowding round me and clapping me on the back, and my mother, smiling and tearful, embracing me, and Ben Gunn hanging heel in the doorway, grinning and bobbing his head like a bird.

'It was the Doctor's notion, Hawkins,' says the Squire, as they hauled me, still dazed, into the parlour, 'and a capital fine one, to muster the old ship's company of the *Hispaniola* to welcome Jim Hawkins home from Oxford.'

Here, Ben Gunn croaked out again, 'Pieces of eight!' in imitation of Silver's parrot, and most horribly life-like!

'Hah!' says the Squire, breaking into fresh laughter, 'that was my own jest, what?'

'And like too many of your jests,' Dr Livesey replied, in his dry, crisp manner, 'it very nearly went too far.'

As he said this he cast a meaning look at me, or rather at the pistol which I still held in my right hand and had clean forgot!

'Gad yes!' cries the Squire, laughing again. 'Better put it away, eh, Hawkins!'

Then Captain Smollett, sharp-looking and sailorlike as ever, though he was long retired from the sea, steps up and grasps my hand, and says, solemn and serious, in his way; 'Jim, you're a man, and a scholar, so they tell me. Handy with a firearm, too, which is no bad thing in these times.'

I expressed my heartfelt delight to see them all, and then my mother ordered us to table, where there was a feast laid such as the Admiral Benbow never saw before, for besides the good soups and roasts prepared by my mother, there were all manner of dainties and luxuries – hot-house fruits, and nuts, and chocolate – provided by the Squire, and fine Burgundies from the Doctor's cellar. But I truly believe that had we dined on husks we would have accounted it a banquet for the good fellowship and delight to be in one company again that warmed us better than the wine.

Naturally, the talk turned on Treasure Island and our chief antagonist in that affair, Long John Silver.

'There's a man I'd like to meet again,' said Captain Smollett, grimly.

'I too, sir,' the Squire replied, his mouth something full of pigeon pie. 'I'd like to meet him, sir, clap him in irons, sir, and personally escort him to Execution Dock, sir, for the bloody murderer and mutineer he is!'

'He should swing, for certain,' Smollett continued, 'but he was a man of remarkable qualities, all the same.'

'Satan hisself,' I heard Ben Gunn mutter as he charged the Squire's plate anew.

'I side with Captain Smollett,' said I, unable to resist the temptation to twit our bluff old Squire a little. 'There is some good in John Silver.'

'Good?' cries the Squire, astonished. 'Stuff and nonsense. Name me one good thing to lay to the credit of that blood-stained buccaneer.'

'Well, sir,' says I, 'I don't know that you'd call it a particularly good thing, but he did save my life.'

And so he had, you remember, that night on Treasure Island, when I stumbled into the log-house, thinking that our party was still in possession, only to stop dead in terror at the scream of Silver's parrot crying 'Pieces of eight!' out of the dark.

'Mrs Hawkins,' said the Squire, half-turning to my mother and looking somewhat chagrined, 'your son's become as sharp as a Lincoln's Inn lawyer,' which was saying much, since Mr Trelawney greatly abominated lawyers, having had a long suit against his cousin about certain properties.

'That he has from me,' my mother spoke up boldly. 'Fairness of mind – that was his father's gift.'

'Well,' says the Squire, blowing through his nose, but with a good-natured smile in my direction, 'I say Silver should hang – and hang he would if I had my hands on the villain.'

'Enough of Silver,' says the Doctor. 'I propose a toast. I drink to you, Jim. It was you who brought us the map of Treasure Island; it was you who discovered the mutiny and warned us in time; it was you who would keep running off and so saved us all in the end.'

'I'll drink to that,' says Captain Smollett, raising his glass.

'And I, with a will,' says the Squire.

So they all pledged me, and drank my health; then the Squire, greatly excited, stood up and called for silence.

'I'll go better,' he said. 'I'll ask you gentlemen to drink to a piece of news I'll tell you.'

At this I protested, for I was sure Mr Trelawney meant to disclose our business, of which I had said nothing to my mother; but there was no stopping him.

'No, no, Hawkins,' he cries, 'I've bottled it up for a month 'til I'm ready to burst. Gentlemen,' he continued, very important and red about the cheek, 'I have appointed young Hawkins here Agent for my plantations in Jamaica. He sails within the month.'

I looked at once to my mother and saw that she took it very bad. She stared a moment at the Squire, then caught my eye, and darted me a look of accusation. Mumbling some excuse about a pudding, she hastily quit the room.

The Squire, meanwhile, oblivious of the upset he had caused, was explaining to Livesey and Smollett how he suspected that the steward of his Jamaica property, one Joshua Hallows, was cheating him. 'I've seen no profits for a twelvemonth,' he boomed, 'and Hawkins is the man to find out why!'

I was about to beg their pardon and go to my mother when a scream from the kitchen had us all tumbling out of our chairs and running to see what was to do. My mother was standing by the kitchen window, white in the face, holding a wooden spoon. Upon our urgent enquiries she declared she had seen a face in the window – a villainous, man's face.

'A thief or a smuggler, by Gad!' thundered the Squire. 'Come, gentlemen, let's rout him out!' and before we could think, he was striding through the parlour, taking up his great stick, and it seemed best to follow.

We all went out, the Squire trumpeting orders in a voice loud enough to send any miscreant scuttling over the hill and away.

'Hawkins, search the stables! Livesey, Smollett, the road! Rout him out! Scatter!'

The Squire had a boy's delight in a chase and was a terrrible scourge of poachers, and we needs must humour him. So we split up and I went round to the stables that had been new built behind the inn, rather nettled with the Squire for turning us all out to no purpose.

But when I came into the stable-yard I smelt danger in the air as strong as the wood-smoke blowing about the chimney. You'll say I'm being wise after the event, or that my mind was still running upon our table talk, but I swear I felt the presence of Long John Silver in that yard as a tangible thing. The storm had blown itself out, leaving a squally, confused wind that seemed to blow from all quarters at once. The sky had partially cleared, showing a full moon, across which the clouds scudded, making every shadow in the yard leap and dance, while the wind rattled the latches of the doors and moaned about the stable roof.

From the harness-room came a sound of stealthy movement, as of a one-legged man shifting about within – or so I fancied.

For the second time that night, I drew my pistol and advanced upon the door, determined to atone for my former fright. I flung open the door, with what I hoped was a confident challenge, and saw the object of all my bravery: an old piece of sacking nailed up by the window, and flapping in the draught let in through a broken pane!

At that moment I heard a great 'Hulloa!' from the direction of the bridge and ran off, meeting the Doctor and the Captain in the lane. From the little wood beyond the bridge we heard the Squire's voice, loud as a fog-horn:

'Livesey! Smollett! Hawkins! To me! I have him!'

We ran forward, the Captain with a lantern, and found the Squire sitting athwart his victim, who lay face down on the ground, twisting like a gaffed eel.

'Light! Give me light!' roared the Squire, and as the Captain came up with the lantern, 'Now we'll see what I've bagged here!'

He hauled the man to his feet and the Captain shone the lantern to reveal the frightened, gibbering countenance of Tom Pearce, Mr Trelawney's own coachman!

The Squire's face was a study in mortification and disappointment.

'Deuce take it! Tom! What the devil are you doing, Tom?'

Tom, who was simple in the head, though he had a wonderful way with horses, was far too affrighted, of course, to make any coherent reply, and while the Squire fumed and blustered, we concluded that it must have been the coachman's face my mother saw in the window, and the Squire at last sent him off, with a flea in his ear, to fetch his coach from the hamlet.

We went back indoors to finish our supper, and while the Squire and the Captain lit their pipes with spills at the fire, Dr Livesey took me aside, and taxed me about my commission from the Squire, pointing out my duty to my mother.

Now the Doctor had been as good as a father to me and I was bound to hear him out – though determined that nothing should persuade me out of voyaging to Jamaica. I think that the Doctor, though he never said as much, always hoped that I should follow him in his profession, and this proof that I had no such intention, disappointed him.

Nor was the Doctor the only one to raise the subject with me that night. Immediately after the Squire's great coach rumbled away, taking the Doctor and Captain Smollett, Ben Gunn plucked at my sleeve.

'Jim, Jim mate,' says he, very awkward and confidential, as he was when he had a favour to ask, 'may I speak wi' you, private like, man to man?'

Emboldened by my smile and nod, he went on: 'Now Jim, you won't say nay to Ben Gunn, will you? Not to your old shipmate, Ben.'

I asked what it was he wanted. The question threw him into confusion.

'What is it? –' and at length '– Well, what it is, is this.'

He gripped my sleeve again and squinted at me sideways from under his shaggy, grey brows.

'It pertains to this here cruise o' your'n, Jim, to Jamaicy,' adding with an air of triumph, '*That's* it.'

'That's what?'

'Well, what I were thinking,' he went on, greatly agitated, 'what I were a-pondering, like—' He fell silent for a moment, then in a great rush of words: 'Take me alongside o' you, Jim. I'll be servant to you, whatsoever suits, mate, but only take me along!'

Ben Gunn, you should know, had lived at the Admiral Benbow upwards of six years. He had spent, or drunk, or been cheated of his share of the treasure – a thousand pounds – in nineteen days precisely, from date of receipt, and the Squire had given him a lodge to keep. But though, as he so often told me, he'd taken to seafaring by accident, he was seaman enough to sicken without at least a daily sight of the billows. So we had taken him in, and he proved himself a most excellent servant and companion to my mother, so long as she kept the rum locked up.

'Ben,' says I, 'you don't want to go to sea again. You've told me a hundred times, the Admiral Benbow's Ben Gunn's last anchorage.'

'Aye, aye – and a snug berth she is, no complaints. But, Jim, it's been near ten years since I tasted salt on the breeze and felt the roll of a ship under me pins.'

A wistful, longing look came into the old maroon's eyes.

'Jim,' he went on, quietly, 'some days when I takes my stroll out along the cliffs I stops, and I closes my eyes, and I listens to the sea – and she sings to me, Jim, like a blessed psalm she sings, calling to me.'

He fell silent, and I was silent myself, touched to the quick by what he said, since it exactly represented my own feelings. Telling him that I would think it over, and bidding him to see to the horse, I went back into the inn.

My mother was in the parlour, clearing up, and from the way she banged about the plates and dishes, and by her silence, I could tell she was in a fury. Without a word, I began to help her, as I used to do when I was a boy, and at length she burst out:

'Tell me why, then! Will you tell me why?'

Before I could make any answer, she continued in the same style: 'You've got money, an education, you could do anything.'

Lamely enough I attempted to explain myself, and made a hash of it, for this restlessness, this desire, deep in the soul, for new horizons and the wide world, is not a thing that will go into plain words, but only into poetry – and I'm no poet.

'This is the Old World, Mother,' I concluded haltingly, 'out there is the New World.'

'I'll tell you what's out there,' says she, quite fierce. 'The sea. That's what. You think I don't know that rover's look in your eye, Jim? Thirty years I've kept this inn, and I've seen that same look in the eyes of a thousand men – sea-faring men.'

Picking up a platter, and burnishing it round and round

with a cloth, she went on: 'Oh, it's all home sweet home when they're drinking their rum, but their *hearts* are out there, on the sea, and –' setting down the platter with a clang, '– mostly their bodies end up at the bottom of it.'

She laid a hand on my arm and looked at me direct.

'I lost your father, Jim. Must I lose you too?'

I cannot recall what I replied, and I fear it was feeble enough, though it softened her, and she gave me a cuff on the shoulder with, 'Off to your bed, now.'

And to bed I went, feeling like a scolded child.

Tired though I was, I could not sleep. At last, however, I fell into a doze, and then into a dream, or a nightmare rather, for I began to live again the worst moments of the Treasure Island adventure.

I lay trembling in the bottom of the apple barrel aboard the *Hispaniola*, listening to the first evidence of Long John Silver's treachery; I cowered under cover of a live-oak on Treasure Island, and saw Silver murder Tom Redpath in cold blood. Finally, came the worst event of all, when I stumbled into the very bastion of the mutineers. Silver was drawing me close, as George Merry led the others out to decide our fate. He was hissing in my ear: 'Jim – Jim –,' and of a sudden I knew I was awake and that the voice was a real voice.

My heart leaping into my throat, I opened my eyes and there was Long John Silver in the flesh, looming over my bed, his crutch tucked up under his left arm, and in his right hand, a pistol pointed at my head!

Chapter II

Silver's Confederates

As you may suppose, I lay for a moment, paralysed, my wits in a fine disorder from waking suddenly from one nightmare into another! Then I tried to rise.

'Stay, Jim,' Silver says, very low, 'lie easy, mate.'

Strong moonlight was flooding in at the uncurtained window, and I saw him well. Though he was recognizably the same John Silver, he was yet much changed. The broad, plain, open face was thinner drawn, and a thick stubble, very ragged and unkempt, covered the lower part of it. He was paler than ever, almost white, and about his glinting, intelligent eyes I perceived lines of suffering. I concluded that the past ten years had not treated him kindly, which was to be wondered at in a man of such formidable talent, commanding personality, subtle cunning, and in one who was always so careful with his money.

While I observed him, he was speaking, still in a low voice, but quite natural and conversational.

'Aye, Jim,' says he, 'Long John it is, and no sperrit, come for to see his old shipmate – and a sight for sore eyes you are to be sure, Jim. Why, I'd hardly ha' recognized you, mate, you're that grown.'

I noticed that his coat, which was a poor garment and very patched and make-mend, was soaked through with sea-water and it occurred to me that the lantern flash I had seen in Kitt's Hole had not been to do with smugglers after all but with Silver's own arrival (which I afterwards found to be true) and that it was Silver's face my mother had glimpsed in the kitchen window, which Silver immediately confirmed.

'And sorry I am to be the cause o' commotion,' said he, very pleasantly, shaking his head. 'Does my old heart good to see you, Jim. Didn't I always say as how you'd grow into a fine man and a gentleman? I'm as proud of you as if you was my own son, my affy-davy on it!'

'Then listen to me,' says I. 'Get out of this now. If they catch you, they'll hang you.'

Silver nodded. 'That's sound advice, I reckon,' he says, and then with a smile and a narrowing of his eyes, 'but first they've got to catch me, eh? And maybe you recall that Long John can hop nimbler on his one pin than most men can on two?'

I confess that, after the first shock of seeing him had passed, my recollections of Silver had tended to the pleasant side of his nature, but his words, and the shifty, crafty look that accompanied them, put me in mind of that other, stronger, darker side, and I answered very coldly: 'Yes, especially when there's murder to be done.'

'Hard words, Jim, hard words,' says he, 'we were friends once.'

To this I made no reply and he went on: 'I saved your life. They tipped me the black spot, but I stood by you, stem to stem.'

'To save your own skin!'

'Mebbe, mebbe,' says Long John, scratching his chin, 'but that wasn't all there was to it, no, by Thunder.'

At this I asked him straight out: 'What do you want, Silver? What have you come for?'

He answered in the same style: 'For what's mine, for what's mine by right – for Flint's map.'

I was utterly astonished at this, for the map was valueless, save as a curiosity. Certainly, there was treasure left on the island, the bar silver, and a cache of arms, but all together they were not worth the expense of fitting out an expedition to fetch them. I said as much to Silver and straightway his friendly manner deserted him.

'You just give it to me, double sharp,' he growled, then, in a pleasanter tone, 'and I'll slip my cable and be gone, with no harm done.' He added, with a menace that could not be mistaken, 'We don't want for to give your dear mother no more alarms, now, do we?'

In face of such a threat I had no other course but to pull

my breeches on over my night-shirt – Silver watching me all the time like a hawk – take up a candle, and lead him downstairs.

I had another purpose in this: I thought it might offer me an opportunity to disarm him, for the stair was steep and narrow such as to present a considerable obstacle for a one-legged man. But I had forgotten Silver's amazing dexterity. He hitched his crutch to a lanyard round his neck, freeing his left hand to grip to the stair-rail, and came down behind me, steady as you like, with the pistol in his right never wavering an inch from its aim – and so I preceded him into the parlour.

The proof of how little I valued Flint's map lay in the fact that I had put it in a picture-frame and hung it over the settle by the parlour fireplace!

When this was revealed to Silver he broke into such a laugh as brought tears into his eyes and was, I believe, perfectly unaffected. At length, catching his breath: 'Well, if that don't beat it all. There's a score o' hands has died for a sight o' that map, and there she hangs, like a blessed picture, for all the world to see.'

In this, he was a little out, for the parlour of the Admiral Benbow was not so public a place as it had formerly been. With the building of the new turnpike, our trade, which had been poor enough at the best of times, had fallen away, and I had made the parlour into a sitting-room for my mother. Only the bar was kept open to serve our local customers, who were very few, owing to the excise on ale and rum. Still, we made no secret of the map, and would show it to any passer-by who desired to see this interesting relic.

'Fetch it out of its frame,' Silver barked, his voice now hoarse, and a hungry glitter in his eye.

I obeyed without a word, for I had by no means given up hope of turning the tables. Ben Gunn slept within the inn, and slept light, and since he had been the original means of bringing Long John low on Treasure Island, I thought it likely that, by some diversion, he would prove the villain's undoing once again. As slow as I dared, I took the map from its frame, and was about to hand it over to Silver when from the kitchen door came a flash of powder and a report, in that confined space, like the end of the world, and the pistol in Silver's hand flew into fragments!

In the door stood a man of middle height and middle years, soberly dressed, like a merchant, with one pistol smoking in his right hand, and another, ready primed, in his left.

'That's one sharp shot, you'll allow, John,' says this fellow in a voice curiously high-pitched and sing-song, 'and here's another for any jack that moves.'

So saying, he advanced a little more into the room, and behind him came a veritable giant of a Mulatto, with my own mother, half in a swoon from terror, gripped tightly in his arms.

At this I started forward with an oath, but Long John put out an arm to stop me, hissing low through his teeth: 'Steady, Jim.'

Then he turned to the other and said, very cool:

'Well, you're a cautious man, Silas Gadney, what I don't generally reckon a fault.'

Here, he took the map from me, while my poor mother fainted away in earnest in the arms of the half-caste.

'I'll remind you,' says Silver, 'that this map's no more use than a bucket full of brine without me to read it.'

'I know that,' says Gadney, 'but you'll oblige me by handing it over.'

Long John obeyed, while the half-caste (Mulatto Joe, I soon learned, was his name) dropped my mother roughly into a chair.

Gadney threw a burning glance at the map then shouted out: 'Bill!'

A moment later, a third ruffian entered, from the hall-way, a seaman to judge by the pigtail on his neck. He carried a small puncheon of brandy that he must have got from the bar.

'Get to it,' Gadney growled, and as Bill knocked out the

bung of the brandy-barrel, and began to tip the spirit about, he turned again to Silver.

'Once we're on the high seas,' says he, 'it'll be *Captain* Silver all the way. But we ain't there yet, and if we don't take measures *now*, the cruise'll end at Execution Dock.'

'Measures, Silas?' returns Silver, mild as a curate, 'and what measures would those be?'

'If any party knows we come for this map, then he knows our purpose and our destination,' was Gadney's reply. 'Well, here's two that knows,' indicating me and my mother, 'and there's a space on the wall to speak out if we shut their mouths.'

At once I understood his purpose, and the reason why Bill was tipping the brandy about, which was to murder my mother and me and fire the inn! Though plainly these monsters were Silver's confederates, I could not believe that Long John would condone such barbarous actions and cried to him direct: 'Silver!'

Gadney was sharp, and detected the appeal, for a narrow smile spread across his features, and he said: 'Mebbe you don't know Silver so well, boy.'

Silver turned half towards me and said: 'Jim Hawkins knows me, all right, from cross-tree to kelson, so I reckon,' and I thought I noticed in his tone a hint that he was on my side.

Gadney must have thought the same for he quickly put in: 'Besides which, Long John don't have much of a choice in the matter.'

Here, Mulatto Joe stepped forward, an ugly grin on his face.

'I'm a forgiving man, myself,' Gadney went on, 'but Joe here, well, you know he's a score to settle with you, John Silver.'

'Why,' says Silver, in that same milk-and-water way, 'they'll be tipping me the black spot next!'

This was to me, and showed me, plain as a signal-flag, that Silver would help me if he could, though how he was to do it I could not see.

Turning back to Gadney, and in a voice that now had a flavour of contempt and growing rage in it, Silver continued: 'But that's the way of it wi' whining, creeping fo'c'sle lawyers like you, Silas.'

Then, seeming to lose control of his passion, he smote upon the table.

'Hell's damnation! You stand there like a yard o' bilge-water and dare tell *me* my business!'

He advanced upon Gadney, his rage becoming ever more furious. 'You think Silver's soft? You think I didn't mean to scupper this puppy and his hag of a mother *and* their old hulk of an inn? You think I've hobbled half way round the globe, and lived like a pig, and begged my bread, to let a boy an' a woman put a rope round my neck?'

Gadney quailed before this storm, as any man might.

'By the powers!' roars Silver, 'I'll show you if Long John Silver's soft.'

And with that he seizes Gadney's pistol, which Gadney made no attempt to prevent, and shifting away on his crutch, levels the weapon at *me*.

I swear I looked death in the eye, for Silver's speech convinced me that I was mistaken in supposing him a friend, and reminded me that there was no limit to the man's treachery.

I was utterly wrong. When the pistol barked, the ball struck Gadney – in the shoulder – and instantly all was confusion as Gadney reeled, Mulatto Joe's cutlass sang in the air, and Bill flung a lighted candle into a pool of spilt brandy, that instantly burst into flames.

I hurled myself at Bill, my first thought being to save the inn, and he fell down under the hail of blows I dealt him. Then I twitched a cloth from the table to smother the fire, which had caught at the window-blinds. As I beat at the flames I saw that Silver and Mulatto Joe were engaged in furious combat, their cutlasses clashing with a sound of hammers on anvils. Gadney, staunching the flow of blood from his shoulder, scuttled away through the kitchen door.

And then I was knocked down silly by a blow from

behind, and fell heavily to the slate floor. Through a mist I saw Bill coming at me with his clasp-knife. I thought I was done, for I was too weak and giddy to defend myself, but no, there was Silver, heaving up on his crutch behind Bill, and swinging back his cutlass. Silver struck and down went Bill like a felled tree, and the next thing I remember was Silver's brawny right arm hauling me to my feet.

Bill lay stone dead, and by the hallway door Mulatto Joe was crumpled up in a corner, either dead or wounded.

'That's twice, Jim,' was all Silver said as he helped me to a chair, and then he was at the window, for a bugle call had rung out from outside, followed by the thunder of horses at full gallop. Just then I happened to lower my head, the better to clear it, and saw, lying on the floor not ten inches away – the map!

Silver was still engaged at the window, his back towards me, so I quickly seized the map and concealed it in my night-shirt.

As I rose from my chair, Silver turned.

'Ben Gunn, by the powers!' he said bitterly. 'Will that man never cease from plaguing me?'

I clapped my eye to the window and saw a small cavalcade of riders, with Ben Gunn, Squire Trelawney, and Captain Smollett out in front, pounding down towards the inn.

I turned round – to receive such a blow from Long John Silver's crutch as I swear I can feel to this day, and fell down senseless.

Chapter III

I Honour a Debt

I recovered my senses to find myself back in my own bed, and had it not been for the sight of Dr Livesey sitting at the bedside, and a monstrous ache in my head, I could have believed that all the foregoing had been a continuation of my dream.

I confess, to my own discredit, that my first question to the Doctor was about the map. He confirmed, as I expected, that no map had been found upon me, adding, very cross and disapproving, 'Your mother's taken no harm, in case it should concern you.'

It was broad daylight outside, and the brave sunshine was pouring in at the window, through which I could hear a jingle of harness, and a tramp of many feet, and snorting of horses, and men's voices, which Dr Livesey explained, telling me that the Squire had roused the whole countryside up – militia, revenue men, and all his own people – in a great hue and cry after Silver.

The Doctor pronounced me fit to leave my bed and I went at once to my mother's room and found her sleeping peacefully, Livesey having administered her a draught.

Downstairs there was a tremendous toing and froing with the Squire's voice rising above all the other noise. Before going in to him, I sought out Ben Gunn to learn his part of last night's affair, which he told me at great length and with much meandering away from the point, which was this: that having seen to the horse, and making his way back inside the inn, he had spied the print of Silver's crutch in some soft turf, and had immediately set out to follow his track, only to be struck down by a man he never saw, but took to be Silver. On regaining his senses, he had run to the hamlet, borrowed a horse, and ridden straightway to the Hall to summon aid from the Squire.

I went in to see that gentleman himself and found him in the parlour with his wig off and pipe in hand, bending over a plan of his own estate, on which was mapped, in fine detail, the whole of our neighbourhood, which was mostly his property.

'Hawkins!' he cried, his face all ruddy with excitement, 'we have him! I say we have him! We have the scoundrel encircled' – flourishing a quill with great energy – 'and we'll draw the noose tighter 'til it's round the blackguard's neck, what?'

But I was more interested in the figure stretched out on the settle, and being attended by Doctor Livesey – none other than Mulatto Joe.

Plainly Silver had not killed, but only wounded him, and now he was coming to with not a groan exactly, but a curious kind of choking in his throat.

'Ah, Doctor,' says the Squire, striding over, 'I see you've saved this rascal's worthless life. Made sure the hangman has his fee, eh? Charitable of you!' Then, leaning over the half-caste, 'Now, fellow, let's hear what you have to say.'

'I fear you'll not get a word out of him, Trelawney,' said the Doctor, in a strange voice.

'Stubborn dog, you think? But there, you're a kindly, merciful sort of man, Livesey. I flatter myself that I, on the other hand, will succeed in loosening the villain's tongue.'

'That is precisely what you will *not* be able to do,' returned the Doctor, with a frown, 'because he does not possess a tongue.'

'What?'

The Squire positively gaped.

'It's been cut out, sir – a neat piece of surgery too.'

I turned immediately to the half-caste and asked him: 'Was it Silver? Is that the score you had to settle?' and he nodded, rolling his eyes.

'Gad, it's barbarous,' the Squire exclaimed. 'Silver will pay for this, by Heaven he will.' Then, seeing me turn on my heel and walk to the door, 'Hawkins! Where are you off to?'

'To join in the hunt, sir,' I told him, and so I was determined to do because I was shocked to the marrow by this latest evidence of Silver's crimes.

I marched into the stable, to saddle up the hack, desiring nothing better than to see Silver dance on the gibbet, and found myself face to face with the monster himself!

I could give no alarm, for he had his pistol clapped to my neck in a trice, with, 'Stay a moment, Jim,' whispered low.

Before I could speak a word, he stole the wind from my sail – 'How did I come here?' said he, 'Well, I never left, did I? I've been biding.'

'For what?'

'Why, for *you*, matey. I calculated as how you could shake a reef and haul old Long John out of this.'

'Then you've miscalculated.'

'Have I? I reckon not, my son. I reckon Jim Hawkins is a man what pays his debts.'

'The debt's cancelled,' I replied, touching my head, which the Doctor had bandaged. 'You cancelled it.'

'That don't absolve you none,' says he, quick as a flash, 'you owe me for your mother's life, by Thunder!'

This struck home and Silver saw that it had, for he went on:

'Aye, they'd ha' burned the good lady alive, but for me.'

It was true enough – but I was determined, like iron, that he should not profit from his night's work.

'I'll help you,' said I, 'but on condition you restore the map to me.'

At that, he pressed his pistol harder at me, saying, very fierce: 'That ain't no part o' the Articles.'

'Shoot me if you will,' I replied, cool and confident, 'and bring the whole inn, militia and all, down on you. Or give me the map, and save your life.'

His eyes shifted to left and to right as he sought a way out, but there was none, and after a moment he put away his pistol, plucked the map from a pocket, and gave it to me with a smile, saying: 'Jim, you've learned a sight more'n Latin and Greek, so you have, shiver my sides.'

It was the simplest business to effect Silver's escape. We kept a small cart, that Ben Gunn used to fetch supplies, and into this Silver went, concealed under a tarpaulin.

I saw nothing of the Squire or the Doctor as I flicked the horse into a trot away from the inn, and on the way to Kitt's Hole, where Silver had concealed the cutter-gig in which he had come, I encountered only Supervisor Dance, picketing the coast road with three of his revenue men, who gave me a cheery salute and a 'Good day!'

'Trimly done, Jim, trimly done,' Silver said as I helped him down from the cart at Kitt's Hole. I went with him, down the steep path into the cove, to lend a hand at launching the gig. But as we approached the rock where Silver had hidden the boat, he suddenly stopped, peering, then whipped out his pistol.

'Prints, by Thunder!' he hissed. 'They're laying for me. Tell 'em I forced you, or you'll swing with me.'

For a moment I could not think what he meant. Then I saw what his keener eyes had spotted first – the imprints of boots in the sand.

Just then a cry went up, 'Hold, Silver!' and in the same instant that I recognized Captain Smollett's voice, that worthy himself, armed with a musket, stepped out from behind a rock, and three militiamen with him.

Silver threw down his pistol without a murmur, and saluted the Captain almost as if he were pleased to see him!

'Why, Captain Smollett, sir,' says he, very respectful, 'a pleasure to clap eyes on you again, sir.'

'Has he harmed you, Jim?' Smollett asked me. I shook my head.

'As well for you, Silver.'

'Ah,' says Silver, with all the appearance of cheerfulness, 'you're a sharp man, so you are, sir, and always was. It were your notion, I reckon, to watch out for a boat whiles them other lubbers was scouring the moors and the roads.'

Then he added, with a second salute, 'Permission to say a word to Mr Hawkins, sir?'

Captain Smollett nodded shortly, and Silver turned to me.

'Jim,' he said, 'I reckon I'm on a lee shore. But you'll do one thing more for me, Jim, you owe me that. You'll speak up for me at my trial, Jim, speak up like a man!'

I could not resist his appeal, and promised I would do my best for him.

'I doubt it'll aid you better than a cockleshell in a blow,' says Captain Smollett, very dry. 'It's Execution Dock for you, my fellow, and not before time.'

Chapter IV

I Attend a Trial

Silver was taken away to the lock-up at T—, then to Plymouth, where the assize was just then in session. To compound his misfortunes, Sir Solomon Pridham was on the bench, the famous hanging Judge, whose reputation was fearsome, and of whom it was said that he did not consider a felon properly dressed unless he wore a rope round his neck.

I returned to the Admiral Benbow with Captain Smollett, where we found the Squire rather huffy at the failure of his own drag-net but mightily delighted that the law had caught up with Silver at last, rubbing his hands at the prospect of the evidence he would give at Silver's trial, and in the end commending Captain Smollett's wit with a very good grace.

I gave a fair description of Gadney, and the officer from Plymouth said that he had heard the man spoken of. He was said to have money, though the source was a mystery, and he had been settled in Plymouth for less than a year, having previously (it was rumoured) lived overseas.

'An old buccaneer! I'd stake my wig on it,' was Squire Trelawney's verdict, and he commanded the officer, in his stately way, to leave no stone unturned in the hunt for the man. The officer and his men then left, taking Mulatto Joe away in irons.

Only when the Squire had trundled back to the Hall, hauling the Captain with him, and the Doctor had departed to his own house, did I have leisure to look at the map. I conned it for above an hour, running my eye with infinite care over every contour and mark, searching for some clue that might explain why Silver had risked his neck to recover it, and why Gadney was preparing to sink money in a new expedition to the island. But I found nothing.

I then thought of Ben Gunn, which I should have done before, and spared myself a second headache! Ben, you should know, had sailed with Captain Flint. After Flint's death, he got a berth in a ship that by chance bore upon Treasure Island, and at Ben's suggestion put into the anchorage. Twelve days they searched for the gold and failed to turn up a single doubloon. For a punishment, they marooned Ben on the island, where three years later I was the first to discover him. In that time, Ben had found Flint's cache, all seven hundred thousand pounds.

But, when applied to, he could throw no further light on the mystery, vehemently denying that he could have overlooked anything of value in his incessant wanderings over the island.

That night I was bidden to dine at the hall and expose to all the gentlemen the whole truth of the map and Silver's quest. They were greatly excited and baffled. The Squire was all for fitting out a schooner there and then, only the Doctor pointed out that Mr Trelawney could not quit England for the moment, owing to the lawsuit, and in any case it would be a wild goose chase.

'Then we'll have the truth out of Silver!' cried the Squire.

'As likely to get a sonnet out of a fo'c'sle hand,' said Captain Smollett.

But there was Gadney, who must know something, and we agreed that when he was caught, he should be induced to spill, and then, perhaps, we could carry the matter further.

On the day appointed for Silver's trial I set out, soon after dawn, for Plymouth, which was not more than three hours' ride on a good horse. My mother was heartily opposed to my going.

'Are you possessed, Jim?' she said at the door. 'That devil Silver's got a power over you.'

I told her again that I had given my word and must go.

'Your word! When did he ever keep his? And what of me? I suppose you care more for that black-hearted pirate than you do for your own mother!'

'Ben is to stay with you,' I replied, 'there's no danger.'

'Oh no! With a band of cut-throats still at large who'll stop at nothing to lay their hands on that twice-accursed map!'

I had no fear that Gadney and his crew would attempt a new assault on the inn. Further to reassure her, I showed her that I had the map with me, in my pocket.

This somewhat calmed my mother, but it had the opposite effect on Ben.

'That map's a magnet, mate,' he said as he held my stirrup. 'And what'll she draw? Why *steel*, Jim, cutlass steel, that's what. Better let me go along o' you. Take the mistress to parson's and I'll ride with you.'

But I wouldn't hear of it, and told him to stay where he was, bolt the door, and open to nobody.

I had not been gone five minutes, however, before it occurred to me that perhaps Ben was right. If Gadney was still after the map, it was reckless to have it with me on the open road. So I stopped and hid it behind a stone in a wall, on which I scratched an 'X' with the point of my clasp-knife.

I soon had reason to be glad that I had rid myself of the map. I was passing through a lonely stretch of country, where thick woods pressed down on either side of the way, when I observed a rider approaching from the direction of Plymouth. As he came nearer I saw that he was a rough-looking fellow and I already had a hand upon my pistol when he reined in, blocking the way.

I was about to draw my pistol when a familiar sing-song voice rang out from behind me.

'Do and you're a dead man!'

I twisted my head round to see Gadney standing in the road some six paces behind me. He gestured to me to dismount with the musket he carried, and I had no other choice but to obey. Gadney's henchman jumped down also and quickly disarmed me.

'I won't beat about, boy,' said Gadney. 'I've got a heap o' money sunk in that map – a schooner all kitted out and victualled and a crew a-clamourin' to be on the high seas. So you *talk*, boy.'

And so I would – cheerfully – for the map was nothing to me, only a pistol spoke from the woods nearby and Gadney measured his length upon the ground!

I flung myself at the other fellow but missed my footing and he escaped me. A second pistol shot barked and Gadney's friend took to his heels. I gave chase at once, plunging after him into the underbrush, and for all the good I did, I might just as well have stayed on the road, for he was far fleeter of foot than me, and soon outstripped me.

After ten minutes I gave it up and went back to the road. There I found Ben Gunn crouching by Gadney's body!

'He's pork,' said Ben.

Very excitedly he explained his part in the affair (but you will forgive me if I do not reproduce his exact words!) Having an instinct that I was riding into danger, and on my mother's insistence, he had followed me at a distance and so had seen and heard all.

I took out my pocket-watch and to my consternation saw that upwards of an hour had been lost, and my chance to speak for Silver at his trial more than likely thrown away. Brushing aside Ben's protests, and bidding him return at once to the inn, I mounted up again and rode like the blazes for Plymouth.

I fear I drove that poor horse like a cavalry charger, but I was determined that no effort of mine should be spared to fulfil my pledge to Silver. I had a dreadful business as I entered the town, for it was market day, and the narrow streets were thronged with wagons. In my headlong rush I upset a whole coop full of fat ducks, but pounded on, amid scandalized shouts and flying feathers, and so reached the court-house at last.

Leaping down, and flinging the reins to an urchin, I ran into the court to hear the thin, petulant voice of Sir Solomon Pridham pronounce:

'John Silver, I find you guilty on all charges.'

I was too late!

But perhaps not so, as the Judge went on: 'Before I pass sentence on you—'

I ran down the room to the bench – and a wild figure I must have cut, all covered in dust from the road, and streaming in sweat – and burst out:

'If Your Lordship pleases, my name is Hawkins. I am to speak for the prisoner!'

There was uproar in the court. I heard Silver exclaim, from the dock, 'God bless you, Jim!', and Squire Trelawney, from the foremost row of the benches, 'Hawkins, by Gad!', then two of the ushers ran to seize me.

Only the Judge, seated high at his desk, seemed unmoved. He was an elderly man, thin as a skeleton, his skin pallid and yellowish, like old parchment. He had an air of the profoundest *ennui*, as if all these proceedings bored him half to sleep, and he sniffed at an orange, studded with clove-sticks, that he held to his nose.

'I do *not* please,' says the Judge, and his voice, distant and feeble though it was, instantly brought a hush.

'You are too late, sir. Judgement has been given.'

'I've not come to question the judgement, sir,' says I, 'but to urge clemency in the sentence.'

'*Clemency*!' I heard the Squire exclaim furiously.

'You are out of time, sir,' sighed the Judge, his eyes almost closed.

But they opened wider when Dr Livesey sprang to his feet.

'If your Lordship pleases,' says the Doctor, in his quiet, commanding way, 'I am a magistrate as well as a medical man. I think the King's justice would be well served by permitting Mr Hawkins a hearing.'

The Doctor made an impressive figure in his fine black coat and snow-white powder. Sir Solomon considered him for a moment, then said with a weary sigh: 'Oh, very well. But you must take the oath, Mr Hawkins.'

I did so, and then spoke my piece.

'My Lord,' said I, 'why do I plead for John Silver's life? Because I owe my own to him, not once, but twice over.' I then explained the circumstances, as well as I could, and concluded: 'For these actions alone, he deserves your clemency.'

For the first time I looked at Silver. His manner was remarkably composed and confident for one who stood under the shadow of the gallows. He had got a new coat somehow, and his appearance was clean and pleasant, as of old. He was nodding in solemn agreement with what I had said, and there were murmurs of approbation from the body of the court, mostly sea-faring types, whom Silver must have won over during the course of the trial.

'Mr Hawkins,' says the Judge, in a voice that boded no good for Silver, 'do you recall a shipmate of yours named' – here he searched among some papers on his desk – 'Thomas Redpath?'

I glanced at Silver, who looked very black and shaken of a sudden.

'Well, Mr Hawkins?'

'I do, sir,' I was forced to reply.

'And what fate befell Thomas Redpath?'

'He was killed, sir.'

'You mean *murdered* perhaps?'

'He was murdered, sir.'

'Did you witness it?'

'I – I did, sir.'

'Why was he murdered?'

'Because he would not join the mutiny, sir.'

'An honest man, then,' said the Judge, 'who stood by his duty?'

'Yes, sir, he was.'

'And in what manner was this good fellow done to death?'

'He was – struck down, sir.'

'You mean the murderer struck him down. With what?'

'With – his crutch, sir.'

A low murmur ran through the court, and I heard the Squire exclaim, 'Infamous!'

'And then?' asked the Judge inexorably.

'The – murderer took out a knife and plunged it into his back.'

The Judge repeated what I had just said, lingering over the words, and then with a sudden rasp he cried:

'Name the murderer, sir! Name him!'

'It was John Silver,' said I.

The murmur grew into an angry buzz, and I saw Silver's eyes flick round the courtroom.

'Thank you, Mr Hawkins,' said the Judge, in a mocking, silken tone, 'you may stand down now.'

Then he turned to Silver and in a voice like a freezing north wind gave sentence: 'John Silver, the catalogue of your crimes is without equal even in my experience of man's abysmal depravity. The pity is that you have but one neck to forfeit. But that you shall, fellow, for you will hang at noon on the day next appointed, and may God have mercy upon your soul.'

Chapter V

I Post to London

So the blow had fallen at last, and Silver was to die.

I confess I was heartily sorry for it, and quite sick at heart, for though no man more richly deserved the gallows than Silver, he had been my friend, and for all his black treacheries, I had a strange liking, even an affection for him.

I was sickened by the manner in which the Squire exulted, and even the Doctor pursed his lips when Mr Trelawney said we should all go to the tavern and 'drink a bumper to the blackguard's eternal damnation.' Doctor Livesey said, very frosty: 'This isn't seemly, Trelawney, to be gloating over a fellow creature's doom, Silver or no.'

It was indeed the Squire's gloating that decided me to save Silver's life if I could.

I had a recollection that a new law had lately been added to the statute book whereby the Crown had power to commute a sentence of death into transportation for life and slavery in the Colonies. If this were so, and I could somehow contrive to present a successful petition to the Lord Chancellor on Silver's behalf, I could get him at least a stay of execution.

Thereupon, without a word to the others, I took post to London, having found out that the date for Silver's execution was in ten days' time, and dispatched a note to the Admiral Benbow to tell my mother where I was bound.

Arrived in the capital, I went at once to The Temple, to seek out an Oxford friend, Philip Germain, who was to be a lawyer, and was, moreover, cousin to the Lord Chancellor himself.

To be short about it, Germain readily consented to help me, discovered the precise statute under which the commutation could be sought, found out the best man to write up the petition, obtained an audience for me with his cousin, and in five days I had a paper for Long John to sign, which was very fast work indeed for any matter to do with the Law.

Back to Plymouth I posted, with less than four days to run before the execution. By a small payment to the Governor of the prison, I obtained permission to see the condemned man.

Silver was lodged, not in the dungeon, but in a fair-sized cell in a tower, and though he was shackled to the wall by his good leg, he seemed to be in remarkable spirits. To judge from the remains of an excellent supper on his table, he was faring none so bad either, which meant, for sure, that he was bribing a warder, though where he got the money I could not hazard.

I began to explain my mission to him, but he stopped me.

'Avast, Jim! Transportation! That means slavery. Better the rope.'

'But I've put your case to the Lord Chancellor himself. You've but to sign, and he'll grant your plea.'

'Well,' says Long John, 'I weren't never much of a one for pleas – aside o' which, I seen them plantations – and hell'd be prettier. No, better swing, says I.'

'Where there's a breath there's a hope. I've heard you say so a hundred times.'

'Aye,' says he. Then looking at me straight, 'but I ain't afeared to die. Death and John Silver, they've sailed together many a long year.'

I pressed him again, but he was firm.

'Jim,' he says, 'you're a true man, but I've always knowed the cruise'd end at Execution Dock, knowed it since I were a lad, and so be it.'

Laying a hand on my arm, he continued, with a look in his eye as if he gazed at some far horizon, 'I've stood where you stands now, high up, with a world at your feet, and a sea-breeze in your face, and a call a-ringing in your ear.' Gripping me tight: 'You take the Squire's commission, you heed the call, for that's the call o' *life*, Jim. *Jim*,' he went on, 'you've been a son to me and I ain't got no legacy for you but one; that map o' Flint's, what were always mine by right. It ain't worth two coppers now, but you'll breed sons, Jim, and you'll yarn with 'em of a night, and mebbee you'll blow the dust from that old map to show 'em, and mebbee you'll tell 'em how once you sailed with Long John Silver.'

There was almost a tear in my eye as I shook his hand for the last time, and left him, still smiling at me, and throwing me a salute.

It was only as I rode home to the Admiral Benbow, turning over and over in my mind my last interview with John Silver, that I started to question the way in which he had refused my offer.

The more I pondered it, the more strange did it appear. Silver might fear to be a slave, but as sure day follows night, he would not remain a slave for long, but would contrive some method of escape. Escape! At once I saw all. Silver had refused me because he had a better plan – to escape, through bribery no doubt, from Plymouth gaol. Nor had he even given up hope of recovering the map, since he had made such a point that I should always keep it by me, so *he* should always know where it was!

Marvelling at the tenacious spirit of the man, and half-wishing him success, I reached the inn, to find a note from Mr Trelawney, summoning me to the Hall.

In all my concern over Silver's fate I had almost forgot about the Squire's business, and that I had a passage taken on the *Saracen*, due to sail for Kingston, Jamaica in three days' time!

The Squire received me in his great library, the same room in which I had seen him close to for the first time, when, as an awestruck boy, I had brought him Flint's treasure map. Some of that feeling of awe returned as he burst out, before the servant had closed the door: 'Confound it all, Hawkins! Did you have to defend the blackguard in public?'

'It was of little use in any case,' I replied, but he hardly heard me.

'And dashin' off to London, without a by-your-leave! The Lord Chancellor! Petitions! What the devil are you playin' at, Hawkins?'

Now I had been taught from the cradle to look up to Squire Trelawney as a personage whose importance ranked half-way betweeen that of God and the King, with a shade in favour of God. His present temper might have dismayed me but for the reflection that it probably stemmed from the fact that Silver (so I had heard) had made an ass of him in court. So instead of begging his pardon, I stood firm.

'If you feel that you must cancel my commission, sir,' I said.

He gaped at me.

'Are you drunk, Hawkins?'

'No, sir.'

'Then cease babbling, man. Cancel, indeed!'

He looked at me a moment, very shrewdly, then grinned, and clapped me on the shoulder.

'I'm as famished as a kestrel. For the love of Heaven let's dine.'

Over dinner, we settled all the final arrangements between us very amicably, the Squire offering to take me to Plymouth in his own carriage.

The sole remaining impediment to my departure was now my mother. To my surprise, when I approached her on the subject next day, she was sorrowful but quite reconciled to my going.

'Seems a body isn't safe in his own house in England,' says she, 'what with cut-throats and villains; maybe that Jamaica's more peaceable!'

She made only one condition, that I should take Ben Gunn with me as my servant, for his rescue of me from Gadney had made a profound impression on her, and I think she had a superstition that old Ben was a sort of talisman, and that so long as he was with me no harm would come to me.

Next day, I bade farewell to my dear mother, and to the Doctor, who came to wish me God speed and to present Ben Gunn with a piece of parmesan cheese for the voyage, and the Squire took me off, with Ben, to Plymouth.

He left me at the quay, where the *Saracen* was berthed, wrung my hand heartily, wished me British luck, and went off to the gaol, for he had another reason to be in Plymouth, which was to see John Silver swing.

I stepped aboard, made myself known to the Captain, and went below to my quarters.

Now I had noticed a slight breeze blowing atop, which was causing the ship to roll a little at her hawsers, and as I followed the boatswain along the companion, my eye was caught by an object hung on a nail, that was swinging gently with the motion.

It was a crutch!

Pushing past the boatswain, I dashed into the fo'c'sle

hold on the larboard side, and there, chained to the bulkhead with ten or twelve other prisoners, was Long John Silver!

He raised his head as I stood staring stupidly, like an ox, and smiled as if he had been waiting to see me.

'Ah, Jim,' says he, 'shipmates again at last!'

Part II

The Cruise of the *Saracen*

Chapter VI

I Make My Bow to a Lady

'Where there's a breath, there's a hope,' said Long John Silver.

'Them was your words, Jim,' he went on, 'aye, and they would keep ringing in my head. "Silver," says I to myself at last, "Jim Hawkins has driven the nail! That's been your Bible and Creed, and you're a fool to forget it!" '

His manner was very solemn and sincere, but I was not taken in for a moment. I was sure that his plan of escape had failed, forcing him to seize the straw offered by the Lord Chancellor's petition. I accused him of this straight out, but he only smiled, and shook his head, and said: 'Ah, Jim, why go robbing yourself o' the credit for saving Long John's neck?'

Here, the boatswain, Gridley by name, stepped between us and said very gruffly: 'Captain's orders. No talkin' wi' the prisoners.'

I did not like the look of Gridley. He was a sour, glowering fellow, with a hot, cruel glitter in his eye, and had more the air of a prize-fighter than a seaman. I followed him to my cabin, amidships, and here I should say that I had Flint's map with me, having retrieved it from its hiding-place. I had a half-formed notion, you see, that my travels might one day lead me near Treasure Island, and I might step ashore and go a-treasure-hunting. How many times, in the months to come, did I wish that I had left the cursed parchment to rot away behind a stone!

My residence for the next month or two was a three-berth cabin no bigger than a broom-closet which I was to share, so the Captain had told me, with a Welsh parson, Rev. Morgan, and a Dutchman. A single berth, with lockers above, was built into the aft bulkhead, and was occupied by a great heap of Bibles, in a cheap edition. Opposite, there were two berths, one above the other. The lower, where I was to sleep, was almost wholly taken up by a massive sea-chest, strapped with iron, very battered, and with the name of its owner, 'H. Vanderbrecken', burned into the wood with a poker's end.

The upper berth was most completely taken up by the largest man I have ever seen in my life. This giant lay on his back, fast asleep, his hands clasped behind his head. One elbow projected out like the bough of an oak-tree while his legs, which were far too long to be stretched out straight, dangled over the edge of the bunk. He wore a pair of sea-boots that could have accommodated an elephant, and leather breeches and jerkin that must have swallowed up a whole herd in the tailoring. It was no great feat of deduction to match the huge sea-chest to the sleeping Goliath above.

I cleared my throat politely in the hope of waking him. This hope was not fulfilled, so I coughed rather louder.

The giant snored on.

'I beg your pardon, sir,' I said in a voice loud enough, I thought, to penetrate his slumbers.

It had no such effect; so I shook his elbow.

This worked the trick. He snorted through his nose, shifted his limbs, turned his head, and opened his eyes, which were of a startling, clear blue, and very angry!

'I beg your pardon, sir, for waking you,' says I, 'but I believe that to be my berth,' indicating the lower bunk.

He let out a grunt, then rolled towards me, with much creaking of his leather jerkin, lowered his head to peer at the bunk below, let out a second deep grunt, which I took to be a confirmation, and resumed his former position.

'Is this your sea-chest?' I asked, whereupon he went

through exactly the same manoeuvre as before, agreeing, with another grunt, that it was. Such insolent behaviour seemed calculated to provoke me, but I decided not to be provoked, for I thought I had detected, deep down in those blue eyes, a teasing sparkle.

'Then I'd be obliged if you'd remove it,' said I, very steady. This apparently astonished him, at least that was the way I interpreted a third grunt.

'Immediately – if that's convenient to you,' I said.

Then the giant rose up, swung his legs over the side, jumped down with an impact that shook the ship, and towered over me.

'I haff long legs,' said he, in a profound, guttural bass.

'So I observe.'

'I must – *stretch*!'

'I've no doubt that the Captain can find room in one of the holds.'

'*Huh*? In the *hold*?'

'For your sea-chest,' I added, sure by now that the Dutchman was playing a game to test my mettle.

'Also,' says Vanderbrecken, 'I am very *strong*,' flexing an arm like the hind-quarter of a bull.

'Then it'll be no trouble to you to shift it.'

'*Very* strong,' he repeated, and with as little effort as you or I have to pick up a mug, he lifted me off the floor by my coat-front. I was ready, however, for some such trick, and had my pocket-pistol out in a trice.

'But unobservant,' said I, suspended six inches above the floor.

He saw the pistol, and let me down gently enough, and at that instant the door opened and a smallish, thickset, harried-looking man in very shabby clerical clothes stepped in and stopped dead, his eyes popping at the pistol in my hand.

'Gentlemen!' says he, 'Mr Vanderbrecken!'

At this, Vanderbrecken broke into a bellow of laughter loud enough to rattle the caulking in the planks, and I turned to the newcomer, assuring him that there was no cause for alarm, and that the pistol was not loaded.

'This gentleman and I were making each other's acquaintance,' I said, and introduced myself to him, adding that I thought he must be Mr Morgan, and was acquainted with Squire Trelawney.

'What? Oh! Ah! Yes, indeed. Mr Trelawney,' says Morgan, scratching his grey locks, 'a most charitable gentleman, generous and charitable, though – I say it – quite wrong-headed, wrong-headed on the slave issue.'

Vanderbrecken then grasped my hand in a grip that caused my eyes to water, made himself known to me, and said: 'I joke with you. You like a joke. That's good. We are friends.'

And so we were, from that moment on, for I have no prejudice against the Dutch, and Vanderbrecken was the finest specimen of that slow, silent, intelligent, and adventurous race I ever encountered. He was a man of some forty summers, a very Colossus, as I have said, clean-shaven, with a lion's mane of yellow hair.

Morgan was fifty or thereabouts, and looked as if he slept in his clothes. His manner was extremely diffident and distracted, as if he lived in a daydream, but although he looked poor and shabby and of no account, you could see that he was bar-gold.

Vanderbrecken, still chuckling, picked up his sea-chest as if it was a feather pillow and carried it out of the cabin, saying as he went: 'You see, my friend. *Strong*!'

I disposed of my books and clothing as best I could, then went on deck, which was in a fine bustle of Jack Tars stowing and battening down ready for sea.

Captain Parker was up on the poop, taking a letter from a gentleman who had just arrived on board in a great hurry. Drawing nearer to them, I overheard the following conversation:

'My name is Moxon, sir,' said the latter, bowing to the Captain.

'Well, Mr Moxon,' said Parker, 'and how can I be of service to you?'

'Has the news not reached you?' says Moxon, rather put out.

'News? What news?'

'I'm appointed second officer, sir.'

'I've heard nothing. What on earth's become of Gray?'

'He was thrown by his horse. Near Shrewsbury, I believe. Broke his neck, poor fellow.'

'What a shocking business,' says the Captain.

'The owners engaged me to replace him – at short notice, as I believe they say in their letter to you.'

The Captain now opened up the letter and scanned it. Apparently satisfied, he offered his hand to Moxon.

'They sing your praises,' says he, 'I'm glad to welcome you aboard the *Saracen*.' Then, with a shake of his head: 'Poor Gray. It's an unhappy start to a voyage.'

They talked for a few moments more, then Moxon took his leave, and passing me, made me a bow, and wished me 'Good day.'

He was older than me, twenty-six or twenty-seven I guessed, with hair and eyes as black as jet, like a certain type of Cornishman who has Spanish blood in his veins from Armada days. He was lean and tall, and bore himself like a seaman, though his coat was of a better cut than most sailors affect. He went below, and I strolled to the rail to observe a fresh arrival.

A dilapidated hackney-coach, very down in the springs, was drawing up at the foot of the gang-way. From this decrepit equipage stepped an old woman so wrapped about with plaids and shawls, it was a wonder she could move at all, and wearing on her head a monstrous black bombazine bonnet. She was as squat as a bulldog, and under the bonnet looked not unlike one. She certainly behaved like the worst-tempered old bulldog you ever saw, for she immediately began to berate the coachman, threatening and complaining, in a broad Scotch dialect.

But by now I had no eyes or ears for Black Bonnet, for a second and much more interesting figure had emerged from the coach, a young lady of about my own age, the most bewitchingly beautiful young lady I had ever seen.

She was tall, and slender, and under a Spanish lace veil her lustrous black hair fell in long ringlets. She was dressed altogether in the Spanish style and her gown, when new, must have been very fine, though it was now much the worse for wear.

I stared at her, completely entranced, and she must have felt my gaze for she looked up at me suddenly with eyes of dark amber. I blushed to the roots, and she smiled. I returned her smile but she seemed suddenly to recollect herself and turned her head away, proud and haughty, 'nose in the air' as the saying is. I very nearly burst out laughing for her manner reminded me exactly of those genteel Oxford landladies who never cease to boast of their important connections and former affluence while letting rooms at five shillings a week, and woe betide if you're a day late with the rent!

The old Scotch scold and her grand companion now mounted the gangway to where Captain Parker was waiting to receive them. He bowed, and a word of welcome was forming on his lips when Black Bonnet said very imperiously and rudely: 'Are you the Captain?'

Parker admitted it.

'Then ye'll have had my letter, no doubt,' says Black Bonnet. 'McPhail's my name, governess to Señorita Isabella Zorilla' – with a gesture towards her charge – 'and *personally responsible* to her uncle, His Excellency Don Jaime de Pachero, for her well-being.'

'She could not be in safer hands, I'm sure,' returned the Captain drily.

Black Bonnet darted him a suspicious look then declared that she'd be glad to inspect her quarters – immediately!

The Captain shouted for Gridley, catching my eye as the boatswain made his way from the foredeck.

'Madam,' says he to Black Bonnet, taking up his cue, 'may I present Mr Hawkins, a fellow passenger.'

Black Bonnet, turning suddenly, and, I suppose, seeing the direction of my own eyes, which was towards Señorita

Isabella, said: 'No! Ye may not!' And with a 'Come, my girl,' to her charge, off she stalked behind Gridley. I caught the Captain's eye again and we both burst out laughing.

Then I went to look for Ben, but could find him nowhere, and was told that he'd run ashore on some errand, which surprised and annoyed me. I went back on deck in time to witness yet a third arrival, the most dramatic of all. A tumult of shouts all along the quay – 'Make way!' 'Stand aside!' – heralded the arrival of a horseman.

Pulling in his mount, and jumping down at the gangway, he ran up on to the deck and hastened towards the Captain, who was on the poop. From the livery and badges he wore, I could tell that he was a King's Messenger.

He spoke low and rapidly to the Captain, handed over a leather wallet, then marched back down the gangway, mounted his horse, and vanished as fast and mysteriously as he had appeared.

Many eyes had observed this exchange, none more keenly than those of Moxon. He saw that I was watching him and gave me a smile and a nod with a carelessness that was just a shade too studied to be real. The Captain ordered Moxon to muster the hands for sea, then went below to his cabin, with the wallet tucked into his coat.

Since we were so imminently to set sail, I inquired urgently after Ben and was told that he had slipped aboard and was slinging his hammock aft.

When I questioned him about his errand ashore, Ben was so incomprehensibly long-winded and obscure that a child of three could have told that he was hiding something.

On a sudden inspiration I asked him if he had seen Silver. 'Silver!' says he, with a great start, 'I ain't no friend to Silver, nor ain't he been no friend to Ben Gunn. I be *passenger* aboard this ship, Jim, and don't owe no "Aye, aye, sir" to no man, and not to John Silver neither!'

Which told me that Ben had performed some service for Long John, who had a hold over his old shipmate like that of a snake over a bird. But it was not the time to press him for the men were at the capstan, with a 'Yo, Ho, Ho!', warping the ship off the quay, and hands were swarming on the bowsprit, shaking out the jibs to catch the offshore breeze.

My voyage had begun, and I was too full of emotions, both joyful and sorrowful, to worry about Silver's machinations.

We beat up the sound in a spanking breeze, with royals and t'gallants set, and I stood at the rail as the Devon coast slowly receded from view. I thought of the Admiral Benbow, and my mother teaching the new manservant the ways of the house, the Squire in his Hall, the Doctor in his house nodding over his book, and looked my last upon England for many, many months.

Chapter VII

Man Overboard!

I will not labour the first part of our voyage, which was prosperous enough, though the Bay of Biscay lived up to its reputation with a furious blow, during which some of the hands swore they heard Mistress McPhail's voice raised in prayer through the locked door of the ladies' cabin.

But before proceeding to the two mysterious deaths that presaged events still more violent, I should give some account of life on board the good ship *Saracen*.

She was a well-found barque, very cramped as to quarters, but a weatherly vessel. Captain Parker was a most excellent master, who thoroughly knew his trade, would have everything Bristol fashion, but was nonetheless liked and respected by the crew.

Moxon, too, was a good officer, though I liked him less than the Captain. He was affable enough, but I could never escape the feeling that he was secretly laughing at everybody; those smiling black eyes of his seemed to contain, at the back of them, a kind of mockery.

But the source of real discord in our company was Gridley, the boatswain. Harsh and brutal, he was hated and feared by the crew, though, I heard, most of his cruelties were reserved for the prisoners. Of these, including Silver, we saw nothing at all, for the Captain was strict about their segregation. He had, he told me, had a fine old racket with the owners when he heard that he was to transport felons, for he anticipated nothing but trouble. However, the government was paying a pretty penny for their passage, and a shipowner loves a profit more than a Mincing Lane money-lender.

Mr Morgan, when he was not chewing his quill over a sermon for the services which he regularly conducted, was scratching his head over the plans he was drawing for the church he was to build on the Squire's plantation. Mr Trelawney had given him a piece of land and a contribution of money for this project, and when Mr Morgan discovered my connection with his benefactor, and that I was Agent to the plantation, he eagerly involved me in all the perplexities of roof-trusses, foundations, and thatching.

Vanderbrecken, though a man of very few words, was a fine companion, who loved nothing better than to watch the dolphins cavort in the foam streaming from the bow. He was a trader in rare timbers, and had a great forest in Mexico, to which he was returning *via* Jamaica, where he had left his boat.

'Wood, yes, fine wood,' he said 'to make pretty things for Lords and Ladies, and Princelings, and Bishops. It is very ridiculous, I think.'

When I asked him why, he laughed.

'Because it is hard, my friend. The earth guards its treasures well. It does not yield them up so easily – no. I trek through wild places, dangerous places, I risk my life – and all to adorn a great lady's commode! Ridiculous!'

The mention of great ladies leads me naturally to Señorita Isabella and her Guardian Demon of the black bonnet. For the first several weeks we saw nothing at all of these ladies: they never left their quarters – through sea-sickness we supposed. But later, when they had found their sea-legs, we had to revise this opinion, and conclude that their want of sociableness was due to pride.

After Biscay, they would appear upon deck twice in the day, at regular hours in the morning and evening, to take the air. Black Bonnet would exchange a few words, very uncivil, with the Captain or Mr Morgan, but the Señorita never opened her lips. Nor would they ever consent to dine in the Captain's cabin, as the other passengers did, but took their meals in their own quarters, Black Bonnet never failing to complain about the quality of the victuals.

In this she would have had the support of the whole ship's company, for the cook, a waddling, greasy hog's lard of a man, was the very vilest manufacturer of rancid soups and pestilent stews I ever encountered.

It was at a dinner, prepared by this poisoner, in the Captain's Great Cabin in the stern, that we first heard of Seaman Baker's sudden and strange death.

'Gentlemen, I apologize,' said Captain Parker as we attacked our soup.

Moxon winced as he tried his, and Vanderbrecken made a grimace; only Mr Morgan, whose taste was invulnerable to the most noxious products of the galley, fell to with an appetite.

'Horrible,' said Vanderbrecken. 'But many times, in the forests, I haff been starving, so always, if I haff food, I eat.'

'If they're serving this slop to the hands,' said Parker, 'I'll have a mutiny!'

Moxon raised his glass.

'I propose the traditional toast, gentlemen. Damnation to Spain!'

'I drink to that,' said Vanderbrecken heartily.

'Mr Moxon,' said the Captain frostily, 'I'd remind you that we're at peace with Spain. In any case, we have more to do with the French these days.'

'At peace! Yes!' says Vanderbrecken, sarcastically, 'with

every Spaniard looking for an English throat to cut and every English looking for a Spanish ship to sink!'

'We'll have no peace in the New World until every last Spaniard has been extirpated,' Moxon returned, surprisingly passionate, for cool and collected was his usual style.

'There'll be no peace,' says Mr Morgan suddenly, 'until God's word has been proclaimed in every continent and island, sir,' – this to Moxon, of whom he disapproved, for the second officer was no great attender of religious services.

'If you'll forgive my saying so, Reverend,' returns Moxon, rather sneering, 'religion would appear to be the cause, rather than the prevention of war, Catholic against Protestant.'

'No, sir,' replied Morgan hotly. 'Religion is made the pretext, God forgive us. The root of all strife and bloodshed between nations is the greed for land; Englishman, Frenchman, Spaniard, Dutchman at each other's throats for possession, as if God's creation was a joint of meat to be carved up between them.'

At this interesting point, Gridley came in, his unpleasing features more grim than ever, and whispered something to the Captain. The Captain started, and, looking very solemn of a sudden, rose, and summoned Moxon. With no further explanation, he, Moxon, and Gridley quit the cabin.

They returned five minutes later with bad news. Baker, one of the hands, had been found dead with a broken neck at the foot of the fo'c'sle ladder.

It seemed that the man had got at the rum rations, for there had been a reek of grog about him.

'He must have missed his footing,' said Moxon. 'Well, he's paid the price for his drunkenness, poor devil.'

But the Captain seemed dissatisfied.

'A seaman of twenty years' service may be as tipsy as an Irish fiddler,' says he, 'but he don't fall down a ladder.'

Baker was buried at sea the next day and the whole ship's company turned out to hear Mr Morgan 'commit his body to the deep, to be turned into corruption, looking for the resurrection of the body, when the sea shall give up her dead.'

From the enquiries I heard that the Captain was making, it was plain that he suspected foul play, and there was another of like mind, a most unlikely investigator – Ben Gunn.

Now I had wormed the truth out from Ben about his mission ashore before we sailed. It was, as I thought, at Silver's bidding, but Ben swore by every Saint in the Calendar that it had been only to procure Long John a bottle of rum. Ever since this confession, however, he had been shy of me, nursing, I supposed, a troubled conscience. But now, directly after the rites were over, he drew me aside, very confidential and important, and gave me to understand (or so, in the end, I understood) that murder had been committed.

'Shipped a nip too much o' the grog! Two sheets in the wind! That's *their* notion,' says he, 'but it ain't Ben Gunn's. For he weren't no tippler, Baker, not he, leastways not in my way o' reckonin'.'

'I think the Captain's with you there,' said I.

'Mebbe he is,' says Ben, and then with a solemn wink, 'but 'e don't know what Ben Gunn knows.'

'What's that?'

'Ah,' says Ben, 'I seen what I seen.'

'What have you seen?'

'Him with the Evil Eye!' was the mysterious reply.

I established eventually that he meant Moxon. He had, he said, seen Moxon and Baker together, talking privately, and in no very friendly way. Creeping closer, he had heard a snatch of their conversation, a few words only: 'The Great Cabin,' and 'I advise silence,' – both from Moxon.

I thought I should communicate this to the Captain straight away, but he was already aware of it, Moxon himself having told him. The explanation was that Moxon had discovered Baker in the stern cabin, plundering the Captain's strong drink, it was supposed. Wishing to spare the seaman a punishment, for he was a good hand, Moxon had given him a private warning.

'And do you believe it?' I asked the Captain.

'I am forced to,' he replied. 'For what possible reason could Mr Moxon have to harm Baker?'

The incident was closed; but it continued to have an effect, for most of the crew thought that their shipmate had been done to death, and there was suspicion and discontent where once harmony and good fellowship had reigned.

Less than a week later, the second death occurred.

I remember the night it happened better than what I had for dinner yesterday, for it was the first time I spoke to Señorita Isabella Zorilla.

We were now passing rapidly into the Tropics and the weather was blazing hot by day, and sultry by night, and the winds were less favourable than previously. Late one night, unable to sleep because of the stifling heat in the cabin, I decided to take a turn on deck. There I found Señorita Isabella, alone, gazing up at the velvet Heaven, which seemed magnified to an immensity, and was all lit up with the dancing scintilla of a myriad of unfamiliar constellations. It was very still and peaceful, the helmsman nodding at the wheel, the watch half dozing. The breeze was slight, and hardly filled the sails, and the creak of the rigging was muted to a gentle slap, like the quiet rocking of a cradle.

'Good evening, Señorita,' I said, making my bow as she turned. 'A beautiful evening.'

She favoured me with a cold, disdainful look, drew her shawl tighter round her and said: 'I am cold. I think I will go below.'

Her voice was light and musical, and its Spanish inflexion gave to it a lilt that was wholly delightful.

I stood aside, bowed again, and very coolly wished her a good night. She could not disguise her surprise at this, and stopped.

'It is good, sometimes, to be *alone*,' says she.

I agreed that privacy was a rare commodity at sea,

adding: 'Still, we all regret that you and your companion cannot share our table.'

'Ah,' says she, with a very superior smile, 'but you see I am spoiled. In my father's palace in Sevilla I learned to appreciate the conversation of noblemen, poets, scientists.'

'It's from fear of being bored, then?' said I, and she inclined her head like an Infanta, and it was all I could do to stop myself laughing.

'Perhaps *you* would not bore me,' she said after a moment. 'You have been at Oxford.'

'You've been enquiring about me?' I said, my interest reawakening.

She ignored this and said: 'Your father is perhaps a man of importance?'

'He's been dead many years,' said I, 'but you are right. He was the *most* important man in our part of the country.'

'The Seigneur?'

'Oh, much more important than that. He kept the only inn for miles about.'

This revelation shocked her.

'An innkeeper!' she said with a shudder. 'You don't have the appearance of an innkeeper's son.'

'How many such do you number among your acquaintance?'

'I number only *gentlemen* among my acquaintance. I mistook *you* for a gentleman.'

I was about to observe that she was wiser now when the peace of the night was rent by a howl of terror and a mighty splash.

I ran at once towards the foredeck, whence the sound had come, and almost collided with one of the watch, who cried: 'Man overboard!', then jumped to the ship's bell and rang it furiously.

I peered out over the rail and thought I saw a dark shape, like a porpoise, in the sea, and heard faint cries. By now all was confusion as the hands came tumbling up from the fo'c'sle, and the Captain strode forward, rubbing the sleep from his eyes, shouting to the helmsman to heave to.

With the sails full aback, and cracking like pistol-shots over our heads, the Captain called over the muster, while Gridley and two hands cut loose the jolly-boat to attempt a rescue. But this action was called off when the cook failed to answer to his name, for it was known that he could not swim, and since he had been in the water for ten minutes, it was certain that he was drowned.

A low whispering and muttering now started up among the crew assembled amidships. I heard one old salt growl, 'This cruise be accursed,' and another, rolling his quid, 'There's the furies loose as'll see us all to Davy Jones,' for your ordinary Jack Tar has more superstitions than a Gaelic grandam. Nor are these sailors' fancies – Mermaids and Harpies and the rest – a matter for mirth merely, for dread of them can spread like a plague below decks and rot a good crew faster than the scurvy.

Our Captain knew this well enough, and swiftly applied the best remedy, which was to order hands aloft, and luff alee to catch the freshening breeze. In a moment the ratlines were aswarm, and men were bending to the sheets with a will, the Captain himself leading them in a shanty, and Moxon raising a laugh from the harder-hearted by telling them that the sharks would dine well off our late cook – and would all be poisoned. I looked about to find Señorita Isabella, only to a meet a basilisk glare from Black Bonnet as she shooed her charge below. Reflecting that there was at least one fury loose aboard, I turned in.

I awoke early next morning and went on deck. Immediately, my nostrils were assailed with the most glorious fragrance of frying pork and new-baked bread from the galley, which was built under the poop.

I had only ever known one sea-cook to create such succulencies in a ship's galley, and sure enough, there was Long John Silver, leaning on his crutch and burnishing a pan until it shone, very grey from his long confinement in the prison hold, but grinning cheerfully.

'Top o' the mornin' to ye, Jim,' says he.

Chapter VIII

In the Doldrums

Now anyone even distantly acquainted with Silver's true character, would have accounted it a very fortunate coincidence indeed that the ship's cook should have gone overboard and that Long John should have replaced him so immediately, thus gaining for himself not only a respite from his dismal confinement, but a fair degree of freedom to move about the decks and to fraternize with the crew.

Long John read these thoughts of mine like a book.

'Aye,' says he, 'I never thought as how I'd thank my stars for bein' clapped in irons, but if so as I hadn't been, why, I reckon there'd be folk as'd be entertaining dark suspicions of John Silver.'

Here, the Captain and the boatswain stopped by the galley, and Parker asked to taste the bread.

'Remarkable,' says he to Silver, positively smacking his lips. 'Well, the berth's yours if you want it. It confers no special privilege, mind. And if you abuse my trust—'

'No fear o' that, sir!' chirps Long John with a respectful salute. 'A whiff o' sea breeze, that's privilege enough for me.'

'I should think it is,' says Parker. 'But in case it isn't, Mr Gridley has orders to watch you like a hawk.'

'God bless ye, sir,' said Silver, as the Captain walked away.

I accompanied him, for I had half a mind to warn him about Silver. But he forestalled me, saying: 'Every instinct tells me that man is an incorrigible villain.'

I provided him with some choice examples of Long John's past villainies, but he only sighed and declared: 'Ah, but he cooks like an angel.'

I said no more, but took a resolution to put the Captain wise at the first opportunity, for he had no idea that Silver was capable of stirring up a company of archangels to mutiny against Heaven itself, and that nothing less than mutiny would serve his turn.

I confided my fears to Vanderbrecken, but he pooh-poohed them.

'Mutiny!' says he. 'Bah! This crew purrs like a cat by a fire! They grow too fat for mutiny!'

This was a fact. With Silver's arrival in the galley, the whole atmosphere of the ship was transformed. It was not just that the hands were now better fed; Silver's arts only began at the stewpot. He had a cheery word, or a joke, or a sea-song for everybody, high and low. He could spin a yarn better than an Irishman, and the younger hands were spellbound by his tales of Spanish plate-ships, and keel-haulings, of legendary pirates like England and Flint, of desperate deeds, and gold to swim in, and rum to drown yourself in the taverns of Tortuga. Why, he even won over Black Bonnet herself, for I saw her one day at the galley door chuckling and wheezing at some jest of Silver's until I thought she'd burst her stays.

'That man's a tonic!' said the Captain. 'He's worth duff and double grog to any ship's company.'

In other words, Long John Silver was doing exactly as he had done aboard the *Hispaniola*, ingratiating himself with one and all, and fooling them to the top of their bent! But nobody wanted to listen to me and I told myself that even Silver could hardly prevail against an honest crew, and well-armed officers, without allies. In any case, I had other business to occupy me.

One evening, Ben Gunn drew me aside with a new piece of evidence about Mr Moxon. It was a very rambling narrative but it came down to this: that during the night watch, when Moxon was on duty, he had sent away the helmsman on some pretext, and had then got out a lantern, which he used to make signals to some other ship. I could make little of this tale, and was inclined to think that Ben had been at the rum, so said nothing to the Captain. But I began to watch Moxon closely, and the closer I observed him, the more convinced I became that there was something false about the man. It was only an impression, however, and I kept it to myself.

A few days after this the weather changed. The breeze died, the air grew as hot by night as by day, the sea was flat and oily, and seemed to sizzle like porkfat in a pan. The Captain declared that he had encountered such doldrums before, and that they were always shortly relieved by a violent squall. But day after day crawled by, with the sails flapping dismally, the pitch bubbling in the timbers, and the tempers of everybody on board becoming uglier and uglier in the unendurable swelter. To make matters worse, it was discovered that over half our casks of fresh water were foul, and we were all, passengers not excepted, put on quarter rations, so that thirst was added to our other torments.

'I don't like it, gentlemen,' said the Captain. 'I don't like it at all. Doldrums turns any ship's company into a powder keg.'

Ah-hah, thinks I, here's your chance for a mutiny, Silver.

But on the contrary Silver was a positive boon, an inexhaustible fountain of cheerfulness, tirelessly rallying the down-hearted, and contriving to produce victuals we could all stomach, which seemed miraculous, and which earned him the right, not questioned even by Gridley, of coming and going much as he pleased.

But still I felt that the Captain was right and that we lived on top of a powder keg which wanted only a spark to light it. That spark came through the agency not of Silver but of Gridley and Moxon between them.

It happened like this.

The fresh-water barrel for the hands was lashed to a stanchion near the galley, with one of the mates, armed with a musket, standing guard over it night and day. I was lolling nearby, late one afternoon, trying to persuade myself that I could feel a whisper of a cooling breeze, when I saw two of the hands, Simpson and Roberts, approach for their ration.

Roberts was a young fellow, about my own age, a great admirer of Long John, whom he called 'a true old sea-dog,' and very popular with his mates. Simpson was the oldest, steadiest hand aboard, and deserved the epithet 'old sea-dog' better even than Silver.

Roberts drew his ration and took a gulp. At once he spat it out, with an oath.

'It's brine!' he gasped, half choking on it.

At this, Gridley stepped out from the shadow of the mainmast, where he had been watching.

'Foul my deck would you, Roberts?' he snarled, striding forward. 'I'll have the skin off your back if you do.'

Now the boatswain's temper had been shorter than ever of late, and he had been spoiling for some trouble. Roberts knew this and replied, very fair: 'Meant no disrespect, Mr Gridley, sir, but this water ain't fit to drink.'

'That's you, Roberts,' returns Gridley, 'forever griping and grousing.'

He thrust out a hand for Roberts's mug, seized it, and took a sip of water.

'A mite brackish,' says he, 'but sweet enough for fo'c'sle scum.'

Handing back the mug, he commanded Roberts to drink it off. At this, old Simpson attempted to pour oil.

''E means no 'arm, sir,' says the old man, 'but truly it's tainted.'

Gridley ignored him and said to Roberts: 'I'll see no wanton waste on this ship. Drink it, you swab.'

'I won't,' Roberts replied through his teeth.

'Won't you, so?' says Gridley very softly. Then, with complete suddenness, he lashed out, knocking the mug from Robert's hand, and sending it spinning across the deck.

'Then you can scrub your filth off my deck,' the boatswain roared, 'and drink nothing 'til you knows your dooty!'

I could see plain murder in young Roberts's eyes and so could Simpson, for he attempted to lay a steadying hand on his mate's arm. But Gridley brushed him aside and stepped right up to Roberts, determined, it seemed, to provoke a breach of discipline.

'You won't talk so saucy,' says Gridley, 'when your tongue's cleavin' to your mouth.'

'No, Joe!' cries Simpson, but too late, for Roberts's fist shot up, delivering a blow to Gridley's jaw that sent the boatswain reeling.

Gridley picked himself up off the deck, wiping a smear of blood from his lips, which were twisted into a smile of triumphant cruelty.

'You'll pay for this with your hide, Roberts,' he snarled.

Roberts pulled out his clasp-knife and advanced on Gridley.

'I pay wi' my neck,' he panted.

'*Roberts!*'

Moxon's voice rang our clear as a clarion from the poop-rail. Roberts hesitated, stopped for a moment by an officer's command. But his blood was up, and shaking the sweat from his brow, he continued his advance on the boatswain.

'Mr Mate!' raps Moxon. 'Your musket! Shoot him down!'

The mate raised his musket and was about to fire when old Simpson darted forward and threw his arms round Roberts to spoil the other's aim. Moxon, meanwhile, had run forward, summoning hands, and in a few moments, but not without a struggle, Roberts was secured.

'Did he strike you, Mr Gridley?' Moxon asked the boatswain.

'He did, sir.'

''Twere he provoked it,' Roberts shouted.

'That's the truth, sir,' says Simpson.

Moxon paid no heed to the old man.

'Fifty lashes, Roberts. Dawn tomorrow, at eight bells. Take him below and put him in irons.'

Roberts was dragged away, still protesting that he had been deliberately provoked, and Moxon turned on his heel and stalked back to his post on the poop.

I too moved away but not before I saw Silver beckon to Simpson and hale him into the galley.

Captain Parker was in a rage with Moxon and I think half

the ship heard him berating his second officer in the Great Cabin. But of course, for the sake of discipline, he was bound to back him, and sanction Roberts's punishment.

I went to my berth that night in a very troubled frame of mind and slept but fitfully, which was as well because when Ben Gunn laid a hand on my arm, in the small hours, I was instantly awake.

'Jim,' hissed Ben in my ear, 'there's doings!'

Chapter IX

Mutiny

With no more explanation, and gesturing me to be silent, Ben led me for'ard towards the fo'c'sle. Below, the whole ship slept; atop, all was still save for the flap of the sails and the muffled tread of the watch. Moving like a wraith before me, Ben took me direct to the fo'c'sle door, which was closed, and showed me a crack in the planking through which I could see. I put my eye to it and peered inside.

The hammocks were swinging gently to the roll of the ship, but they were all empty. The whole crew, save those on watch, were sitting round in a ragged circle in the light of two smoking lanterns. Seated upon an upturned cask, pipe in mouth, was Long John Silver.

'Be these gentlemen of like mind to you?' says Long John, addressing himself to Simpson.

'They's ready to listen to you,' returned the old salt. 'Listen, mind – I don't undertake no more'n listen.'

'Very prudent, Mr Simpson,' says Long John, 'and wi' me that's a virtue.'

He bent forward, blowing upon the bowl of his pipe, and only then did it occur to me to wonder how he had got free, for he was put in irons every night.

'Well then,' says Long John, 'I'll speak straight. There's a dozen in the prison hold ready to fight alongside o' you for your rights, and you may lay to it.'

There was a general growl, partly approving, partly demurring.

'You'd not take this ship if you had twenty hands,' says one grizzled seaman, with which the majority appeared to agree.

'Takin' ships,' says Long John, 'that's a trade like any other, and I ain't no 'prentice, by the Powers! I got my learning from a master, aye, and his name were Captain Flint!'

The name of the legendary pirate had a great effect, especially with the younger men.

'I ain't sayin' we can't do it,' says Simpson, 'but what then? I ain't lookin' to be no buccaneer.'

There was a mutter of agreement from the older hands, which stopped suddenly at Long John's reply.

'Nor me neither,' he said, and went on in a silence you could touch: 'I'm lookin' to a fortune o' treasure as'll make every jack o' you richer than a Lord.'

'Bilges talk!' said the grizzled one, and there was some laughter, in which Long John joined heartily.

'You've a pretty wit, Billy,' says he, 'for such an ugly old barnacle,' so turning the laugh against Bill, who grumbled and spat while Silver went on: 'There's a passenger aboard this ship goes by the name o' Hawkins. A rich young gentleman – and I reckons I don't have no need to tell you how he came by his blunt. Aye,' and every man was staring at him, agog, 'Flint's treasure!'

'What were all took ten ten year ago,' says Simpson.

'Is that right, Mr Simpson?' Long John replied. 'All, says you. Not a half, says I – who was Flint's quartermaster!'

And then he went on, with an air of truthfulness that would have convinced Squire Trelawney himself: 'Ten long years I've knowed, ten long years I've had the secret, but Hawkins had the map, see, and he has it still, has it aboard – Flint's treasure map!'

At this there was an uproar of excitement, even Simpson and Bill joining in.

'So who's with me?' cried Silver, seizing the moment. 'Who's for mutiny and Treasure Island?'

Amid the cries of 'Silver for Captain!' and 'Silver for ever!' I turned away to see Ben Gunn lying prostrate behind me and one of the prisoners coming at me with a belaying-pin, with which he laid me out on the spot.

I came to my senses to find myself lying in the prison hold, which was deserted save for Ben Gunn, who was prone beside me. We were both trussed up like a couple of fowls for the oven and straitly gagged.

I had no idea of the hour but I reckoned that it might be getting on for dawn; nor could I fathom how Silver had effected his escape, and that of his fellow prisoners, from the stout locks and irons I could see hanging empty around me. But it was idle to speculate; my business was to get free myself, and as swiftly as I could.

Ben was recovered and, by signs of my head, I made him roll over so that his back was towards me, then I shuffled round until we were back to back, and I set to with my fingers to unloose the knots that bound his wrists.

It was a fearful business, for I could not see what I was doing, my hands were restricted by my own bonds, and those knots were as fast as only a seaman can tie. While I sweated and grunted over my task, my ears kept me pretty well informed of what was happening elsewhere.

I heard seven bells rung, which meant that in a half hour the watch would end and Roberts would be taken from his confinement, just for'ard of the Great Cabin, to be flogged with the cat-o'-nine-tails in front of the whole ship's company. It was not likely that any of the mates, or Gridley, or an officer should approach the fo'c'sle or the prison hold until after the punishment, so there was no help to be expected from that quarter. It was all up to me.

I fell on the knots again with a sob, twisting and pulling at the harsh fibres until my fingers were raw. At last, after what seemed like an age, I felt some slight loosening, and redoubled my efforts. A few moments later I had my way; the ropes parted, and Ben was free. He ripped the gag from his mouth, and while he untied me, told me breathlessly: 'Watch out fer squalls, Jim, for they've had the pistols 'n' muskets out of the armoury.'

At that instant, eight bells rang like a funeral knell.

Ben and I crept out of the prison hold, stealthy as cats, and stole towards the fo'c'sle ladder. Three of the prisoners were standing still on the ladder, their heads below the level of the deck, their backs towards us, and armed to the teeth. We moved on down the companion to find that it was the same story at the hatch amidships: four of them, this time, watching and waiting. From atop we heard the drumroll for the muster, and the Captain's clear voice addressing the hands.

I suddenly thought of the gun, for the *Saracen* carried a brass swivel-gun aft of the poop-deck.

There was the armoury to hand with the door shut but not fastened, for the lock had been sundered by the mutineers. In a trice we had powder and a sack of grape-shot and were making our way, swiftly and silently, to the Great Cabin in the stern.

My plan was to climb out of the transom window and up over the stern rail to the exact place where the gun was housed. You may ask why we did not take up muskets and attack the mutineers on the ladders, which we could easily have done; but this would only have given the alarm to the others and, like as not, started off a wholesale slaughter.

It was no difficulty to wriggle through the window on my back, then reach up to grasp the base of the flag-stanchion, and so haul myself up to a level with the poop. And here our luck came in, for the poop-deck was deserted. The wheel was lashed down, and the whole crew assembled amidships to witness the flogging. Better yet, the mizzen boom was yawing to larboard, and the mizzen-sail itself was acting like a curtain to mask most of the poop from the view of those on the lower deck.

I reached down and Ben passed me up the powder and

shot, then I gave him a hand and together we scrambled over the stern rail. Without further ado we had the tarpaulin jacket off the gun, and primed and loaded her.

All this time, Captain Parker had been talking to the men, telling them that Roberts was to receive just punishment for striking his superior, and exhorting them to stand by their duty, for he could see what mood they were in.

'Fifty lashes,' he said finally. 'Carry on, Mr Gridley.'

I crept forward to get a better look, and this is what I saw. Roberts, stripped to the waist, was lashed to the mainmast ratlines. Parker, Moxon, and the mates were standing under the poop, near the galley. Vanderbrecken was by the larboard rail, and the crew was in a big huddle between the mainmast and the foremast. Of Mr Morgan and the ladies there was no sign. Gridley, swinging the cat-o'-nine-tails, was stepping up behind Roberts.

Gridley raised the cat high for the first blow and in that instant a shot bellowed out from near the bowsprit, Gridley fell stone dead to the deck, and faster than my words can describe the prisoners on the ladders sprang out and had knives at the throats of the mates, and Moxon. Silver stepped out of the galley and put a pistol to the Captain's head.

In the profoundest silence I ever knew, old Simpson rolled over to where Roberts was stretched upon the ratlines and cut him down.

Leaving one of the prisoners to guard the Captain, Silver tucked his crutch under his arm and heaved forward to address the crew. In spite of his crutch, he moved like an Admiral on his quarter-deck, and when he spoke his voice rang with eager confidence.

'Listen to me, mates,' he began, and I slipped back to the gun, whispered an urgent instruction to Ben, and got out my tinder to light the torch.

'Gridley's dead,' Silver continued, 'and justice is done. I'm takin' this ship. For any man what's against me, there's a boat, and water, and vittles. For any man what'll join me, there's a swift cruise and a fortune at the end of it.'

At this I nodded to Ben, and he swung round the mizzen boom, as I swivelled the gun's barrel amidships.

'Or a knife in the back, more like!' I cried.

Silver screwed round, the blood draining from his face, while every other soul on board stood as if turned to stone.

I held the flaming torch aloft.

'Here's grape-shot for you, Silver, and any other man who moves,' I shouted.

Silver's voice rang out before mine had died away.

'And here's a pistol shot for Captain Parker!'

Chapter X

Deadlock

A further long silence followed these two declarations. We had reached deadlock, and I could not think what to do. A minute ticked slowly by, and then another, as we all stood fast, without moving, like figures in a *tableau*.

And then a shaggy, grey head appeared in the 'midships hatch and a strong Welsh voice said: 'Whatever's to do?'

Mr Morgan's sudden intrusion tipped Silver off his balance for a vital second that allowed Captain Parker to fling himself desperately at the sea-cook. Silver's pistol went off, but whether he hit Parker or not I could not see, for the whole of the deck amidships boiled suddenly up into violent action. I saw Vanderbrecken pick up the prisoner who'd been guarding him and fling him bodily over the side, and Moxon at grips with another.

Cutlasses were flying amongst the crew, and I picked up my own and ran forward to add my arm to the fray, for it was no use now to touch off the gun. But as I reached the stair, Moxon came flinging up, blood streaming from a cut across his face, yelling: 'Back! Back! Hold the poop! Faithful hands to the poop!'

Just then a stray musket ball grazed my forehead and I fell down, half in a faint.

The clash of steel and the roar of musketry receded and returned again, like waves sucking and hissing at a pebble beach. Vanderbrecken's powerful arms were round me, dragging me back towards the wheel. I saw one of the mates leading a few of the faithful hands on to the poop, and a press of mutineers behind them. Then there was a thunderous eruption like Judgement Day, and the mutineers turned and fled.

Moxon had touched off the swivel-gun.

Led by Ben Gunn, three of the faithful hands were swarming over the stern rail to secure the Great Cabin.

I turned to Vanderbrecken.

'The Captain!' I cried.

Vanderbrecken shook his great head.

'Silver's prisoner,' was all he said.

An hour later, when all was shaken down, we found ourselves still at deadlock. The ship was about equally divided between us and the mutineers. Above decks, we held the poop. Below decks, we had the Great Cabin, the armoury, and all the berths as far as the 'midships ladder, where we posted two guards, as did the mutineers, with three feet of dead space separating the two parties. The mutineers held the whole fore part of the ship, above and below decks, and an inspection of the armoury showed that they had got more than three-quarters of the weapons and powder. Meanwhile, the sun climbed over the horizon into a clear sky, with a promise of another day of merciless heat.

A conference was held in the Great Cabin, to which the ladies had been brought for their own safety, having locked themselves up in their cabin during all the bloodshed. Our position was dangerous. For a start we were outnumbered, one of the mates, and four of the faithful hands having lost their lives in the brush with the mutineers. On our side were Moxon, the First Mate, five hands, and the passengers,

Vanderbrecken, Morgan, and myself, not counting the ladies. The strength of Silver's force was difficult to calculate with complete accuracy, for we did not know how many had fallen during the fight, though Vanderbrecken and Moxon, between them, had accounted for three at least. But on any reckoning, Silver must have more than thirty, and some of them, the escaped prisoners, were desperate men with little to lose and everything to gain from an assault. We did, however, have some important advantages. Most of the food and water supplies were under our hand, and we had the gun, to discourage any attack across the deck.

Our most crippling disadvantage was the fact that Silver had the Captain hostage.

For three or four hours we heard not a word, and hardly a sound from the mutineers. I later found out that Silver had very nearly had a mutiny of his own, led by Simpson, who vowed that no harm should come to the Captain. No sooner had Silver talked Simpson round than he had to put down another rebellion from the former inmates of the prison hold, who were avid to get at the rum kegs.

Soon after noon, however, a white flag of truce appeared in the fo'c'sle hatch, and Silver's voice called out, demanding a parley with Jim Hawkins. Moxon was not pleased with this and was all for defiance, and letting time and the heat do its work, but Vanderbrecken supported me when I said that we should hear what Silver had to offer, and so it was agreed.

I felt the change in the weather the moment I stepped on deck. It was perceptibly cooler, and a thick sea mist was rolling in from the north and east. We'll have a squall before tomorrow, says I to myself, and that'll break the deadlock, one way or the other.

Long John was standing under the lee of the foremast. He took the pipe from his mouth and greeted me in the friendliest manner with, 'Sit ye down, Jim, sit ye down.'

And so we sat down, he on the stern of the upturned gig, I on a cask lashed to the mast.

'Well, Jim,' says he, 'let's not beat about. I've got the Captain, and you've got the long nine,' by which he meant the swivel-gun.

'That's not all we have,' says I. 'We have the water and the food.'

'I've forty against your ten, all desperate men, athirst for blood if it comes to a fight.'

'We don't intend to fight,' said I. 'We can afford to wait.'

With that I looked out to sea, where in the past few minutes the mist had made great strides across the flat water, and was now starting to envelop the ship in an impenetrable fog.

I turned back to catch Silver's eye. He was nodding and smiling, thinking, with some justice, that a fog would stand him in good stead.

'You don't want to wait too long, Jim,' said he. ''Sides, where's the sense, since you and I can settle this business and agree articles.'

Tapping the dottle from his pipe, cool as you like, he continued: 'Give me what's mine, give me Flint's map, and . . .'

'And what?'

'I takes the long-boat an' a crew o' three, and slips my cable, and you has Captain Parker, safe and sound.'

Even I, accustomed as I was to Silver's treachery, was stupefied for a moment by this double-dealing.

'What of the other mutineers?' I said stupidly.

He shrugged. 'Wi' me gone, they'll parley for terms, most likely, an' if not, well, without me to lead 'em they'll be putrid wi' grog — I reckon you'll make pork of them wi' no more trouble than a petrel takes a sprat.'

And with that he leaned back and started to fill his pipe with plug.

I did not know what to think. On one hand Silver's bargain offered a swift way out of our present predicament. On the other I could not stomach the notion of his getting clean away with the map. Besides, there was no guarantee that, once in possession of it, he would not turn his coat again, for a well-found barque would take him to Treasure Island quicker and safer than an open boat.

'Well, Jim?' says Silver quietly.

'I must put it to my friends.'

'Aye, aye,' says he, 'so you must. But they'll listen to you, mate, they'll take your affy-davy, so what'll you tell 'em, Jim?'

I looked him straight in the eye.

'This,' said I. 'That you're no more to be trusted than a Frenchman, and that for my part I'd see you to Davy Jones.'

The blood rushed into his face, and the stem of his pipe snapped between his fingers. Flinging down the broken pieces with an oath, he leaned forward, his eyes burning.

'You mark me well, Jim,' he says, his voice trembling with rage, 'I've a fondness for you, more'n any other living being save one – who goes by the name o' John Silver. Stand against me and by the Powers I'll cut you down, and you may lay to that!'

I continued to meet his eye and for a minute we glared one at another. Then Silver looked away, out to sea – and let out a gasp as if he was taken with a stroke.

'Blood o' the Devil,' he cried, 'Spaniards!'

I whipped round my head to see five or six long-boats darting out of the mist with the sinister speed and silence of sharks' fins.

The boats were crammed to the gunwales with Spanish Musketeers – the scourge of the Caribbean.

Chapter XI

A Secret of State

Silver was up and roaring, 'Attacked! We're attacked! Simpson! Roberts! To arms! Lively you swabs!' and the ring of his voice was proof enough to his confederates that here was no trick, but mortal danger. I pelted to the 'midships hatch, flung myself down the ladder, and heedless of the mutineers on guard, ran to the Great Cabin to rouse Moxon, Vanderbrecken and the others. In a moment that divided ship was at one again, shoulder to shoulder, united by the greater external threat of the Spanish.

But too late.

Before the Captain could assemble a disciplined defence, the Spaniards had boarded, score upon score of them, an overwhelming invasion.

Ask any old soldier to describe a battle and you will get, at best, a series of impressions, without any connecting thread, for, in a battle, your world shrinks down to yourself and the enemy who's lunging at you, and you have eyes for little else.

What with the fog, and the smoke of muskets, and the blood and sweat running into my eyes, my memory is all a blur of thrust and parry, and howling death-cries, and slipping and sliding in gore, from which only three clear pictures stand out: Vanderbrecken laying about him, a giant among pygmies, spitting Spaniards on the end of his long sword with terrible effect; Silver roaring damnation and defiance, parrying with his crutch, and hacking with his cutlass, invincible and devastating; and Captain Parker driving two Spaniards back towards the poop with neat, short jabs, British style, until he was suddenly struck down from behind by his own second officer!

I believe I was the only man aboard to witness this enormity, and it very near cost me my life, for my opponent, a Spanish officer with black moustachios, took advantage of my distraction to have at me with his poniard. I dodged his attack in time, and riposted with an energy that settled my gentleman. Then I tore off in pursuit of Moxon, who had vanished below.

I hacked my way to the 'midships hatch, struggled past two bodies that were half-blocking the ladder, and so down, and towards the Great Cabin. I stopped at the door, which was half open. After the ghastly clamour of the battle raging above, it seemed preternaturally quiet below decks. Moxon was at the Captain's bookshelf, his back towards me. He was rapidly removing the volumes, flinging them aside. I stole closer.

The removal of the books revealed the small, square iron door of a safe, built into the bulkhead. Moxon let out a gasp of triumph, took out a key from his pocket, and fitted it in the lock of the safe. The thought that this must be the Captain's key rifled from his body, made my temples throb with rage.

'Mr Moxon!' I cried.

He jumped like a startled hare and flung round, his face as white as powder. But as I advanced on him he recovered himself and whipped up his rapier.

At the first clash I knew I had to deal with a swordsman, for he feinted and thrust with the elegance and precision of a Bavarian duellist. At the same, I thought I should prevail, for I had been taught by Angelo, the Italian master, which had cost me five hundred guineas – the best bargain I ever made! All his skill notwithstanding, Moxon could not break my guard, and I slowly drove him backwards, towards the transom window. It was warm enough work, for he disputed every inch, but fury at his treachery lent me energy, and at last I hooked his blade from his hand, and had my point at his throat.

'Now,' says I, 'we'll have the truth. Who and what are you?'

'He is Don Esteban de Cordova,' answered a thick Spanish voice from behind me.

Keeping my point against Moxon's throat I turned my head. Standing in the door were two Spanish musketeers, their weapons aimed directly at me, and a richly dressed officer. It was this last who had spoken, and who spoke again, commanding me to throw down my sword. I had no other choice, for though I could have killed Moxon with a thrust, I should have been shot down immediately. As I lowered my blade Moxon sprang to the safe. The key was still in the lock, and Moxon turned it, and opened the safe.

'What is he?' the Spanish officer said, advancing towards me. 'He is a confidential agent of His Most Catholic Majesty, the King of Spain.'

'Amen,' said Moxon, as he took from the safe the leather wallet that had been so mysteriously entrusted to the Captain at Plymouth.

I was taken away by the musketeers to the prison hold, and there clapped in irons alongside the survivors of the rout, for the vastly superior numbers of the Spanish had defeated us, and the ship was in Spanish hands.

There were only ten men left alive, but to my joy they included all my friends, Vanderbrecken, Morgan, Ben Gunn, and Captain Parker, who had not been seriously hurt. Long John Silver was also among the living, and the First Mate, and four of the hands, two of whom had been mutineers. Simpson and Roberts were both dead. Nobody knew what fate had befallen the ladies but since Señorita Isabella was Spanish, and high-born, it was a near certainty that they were safe. I instantly apprised the Captain of what had happened in the Great Cabin, and he looked very grim and solemn. I asked him what the wallet contained.

'I don't know,' says he, 'for it wasn't my business to look inside. Some secret of state, it must be.' Then, shaking his head: 'I should have seen what Moxon was; I blame myself.'

'Pray don't!'

It was Moxon's voice. He was standing in the entrance to the hold, and now came forward, smiling blandly.

'I have to inform you, Captain Parker, that this ship is a prize of war and that you and your men – those few who are left alive – are prisoners of war, as are these other gentlemen.'

'War!' says the Captain. 'There's been no declaration of war. It's piracy!'

'True enough,' says Moxon, with a shrug, 'but I merely anticipate, for war there will be. Let me enlighten you as to the contents of the wallet, which you were too delicate to examine for yourself. It contains secret dispatches from the First Lord to the Admiral of the Jamaica Fleet, with instructions highly prejudicial to the interests of Spain, so much so, indeed, that war, I think, will be the inevitable consequence.'

There was a silence, while the Captain glared. Then I asked Moxon right out: 'Did you murder Baker?'

Moxon smiled and shrugged again.

'He disturbed me while I was making a search of Mr Parker's quarters. A pity. It cost a deal of trouble, for there's been a Spanish man-o'-war just over the horizon since Biscay, ready to obey my signals.'

'And the cook?' cried the Captain.

Moxon shook his head. 'I cannot claim the credit for that. As I said before, you must not blame yourself, Captain. High politics is not for simple seamen.'

'Tell me you're Spanish-born,' said the Captain.

Moxon regarded him for a moment as if he was a strange fish at a fair, and then replied: 'My mother was a Spanish lady, but my father English.'

'Then you are a damnable traitor, sir!' thundered Parker.

'I think not,' returned Moxon, with another smile. 'When loyalty must be divided between mother and father, the lady surely takes precedence?'

And with that he turned on his heel and went away.

'Politics!' boomed Vanderbrecken, with a sulphurous Dutch oath. 'All the trouble in the world comes from politics!'

'Very true,' said Mr Morgan.

'We must act!' cried the Captain.

'Huh!' grunted Vanderbrecken, putting a volume into it.

'If we could but get free,' the Captain went on, very agitated. 'They've only a prize-crew aboard! Night! A surprise attack! We could do it, gentlemen! I know we could do it!'

'Ja,' says Vanderbrecken, with a rattle of his leg-irons, 'but how do we get free?'

At this, Silver spoke for the first time.

'Humbly cravin' your pardon, Captain,' says he, 'but would it be accordin' to orders for me to speak a word, sir?'

The Captain turned a cold and contemptuous eye on him.

'You'd best hold your tongue, fellow,' he said, 'for I've not forgotten your part in this, and by God, if we come out of it, I'll see you at the yard's end for mutiny, and if we don't, I'll follow you down to Hell and see you swing there!'

'Well now, there ain't no call to go that far,' says Silver, utterly unabashed. 'We're in a fix, right enough, holed and sunk, as you might say, but not so as John Silver mayn't contrive to warp us away.'

'Well, say on, man,' said the Captain, in some exasperation as Silver fell mute.

'Well, sir,' says Silver, 'it seems you requires arms. You'll find a handy store not a yard from where you're standing, what was concealed for – a purpose, and what the Dons ain't struck.'

'Purpose! I know very well what the purpose was!' says the Captain furiously. 'And what the devil's the use of arms while we're in irons?'

'Appertainin' to that, sir,' says Silver, 'it may be that I can answer you.'

And again he fell silent.

'Speak out, man!' roared the Captain.

'So I could,' returned Silver, with an insolent coolness, 'but you talks o' yard-arms, and swingin', and that don't encourage a man.'

Swallowing his fury with great difficulty, the Captain replied that, naturally, if Silver returned to his duty with good effect, it would be taken into account in mitigation for his previous crime.

'Would that run to a King's pardon, now, sir,' says Silver, 'seein' as it's the King's business we're about?'

Wellnigh choking on the words, the Captain replied that he would do his best to obtain a pardon.

At which Silver nodded, and with, 'That's fair, I reckon,' took from a pocket a curiously wrought metal object, like a key. In a word, it was a picklock, such as thieves use. Its production solved, for me at all events, a great many mysteries. It was the explanation of Ben Gunn's errand ashore in Plymouth, for plainly the picklock had been concealed by some confederate of Silver's in the bottle of rum. It destroyed Long John's alibi for the death of the cook, for which I was now certain (though he always denied it) that he had been responsible. It showed how he had released his fellow prisoners to play vanguard for the mutiny.

But, for the moment, the picklock meant salvation for all of us!

Chapter XII

A New Hostage

We waited for night to fall.

Our only hope lay in stealth and silence, and our plan was laid accordingly. We would sally from the prison hold and deal with the Spaniards one by one, using only knives or our bare hands so as to preserve secrecy and surprise until the very last moment. We were, like Gaul, divided into three parties. The first, consisting of Vandebrecken, Mr Morgan, and two of the hands, was to secure the fo'c'sle and the watch for'ard of the mainmast; the second, led by the First Mate, with Silver, Ben Gunn, and a hand, was to take the berths amidships, and then the watch on the poop; the third, composed of the Captain, the fourth hand, and myself, would make sure of the armoury and the Great Cabin.

The first obstacle to be overcome was the guard posted outside the prison hold itself, and Vanderbrecken volunteered for this task, which he accomplished without any one of us hearing a single sound.

'There's your model, men,' whispered the Captain, 'now, lay on, and God save the King!'

And so we stole forth, on our separate ways, to put the Union Jack back at the masthead of the *Saracen*.

All went very well. The Captain and I, with our fellow, made our way swiftly aft, encountering only two Spaniards, whom we settled with no fuss. As we crept towards the armoury, we heard behind us some muffled thuds and a cry, half choked off, which told us that Silver and his party were at their work.

A sole musketeer was standing guard at the armoury.

I lured him forth, by a low whisper from the shadows, and the Captain seized him from behind, improvising a useful garotte from a piece of a lanyard, overpowered him, and lowered him to the floor.

We now made direct for the Great Cabin to recover the dispatches, for which purpose I'd borrowed Long John's picklock, in case Moxon had put them back into the safe. But we had not moved a yard before a pistol-shot tore the silence asunder. In a moment, there was uproar. The Spaniards were roused!

'Up, up aloft!' roared the Captain. 'Fight 'em in the open!'

We tore up the ladder on to the deck, to meet a fusillade of musketry from the poop. The fore-deck was a swirl of flying cutlasses, and a platoon of Spaniards, led by Moxon, was pouring from the fo'c'sle hatch.

'At 'em boys for England!' cries the Captain. 'No quarter!' and down the deck he charged, his pistols accounting for two of the enemy, and his cutlass for a third.

On a sheer impulse I slid back down the ladder, which looks like desertion, I know, but I thought I'd take a leaf out of Moxon's book and go for the dispatches under cover of the fight.

The Great Cabin was deserted, though the meat was still steaming on the table. The picklock had the safe open double quick, and I thrust the precious wallet into my shirt. Then I was off and back up the ladder and on to the deck only to throw myself instantly down as the planks trembled to a roar of powder and grape-shot screeched over my head. Moxon had taken a leaf out of *my* book, and touched off the long nine!

That was the end of the battle, and all our hopes. Three of our hands lay dead, and we were surrounded and out-numbered. When Moxon shouted from the poop to us to lay down our arms, the Captain threw away his cutlass at once. The musketeers herded us together by the mainmast and I saw, with relief, that Ben Gunn at least was still standing, though of Silver there was no sign.

Moxon stalked down from the poop and I could see that he was in a raging passion.

'You're for the sharks,' he said, with a stream of oaths, 'all of you.'

'Avast, Moxon!'

It was Silver's voice, and it rang out sharp and clear across the deck like a bell. Every head turned towards where Silver was standing, on the larboard side, and I think that Moxon and I cried out together when we saw who it was he held in front of him like a shield.

It was Señorita Isabella, and Silver's knife was across her throat. 'If so you wants to see a Spanish lady's heart's blood spilled on to this deck,' says Silver, 'then disobey me.'

For one dreadful moment I thought Moxon would sacrifice the girl to his own vengeance and desperately prepared to fling myself upon him if he moved. But he did not stir, and I breathed more easy.

'Right then,' says Silver, crisp as a commander, 'you'll heave a barrel o' pork, an' two o' biscuit, an' a cask o' water into that long-boat,' indicating one of the Spanish boats still alongside.

Moxon nodded to his Sergeant of Musketeers, and two Spaniards ran off for the provisions, which they lowered into the long-boat. Through all this Silver never said a word, but stood steady as Gibraltar, his knife-blade not wavering an inch from Isabella's white throat. When the Spaniards had done: 'Jim Hawkins, Vanderbrecken, Morgan, you'll do for crew, so step to the side lively.'

I looked to Captain Parker, for I hated the thought of abandoning him, but he nodded shortly, and I followed the other two, at the same time motioning Ben to come with me, for I was bound I'd not leave him behind.

'I gave no orders 'bout Benjamin Gunn,' raps out Silver.

I faced him.

'He goes or I stay,' said I, and Silver could see that I meant it and after a moment jerked his head. Ben and I scrambled down the rope-ladder into the long-boat, where Vanderbrecken and Morgan were already ensconced. I was far from believing, however, that Silver's plan would be successful, for he had himself to negotiate the ladder – tricky enough for a whole man and very hard for a cripple – without once letting go of his hostage. I could not see how he would do it without exposing himself, and for sure Moxon was waiting for him to make a slip. Again, I had underestimated Silver's astonishing skill and dexterity.

He backed along the rail until he was by the ladder. Then he called out, 'Jim, stand by!', and threw down his crutch into the boat, where I caught it. Still holding the Señorita in front of him, and with his back still to seaward, he swung his good leg over the rail, and found the first rung with his boot. Gripping on to the rail with his left hand, he lifted the girl with his right arm, lifted her bodily over the rail, and supported her, holding her close, as if she weighed no more than a rag doll, as he swung down the ladder on his right foot and his left hand. Even Vanderbrecken watched in admiration at this tremendous feat of strength and balance.

Then Silver was aboard and sitting down with a gasp on the stern thwart.

'Ben, cast off,' he panted, 'you others, bend to the oars.'

Three strong pulls together took us away from the *Saracen*'s side, and then I shipped my oar.

Silver let out an oath but I ignored him and asked the lady if she could swim.

She nodded.

'Then let her go,' I said to Silver.

'So as Moxon can blow us all to Davy Jones wi' the long nine? Not me. You bend to your oar, mate, or by the Powers I'll show *you* the colour o' Spanish blood.'

There was nothing for it but to obey.

So we bent to the oars until the water was chuckling under our keel. The masts and yards of the *Saracen* vanished from sight into the mist, and we were upon the broad Caribbean Sea.

Part III

The Island of the Damned

Chapter XIII

Isabella

The predicted squall arrived three hours after dawn. It was heralded by a strongly freshening breeze that blew away the sea-mist in twenty minutes, to reveal the overwhelming immensity of ocean and sky.

The squall was followed by a storm that raged for five days without ceasing.

We owed our preservation to Vanderbrecken's expert helmsmanship and indomitable spirit, for even Silver quailed before the ferocity of the winds, and the monstrous, towering billows, while Señorita Isabella mopped and mowed, and Mr Morgan bellowed hymns and prayers in defiance of the elements, in which Ben Gunn fervently joined.

At last the storm blew itself out, the heavens cleared and we had sunshine and light airs. Vanderbrecken rigged up a jury sail to relieve our muscles, which were tortured into knots from rowing, and we were able to take stock.

We were none so badly placed (except that our provisions were running very low) for Silver had provided himself with a compass, a sextant, and a chart: his original plan, once he had betrayed his fellow mutineers, had been to run for the island of Machado, which Vanderbrecken told us was a sort of pirate republic.

When the Dutchman had taken his sightings and fixed our position, he showed Silver that the storm had blown us hundreds of miles to the east, whereas Machado lay to the west. He proposed that we should set our course for the nearest land, which was the island of Santa Anna. At this Silver blustered and threatened, attempting to maintain the pretence that he was still captaining our enterprise. To my astonishment he was seconded by Ben Gunn.

'Jim, Jim,' said Ben in a whisper, tugging at my sleeve, 'hold hard, matey, hold hard, that island ain't no place for a Christian. Why's that, says you? For the reason it's *accursed*, that's why!'

'Balderdash!' rumbled Vanderbrecken.

'The old fool's right at that,' said Silver.

'The Island o' the Damned, that's what they calls it, Jim,' Ben persisted. 'I wouldn't set foot in that place, not for a Dukedom, for they's all devils and lunatics.'

'Devils! Poppycock!' said Vanderbrecken.

He explained that the ownership of the island had, for a century, been in dispute between Holland and Spain. Under Spanish occupation it had been turned into a sort of Bedlam, where the Spaniards marooned lunatics and dangerous felons.

'They all killed each other, and then the last one killed himself,' said Vanderbrecken, with a grim chuckle, 'and that was twenty years ago, before Holland took it back. Now there are good Dutch farmers. I haff friends there, and they will help us.'

'That settles it, I reckon,' said Silver unexpectedly.

I caught Vanderbrecken's eye and read in it the same apprehension at Silver's sudden change of tune as was in my own mind. I still had Flint's map with me. With the secret state dispatches it was in the money-belt I wore under my shirt, and I would have been a blockhead indeed to suppose that Silver was not planning to steal it and get away. Here I should say that, before the squall struck, Silver had relieved us of our knives, and taken back his picklock from me.

We sighted Santa Anna two days later, and not before time, for our supply of water was exhausted. We made our landfall in the late afternoon, in a small cove of white sand, where the forest spread thickly down to the beach. Now I had paid no heed at all to the dark mutterings about lunatics and devils in which Ben Gunn had been indulging; but from the moment I jumped ashore on Santa Anna I was uneasy. I think I have an inborn instinct for danger, and I felt immediately that danger was lurking somewhere in that tangled, luxuriant jungle.

We secured the long-boat, and shouldering the empty casks, set off to look for water. We had expected to breathe cooler air in the forest but it was hotter and more oppressive than ever. A thin, fetid steam rose from the ground, which was a mulch of rotting vegetation. Strange bird-cries echoed and re-echoed among the dense shadows of the spreading trees, and they sounded uncannily like a lunatic's laughter. Clouds of stinging and biting insects assailed us, and we were constantly aware of a rustle of furtive movement in the dense undergrowth of bushes and creepers.

Half an hour's march brought us to a clearing through which a stream was flowing, and never in my life have I been more grateful for cold, fresh water. All of us, except Señorita Isabella, who was in the sulks, plunged into the stream, splashing like ducks, and soaking up pint after pint of the blessed water. We decided to make camp for the night and Ben volunteered to forage for provisions, for on Treasure Island he had learned to fend for himself and was a more accurate hunter with a sling and stone than Squire Trelawney with a fowling-piece.

He returned at dusk with a wild turkey that could have fed a ship's company, a sack of melons, berries, and tubers, and his pockets bursting with seeds, which he pounded into a pulse that tasted like nothing so much as porridge! A roaring fire and the aroma of roasting turkey completely revived our spirits and we sat down in a circle to feast off the fat of the land.

We made a genial company – except for Señorita Isabella who continued sulky and missish and did not disguise her disgust at our manners; when men are famished they are none too delicate about the way they sink their teeth into a sweet melon or a turkey leg!

'Eat! Eat!' Vanderbrecken exhorted her, his chin glistening with grease and melon-juice. 'It is good!'

'If you would trouble yourself to loan me your knife,' says the Señorita primly, 'I might be able to do so with a semblance of decency.'

(Silver had been prevailed upon to return our weapons to us.)

'Most humble apologies,' replied Vanderbrecken heavily, throwing her his knife. 'Tomorrow Milady shall have silver plate and crystal glasses.'

'We may be in the jungle,' says Milady, 'but we do not have to behave like animals.'

'Or prima-donnas,' I could not help putting in.

She went very white, stood up, and in a voice that quavered on the edge of tears said: 'Forgive me if I prefer my own company. Or am I still your prisoner?'

I instantly regretted my words and begged her to sit down again, but she swept past me and disappeared into the shadows.

'Bah!' growled Vanderbrecken. 'Airs and graces!'

I rose in order to follow her, for I wished to apologize, and I did not think she should be alone in the forest at night.

'Let her be,' said Vanderbrecken, but I ignored him.

She had not wandered very far and I soon found her, sitting upon a fallen tree where the stream bellied out into a pool. Her head was hanging down and her arms were wrapped about her as if she would comfort herself. In that savage, moonlit wilderness she was the very picture of forlorn misery and hopelessness. She did not look round as I approached, but remained still, staring at the ground.

'Señorita,' I said, 'I've come to beg your pardon and ask you to return to the safety of the camp-fire.'

She lifted her head, her eyes blazing with rage.

'I'll not be treated like some – some wench in an ale-house,' she cried.

'I don't think you've been so treated,' I replied, 'but—'

'But what?' she said passionately, springing to her feet. 'But what, Mr Innkeeper? What do you expect from me? I am abducted by a murderous pirate, forced to live like a wild beast – what do you expect of me?'

'If only you would stop playing the fine lady—'

'And play the slut, I suppose!'

'It makes you – ridiculous.'

I thought she would strike me for she raised her arm – but only to clap her hand to her face as she burst into tears. Her distress was terrible and I never felt so ashamed of myself. I put my arms about her and drew her to me.

'Señorita,' I said, 'I take back every word.'

'No,' said she, after a moment, the storm of tears dying away, 'no, you are right. It is all play-acting.'

She gave a little laugh and disengaged herself from me.

'Ridiculous,' she said. 'Yes, it is very ridiculous. I have nothing, you see. Nothing at all. No home, no money, nobody to care for me but my old governess.'

'Your uncle—'

'Is in Mexico – and might as well be on the moon.'

'Nevertheless—'

'I do not ask for your pity, Señor Hawkins, only that you should understand. You see I was born in a palace – that is no make-believe. My father was a grandee of Spain. I lived like a Princess until – until he died.'

She looked away and sat down again upon the tree-trunk.

'He died of shame,' she said very quietly. 'It is possible, you know. He was a gamester. He lived only for the turn of a card or the fall of the dice, and in the end he was ruined.'

She was silent; and I could think of nothing to say. I remembered the death of my own dear father, and how my mother and I had drawn comfort from each other during that desperate time. I understood how completely alone and friendless Señorita Isabella was, and made a vow that from henceforth she should have a friend in me, and that I should see her safe to her uncle, cost what it might. I made her a rather stumbling speech to that effect, at the same time pledging that Vanderbrecken and Mr Morgan would do everything in their power to aid her. Taking her hand, I added, with a smile: 'Remember, it isn't a palace that makes a Princess.'

She withdrew her hand quickly.

'Señor Hawkins,' she said, 'I am grateful for your kindness and glad to think that you are my friend. But please, I beg of you, do not seek anything more than friendship. I have no heart to give away.'

Wondering what she meant, I escorted her back to the camp-fire, where Vanderbrecken begged her pardon in the handsomest way.

We built up the fire, and settled down for the night.

I know not what woke me so suddenly in the small hours; perhaps my 'sixth sense' for danger. I raised my head and looked round. The fire had burned down to a heap of ashes and glowing embers; the breeze had died and it was very still. The others were all fast asleep. I turned my head a little more and then the blood in my veins turned to ice.

A figure was standing just within the circle of our camp, a figure out of the worst nightmare you could conceive. It was a man, or the semblance of a man, for his body was completely emaciated, like a corpse, with every rib and bone visible beneath the wrinkled folds of his skin. His body was daubed with a paint that glowed whitely in the moonlight, and he was stark naked save for a ragged loincloth and a hat.

It was this hat that froze my blood more than anything else. It was in the most extravagant Spanish style, with a monstrous plume of ostrich feathers, such as the most dedicated fop of the Alhambra might hesitate to affect, and under its broad, gold-braided brim a pair of eyes like two burning coals stared madly at me.

I let out a hoarse cry that instantly aroused the others, and with a supernatural swiftness the figure vanished into the forest.

Chapter XIV

Devils and Lunatics

I sprang to my feet to give chase, tripped over a root, and fell sprawling. Vanderbrecken hauled me upright, bidding me to hold hard and tell him what was toward. Ben Gunn answered him, for he had glimpsed the apparition. 'A devil! he cried. 'I seen 'im! Beelzebub i' the flesh!' And he crossed himself, calling loudly upon the Good Lord to deliver us all from the Powers of Darkness.

'Devil! Bah!' said Vanderbrecken, when I had described what I had seen. 'A man! A poor mad creature.'

'One of they Spanish Bedlamites as'll tear out a Christian's throat with his teeth and drink his blood!' declared Ben with terrified grimaces.

'A *man*,' says Vanderbrecken. '*One* man against four.'

This argument he stoutly maintained against Ben and Silver, and was supported by Mr Morgan and Señorita Isabella in a strong veto of my proposal to chase after the apparition.

'We *sleep*,' said Vanderbrecken firmly, 'and I keep watch.'

'Aye, Dutchman,' says Silver, 'you keep a weather eye, for 'twas you brought us 'ere, 'twas you said as 'ow 'twere all good Dutch farmers now in Santa Anna.' He spat and shrugged, and added derisively: 'Beelzebub or Bedlamite, that weren't no farmer!'

'Sleep!' says Ben. 'I wouldn't close an eye now, not fer a seat in Parley-ment!'

Indeed none of us had much rest, I suspect, for the few hours of darkness that remained, though towards dawn I fell into a fitful doze, from which I was awoken by a smell of cooking.

Señorita Isabella was at the fire, with her sleeves rolled up to her elbows, kneading Ben's seed-pulse into little cakes that she was baking in the hot ash.

She caught my eye and smiled.

'Come,' she said, 'break your fast.'

We all made a good breakfast, furnished entirely by Señorita Isabella, then set off through the forest.

I was now certain that we were observed and I had no doubt that our tracker was my friend of the plumed hat. Vanderbrecken agreed with me but refused to be discomposed.

'Let him keep pace with us,' said the Dutchman, 'let him show himself and I'll make him squeal loud enough to prove he's human!'

After an hour we came upon a road, very rough and rutted, which Vanderbrecken recognized and which he said would bring us to the farmstead of his friends, Mr and Mrs Huysmans. We trudged on in the suffocating heat, meeting neither man nor beast, but always aware of a presence dogging us. The road began to rise steeply towards the summit of a considerable hill, from which, Vanderbrecken told me, we would see the Huysmans' farm in the next valley.

We were by now a little ahead of the others for it was very warm work for Silver, and Isabella was failing, and needed Ben's and Mr Morgan's help to get her along. She had refused my arm.

'I make a plan,' said Vanderbrecken. 'The Huysmans will lend me money. I charter a boat for us and we go to Jamaica, where I haff my own boat. Then I take Milady with me to Mexico.'

I thanked him warmly but he shrugged and laughed grimly.

'Very good,' he said. 'That's *my* plan. But what, I ask myself, is *Silver's* plan?'

It was here that I noticed the smoke for the first time. A thin column of black smoke was rising from beyond the summit of the hill. Vanderbrecken saw it too, and cursing under his breath, redoubled his pace.

We were both running at full stretch by the time we breasted the rise. We looked down into the valley and saw below us the smouldering ruins of the farmstead.

Vanderbrecken uttered a great cry and ran like a madman

down into the valley. I tried to keep pace with him but he far outstripped me, and when I gained the curtilage of the farm and stopped to catch my breath, I saw the Dutchman kneeling on the ground, his hat in his hands, and tears cutting rivulets through the dust caked to his cheek.

He knelt by a mound of freshly turned earth surmounted by a rudely fashioned cross and half a plank of wood on which was written, in unformed, childlike letters: 'WILLEM HUYSMANS'. For some time Vanderbrecken seemed oblivious of my presence. Then a shiver ran through his frame.

'We came to the New World together, Willem and I,' he said, 'twenty years ago.'

A pistol barked from some bushes nearby and a shot sang past my ear. With a lion's roar Vanderbrecken hurled himself into the bushes and before I could spring to his assistance he reappeared with what I swear could have been a puppet dancing at the end of his brawny arm.

It was a little black slave-boy, not more than six or seven years old, and a most spirited and courageous child, for all the time his giant captor held him dangling by the scruff of his neck, he kicked and punched and screamed with furious vigour.

Keeping the boy at arm's length, Vanderbrecken spoke some words in Dutch to him. The effect of this speech was magical, for the boy immediately ceased to struggle, and Vanderbrecken let him down gently to the ground.

He then knelt beside the boy, who tearfully and angrily poured out his tale. Since he spoke entirely in Dutch, I could not understand a word, but the expressions that chased across the Dutchman's face told me pretty plainly that the news was as astonishing as it was grave.

The others arrived before the boy had finished his narrative, and stood silently and grimly until the boy stopped and Vanderbrecken stood up.

'The Spanish,' Vanderbrecken said simply, pronouncing the words with a bitterness and hatred that caused Señorita Isabella to cast down her eyes.

'By the Powers,' breathed Silver.

'They have taken the island,' Vanderbrecken went on, 'and driven out the Dutch. Burned their farms. They hanged my friend Huysmans in his own doorway.'

'And his wife?' I asked.

'Shot,' said Vanderbrecken.

'A woman! Shot!' cried Mr Morgan. 'Barbarous, oh barbarous!'

'But she is still alive,' the Dutchman continued. 'She is in hiding. Come. The boy will show us the way.'

Vanderbrecken took the boy's hand and we followed them through a vegetable garden. Skirting a large field of sugar-cane, we climbed a twisting path up through woods to the cave where the Huysmans' faithful little servitor had taken his mistress.

She lay within the cave on a bed of leaves, her eyes closed, her breathing laboured, and a terrible stain of blood upon her front. There was the pallor of death about her worn, weather-beaten face, and I could tell at once that she had seen her last dawn. Vanderbrecken knelt beside her and took her hand very gently.

'Juliana,' he whispered. 'Juliana, it is Hans. Hans Vanderbrecken.'

She opened her eyes and stared up.

'Hans?' she murmured. '*Hans*! It is a miracle.'

She attempted to rise but Vanderbrecken bade her lie still.

'The Spanish,' she said with terrible urgency.

'Hush, hush, be still, rest,' Vanderbrecken replied. 'The boy has told us everything.'

But Mrs Huysmans would not, could not be silent. Raising herself a little, and with her breath rattling in her lungs, she gasped out her story.

'Six months ago they came,' she said. 'They burn the town and kill the Governor. Many of our people flee away in boats. But Willem and Jan, they will not go. Then the Spanish, they catch Jan, they kill him – our only son. I beg my husband, I plead with him that we should go. But he says no. "We have won this land from the wilderness," he says, "it is *our* land." '

A dreadful convulsion of coughing overtook her and she sank back, exhausted. His face very white, Vanderbrecken motioned me to accompany him outside, where the others were waiting.

'We must fetch her a doctor,' Vanderbrecken said immediately, as we stepped into the sunshine. Silver was leaning on his crutch a few paces away, and I could tell by the way his eyes flickered under his brows that his mood was dangerous.

'Ain't no mortal doctor as can save that poor soul now, I reckon,' says Silver. 'Aside o' which, there's the risk o' capture for all of us.'

'The devil with the risk,' cried Vanderbrecken, smiting a fist into the palm of a hand, 'I say she needs a doctor.'

'Well now,' Silver returned, his voice deceptively mild, 'it's my opinion that the time's past for you to be giving orders, Dutchman. A pretty kettle of fish you've led us to, by Thunder. I says we've a boat and we'd best slip our cables 'fore the Spaniards haul alongside.'

'And leave a fellow creature to die alone?' says Vanderbrecken.

'And a woman, too – it's not to be thought of!' cried Mr Morgan.

'Beat about and back to the boat!' Silver roared. 'And if we run up against the Spaniards, well, by the Powers, we've a Spanish beauty to bargain with.'

I took a step towards him and my voice trembled with fury as I told him straight that he'd have me to bargain with first. Silver's hand went to his pistol but he stoppped as Señorita Isabella's voice cut through the air like a whip.

'Are you savages?' she cried.

She was standing in the entrance of the cave, her face tight-drawn and her eyes ablaze.

'She lies dying,' pointing into the cave, 'and you squabble like carrion over a carcase.' Advancing towards Vanderbrecken, she continued: 'I will stay. I will look after her. You, all of you, you must go.'

'No!' Vanderbrecken shouted.

'For the love of God, don't you understand?' cried the Señorita, 'if you are caught you will be killed, all of you.'

'I say we go but take the Spanish wench along of us,' said Silver, again feeling for his pistol.

'And I say you may shoot me now, for I'll not leave this spot,' the Señorita replied in a low, quivering voice. She stood before him, like an avenging angel, and stared him down. After a moment, his hand dropped back to his side, and his eyes darted to Vanderbrecken, to me, and to Mr Morgan.

'Then let's shake a reef,' he muttered out of the corner of his mouth.

Vanderbrecken went back inside the cave to say his last farewell to his old friend, and I drew Señorita Isabella away.

'I'm afraid for your own safety,' said I.

She shook her head, and would not meet my eye, and laughed bitterly.

'I am in no danger from Spaniards,' she said. 'They are my own people, God forgive me.'

Vanderbrecken came out of the cave and walked over to us. He took the Señorita's hand and bowed over it.

'Madam,' he said huskily, 'I thank you for what you do.'

'No,' she replied, 'I deserve no thanks from you. I am grateful to make some atonement for—' and her voice faltered.

Vanderbrecken understood and nodded gravely.

'Come,' he said to me, 'we march.'

I turned to take my leave of Señorita Isabella, prepared to make my bow. But she grasped my hand and very quickly and shyly placed a kiss upon my cheek.

'Go,' she whispered, 'and God's blessing go with you.'

Then she turned away and hurried into the cave.

Without further ado, and in a gloomy silence, we set out to return to the long-boat. It was a weary business. The heat, and the dust, and the flies apart, I think we were all, save Silver perhaps, oppressed in spirit by what we had seen and heard. For myself, I kept thinking of Señorita Isabella, of the courage she had so unexpectedly displayed, of her beauty and her tenderness, and of the fact – which seemed unendurable – that I should never see her again.

Having previously stepped out ahead of the others, Vanderbrecken and I now found ourselves falling behind. Silver was immediately ahead of us, hitting out at the flies with his hat, and cursing under his breath. Mr Morgan was leading Silver by six or seven yards, marching doggedly along, his head thrust forward, and his round shoulders hunched. Ben Gunn was in the vanguard, and often out of sight beyond a twist in the road, for he was still mightily fleet of foot, despite his age, and would have run all the way to the beach to be quit of Santa Anna!

Ben vanished round a new bend in the road and a moment later we heard him utter a shriek louder and shriller than any jungle bird. As we started to run forward, Ben came pelting back into view, as if the Devil was after him. And so he was, in a way, for loping in pursuit of him, with a stride like a deer, was my friend of the plumed hat. In the same instant there was a roar of muskets behind us.

We turned to see a whole troop of Spanish soldiers advancing to take us in the rear.

'Into the trees! For your lives!' roared Vanderbrecken.

I plunged into the jungle as one dives into the sea, for I suddenly remembered the papers I carried in my money-belt and which had already cost me so much trouble to keep from falling into Spanish hands. I rushed blindly forward, creepers and low branches and thorns lacerating my face and hands. I could hear the others crashing about nearby and the shouts of the soldiers, and musket shots. Then I came to a little clearing and stopped, with a pain like a rapier-thrust in my side, to catch my breath. Leaning against a gnarled old tree I sought desperately with my eyes for a line to take through the impenetrable undergrowth, while my ears told me that the pursuit was closing in. And then I noticed a hollow in the trunk of the tree to which I was clinging.

It was a good round hole about the size of a puncheon's

end, and deep; when I ripped my money-belt from my waist and thrust it inside, my arm went in up to my elbow.

The precious papers safely deposited, I ran off across the clearing to where I had seen the semblance of a path. A path it was, though very overgrown, but I was able to make a better pace than before. Indeed I went too swiftly for such treacherous terrain, missed my footing, and measured my length upon the ground. The fall punched the wind from my lungs and I had to wait a moment before I could rise. When I did at last scramble to my feet it was to see four Spanish soldiers standing in a circle round me with their muskets raised.

Chapter XV

The Captain-General

The Spaniards bound my wrists then marched me along the path – which led back to the road. There I found Vander-brecken and Silver both prisoners, but no sign of Ben Gunn or of Mr Morgan.

The gentleman with the plumed hat, who looked very much less frightening in broad daylight, was tittering and hopping from one foot to the other while the Major in charge of the troop counted out some gold coins to him. Having received his blood-money, the creature moved towards us, and sweeping off his hat with an extravagant flourish, made us a theatrical bow. I could see that he was of mixed Spanish and Carib-Indian blood, and though every-thing about him – his wild eyes, falsetto laugh, and painted skin – suggested the lunatic, he plainly had sense enough to have made a good bargain out of our capture.

We waited in the broiling heat, forbidden to speak to each other, while the Major paced up and down (Moreda was his name, I presently learned) and the troopers straggled in from the forest, singly or in pairs, having abandoned the chase. My spirits began to rise as it became more and more likely that Ben and Mr Morgan had made good their escape. And then the last troopers appeared, three of them, carrying between them the body of a fourth, whose head had been stove in, and who was dead.

Major Moreda examined the corpse then stalked up to us. He was a burly fellow, with a stomach that stretched his belt, and greying moustaches and beard. His eyes were very small and black, and were set in his fleshy face like currants in a bun.

'This,' he said to Vanderbrecken, pointing to the dead trooper, 'you will pay for with your necks.'

They marched us down the road at a killing pace. Silver, who could barely keep up, was cursed, belaboured with a musket's butt, and spat upon. He hunched his shoulders, gritted his teeth, and kept his eyes on the ground, but I could see the rage building up inside him, like steam in a kettle, and imagined the carnage there would be if he got free.

Towards sundown, utterly exhausted and half dead with thirst, we came to a substantial plantation house, in the Dutch style, surrounded by makeshift barracks and stables, and with the flag of Spain hanging limp from a pole over the portico.

We begged the Major for a drop of water but he merely glowered, ordered us to be locked up in a guard room, and said that we should presently go before the Captain-General of the Spanish forces, and thereafter would have no need of drink or food in this world. Ten minutes later, the ropes around our wrists having been replaced with irons, we were pushed along a passage and into a large room at the back of the house.

Lamps were burning on either side of the door through which we had entered, but towards the end of the room, where a stout oak table was placed in front of a window, the light was dim. I could see the figure of a man, however, sitting at the table, busily writing.

The scratch of his quill was almost the only sound in the room, for the four troopers who were guarding us stood perfectly rigid and still. At length the scratching ceased, the man at the table yawned, stretched, and rose. He sauntered towards us, and as he came into the light I saw with astonishment that he was young, a very little above my own age. I was wondering whether this slim, dark-haired youth could possibly be Captain-General of Santa Anna, when it was immediately confirmed by the Sergeant of the Guard, who saluted most respectfully and declared: 'The prisoners, Your Excellency.'

The Captain-General came closer. He was richly dressed in a suit of black, trimmed with cloth-of-silver, and with a foam of fine lace at wrists and throat. He had the merriest, most twinkling eyes you ever beheld, which brimmed with sardonic humour.

'So-ho,' says this fop in excellent English, inspecting us in turn, 'we have a Dutch ox, an English spy and' – coming to Silver – 'and what?'

Silver raised his head and looked the Captain-General squarely in the eye. A slow smile spread across the young Spaniard's face and was almost immediately reproduced by Silver.

You have heard the expression 'like recognizes like'. It is graphic enough but it does not begin to describe the look of recognition that passed between the Captain-General and Silver as each read in the face of the other the exact same qualities of duplicity, treachery, and utter lack of scruple.

I decided that the Captain-General, Don Pedro d'Aquilar y Montilla, was a very dangerous man.

'You are – Silver?' he says to Long John at length.

'John Silver, sir, beggin' your pardon, sir,' returned the other.

'And which one of you,' Don Pedro addressed us all, 'killed my trooper?'

Vanderbrecken and I said nothing, but, Long John chirped up: ''Tweren't I, sir! My affy-davy!'

'Señor Hawkins? Dutchman?' says Don Pedro.

We stayed mum.

'Silence is no defence, you know,' Don Pedro said in the most friendly tone, as if he was our advocate. 'Quite the opposite, indeed. In Spanish justice it amounts to a plea of guilty.'

At this Vanderbrecken burst forth: 'I don't waste my breath on Spanish justice.'

Don Pedro's eyes danced cheerfully.

'Waste?' says he. 'Whatever are you saving it for, my bold Dutchman? You're bound to hang tomorrow noon.'

I thought it was time to tell him the truth, though I had no great hopes that it would help us. As briefly as I could I described our adventures since the mutiny, placing the most emphasis on Silver's abduction of a noble Spanish lady, and omitting all reference to Moxon, the State Papers, the attack by the Spaniards, and even the name of the *Saracen*.

Don Pedro heard me out, chuckling a little as I described Silver's infamous doings, and when I had finished he complimented me in his sarcastic way.

'Spoken like a true Englishman,' says he. 'Straight and strong as oaks, the English – and as thick. It's a pity you're an accessory to murder – but there it is. You'll have to hang.'

'Beggin' your pardon, your Excellency,' Silver piped up. 'Would it be respectful, sir, for me to offer a word?'

'Pray do,' said Don Pedro.

'Well, sir,' says Silver, 'it's this way. Mr 'Awkins'll pardon me for sayin' it, I have no doubt, what he wouldn't be forward enough to say for 'isself, but the fact is, sir, Mr 'Awkins is a very rich young gentleman, and I doubt not he'd ransom princely, and mebbe account for myself, sir, and the Dutchman, in the tally.'

'Rich is he?' say Don Pedro.

'As a Bishop!'

Don Pedro sighed.

'Then it's all the more regrettable that he must hang, for I have a great affection for rich people, hoping, you see, to become one of them very shortly. Alas, though, there can be no question of a ransom where the death of a Spanish soldier is concerned. A very uneconomical regulation, in my opinion, but sacred.'

'Well, sir,' Silver persisted, 'it may be that there's more than money to it.'

I saw at once what Silver was at. He would use his knowledge of the State Papers to purchase his life. I tried to spring at him, which was foolish of me, because I was immediately seized and overpowered by the guard, and my action alerted Don Pedro.

'Say on,' said he to Silver. 'You interest me.'

At which that ineffable traitor spilled all, omitting no detail, and concluding with: 'Them papers, I reckon they'd be worth untold gold to the King o' Spain.'

'Without a doubt,' says Don Pedro.

'An' a whole heap more – to the King of England,' Silver added with a sly wink I cannot hope to describe adequately. Don Pedro laughed delightedly. (The guards, of course, understood nothing, for we spoke in English.)

'What a very intelligent man you are, Señor, or perhaps I should say *Captain* Silver.'

Turning towards me, he ordered the guards to search me for my money-belt. I offered no resistance and was able to smile at their disappointment. Here, we were interrupted by a commotion from the next room. I heard Major Moreda's voice raised, and then, to my despair and delight in about equal proportion, the imperious tones of Señorita Isabella Zorilla declaring that she was the daughter of a grandee of Spain and would see the Captain-General immediately!

If I had been startled by the sound of the Señorita's voice, it was nothing to the effect it had on Don Pedro. For a moment he simply gaped and then he whispered: 'It cannot be true. It's too strange, too wonderful, too utterly delectable.'

As a confusion of footsteps approached the door, Don Pedro darted swiftly towards his table, into the darkness.

The door was flung open and Señorita Isabella swept into the room, with Moreda attempting unsuccessfully to restrain her. She stopped abruptly when she saw me and the others then pressed on towards the shadowy figure of the Captain-General.

'Your Excellency,' she began, 'I wish to—'

'Protest!' cried Don Pedro. 'Of course you do, my dear,' he added, stepping into the light. 'When did you ever do anything else?'

Señorita Isabella stood utterly transfixed with astonishment.

'*You!*' she gasped at last.

'You were always protesting about something or other,' said Don Pedro lightly, moving closer to her and favouring her with a most elegant, courtly bow.

'*You* are Captain-General of Santa Anna?' said the Señorita in a faint voice.

'Unfortunately yes,' returned the other. 'The very last place you'd expect to find me, my dear Isabella, and, to be frank, the very last place I'd expect to find *you*.'

This speech of Don Pedro's had allowed the Señorita to recover herself a little. She now turned towards us and said: 'Pedro – these, these gentlemen—'

'Yes, my dear? What of them?'

'I beg you to release them.'

'Release them? My dear girl, I am about to hang them! That is – when I have settled a little matter in which you may perhaps be able to assist me, a matter of some documents.'

The Señorita laid a hand on his arm. 'Pedro,' she said, 'I beg you to release them.'

She would have said more but Don Pedro interrupted her.

'My dear, hard though it is to refuse any request from my betrothed—'

'Betrothed!' cried the Señorita so angrily that I thought she would strike him.

'Well,' says he, perfectly collected, and with a charming

smile, 'our engagement was never formally broken off.'

'No!' she returned furiously. 'You just vanished. Without a word! Not even a note!'

'Whose fault was that? When my creditors learned that your sainted father had diced away your dowry' – here he shrugged eloquently – 'well, you understand.'

'Oh yes,' blazed the Señorita, 'I understand. *Now*. But at the time I was under the absurd illusion that you loved me.'

'So I did,' says he. 'You were, and you are, the most beautiful girl in all Spain. But love, alas, does not pay one's tailor's bill. Happily all that has changed now. I have – prospered in the New World.'

'If there's profit in robbery and murder,' says she, 'you must have made your fortune.'

But he only smiled and moved past her, towards me. 'If you'll forgive me, my dear,' says he, 'Señor Hawkins was about to enlighten us as to the whereabouts of these interesting documents when you made your entrance. Señor Hawkins?'

I said nothing.

'Dear me,' said Don Pedro with a sigh, 'I feared this. Something about you, Señor Hawkins – the set of the jaw perhaps? – persuaded me that you would want to play a heroic role. Oh well,' he went on as cheerfully as a man orders his dinner, 'we have a rack, I think, and a thumbscrew, a little rusty but serviceable I'm sure, and any amount of bastinados, branding-irons—'

'*Pedro*, for the love of God!'

Señorita Isabella clutched his arm.

'Ah-hah!' says Don Pedro. 'I thought as much. I have a rival! Yes! I see what has happened! Thrown together by Fate! United by common perils! Very natural and understandable. I congratulate you, my dear. Señor Hawkins is colossally rich, I hear.'

'You are utterly despicable,' cried the Señorita and she swiped him across the face with her hand – or attempted to do so and failed, because he caught her hand easily and held it fast.

'You should avoid these displays of emotion, my dear,' he said mockingly. 'Now I shall witness Señor Hawkins's agonies with a positive pleasure.'

Long John Silver cleared his throat quietly and meaningly. Don Pedro turned to him at once, releasing the Señorita.

'My dear Captain,' says he to Silver, 'do you have something else to contribute to these affairs?'

'Only this, sir,' says Silver. 'I knows where Jim Hawkins hid them papers.'

'Do you indeed? Then speak – I'm all ears, as you say.'

'Ah well, sir,' says Silver, 'it ain't no easy thing, sir, for a man to speak when 'is tongue be a-cleavin' to his mouth wi' thirst an' 'is belly flappin' like a spanker for want o' vittles.'

'My dear Captain,' says the other, 'speak and you shall drink like Cyrano de Bergerac and dine like Lucullus.'

'Handsomely spoke, sir, if I may make so bold,' says Silver, 'but the thought o' Jim Hawkins and the Dutchman dancin' at a rope's end, well, sir, it inhibits a man's tongue.'

'Then dismiss it from your thoughts,' says Don Pedro. 'They shall be ransomed after all, you have my word on it.'

To my bitter chagrin Silver then revealed that he had seen me deposit my money-belt in the hollow of the tree.

'I knows the exact spot, sir,' says he, 'and if you can see your way to gettin' me a boat, sir, all provisioned, well, I reckon I ain't in no position to drive a hard bargain, sir, and what I says is as that'll satisfy John Silver.'

'You shall have a galleon to yourself, Captain,' cried Don Pedro, 'and tomorrow you'll show me the spot. Moreda, lock up Hawkins and the Dutchman. Isabella, my dear, you'll dine with me, I hope, and I dare say that Captain Silver will favour us with his company.'

Without further ado Vanderbrecken and I were hustled away, out of the house, and across a palisaded square at the rear. Our irons were removed and we were thrown like two sacks of meal into a sort of cage. A hunk of stale bread was tossed in after us, and we found a pail of water, so we were able to eat and drink after a fashion.

A pile of noisome straw in a corner was all the bedding we had, but we made the best of it, and settled down for the night. Exhausted though I was, I knew I would not sleep, for I was tormented by thoughts of Silver's treachery and Señorita Isabella's horrible predicament – at the mercy of the man who had treated her so infamously. I now understood completely what she had meant when she told me that she had no heart to give. Don Pedro had broken it. I made a vow to myself that if ever I should get free I would do everything in my power to mend it.

And so I tossed and turned on my wretched bed and ground my teeth as I imagined Silver wallowing in down pillows and linen sheets in Don Pedro's best bedchamber.

Chapter XVI

A Parting of Ways

In the event, I slept like a tree, and awoke soon after dawn completely refreshed in body and spirit. Vanderbrecken was up and testing the bars and the lock of the cage. There was no hope to be looked for there, since they were all of the stoutest iron, and there were, besides, sentries patrolling inside the palisade.

This was, as I have said, roughly a square. One side was taken up by the rear of the plantation house, and the other three were of rough-cut timber, eight or nine feet in height. In the wall opposite the house was set a gate. Inside the enclosure were two more iron cages for the confinement of prisoners, at present unoccupied, and in the very centre, a gibbet mounted on a platform.

'Silver's a fool,' said Vanderbrecken, pointing to the gibbet. 'That's his destination as well as ours.'

'If you can see that, why so can Silver,' said I. 'He has

some plan to save his skin, you may be sure of that!'

'So he may,' said the Dutchman, 'but what of us?'

'You forget – Ben Gunn and Mr Morgan are at liberty, and we have Señorita Isabella within the enemy's camp and she will help us if she can.'

'*If*,' said Vanderbrecken. 'And what can the pastor and the old fellow do?'

'Well,' says I, 'I don't know. But Ben Gunn has been the saving of me once before and I trust him to contrive something.'

Vanderbrecken grunted. 'I know the Spaniards,' said he. 'They'll hang a Dutchman for the pleasure of it.'

Not long after this, the guard was changed, and our breakfast brought to us – some thin gruel and a pannikin of water. We had scarcely finished this banquet when a door of the house opened and Silver appeared, escorted by Major Moreda. They made directly for us and Vanderbrecken growled and muttered curses.

Indeed the iron entered into my own soul at the sight of Silver all spruced up in a new coat and hat, with his face and beard freshly washed. He heaved up to the bars of the cage with a cheerful smile, and rested on his crutch.

'Jim,' says he, 'I've come for to bid you farewell, mate, for I doubt I'll clap eyes on you again, once the business is done.'

'I've nothing to say to you, Silver,' I returned as coldly as I could.

'Now, Jim,' says he with a sniff, 'is that friendly, I ask? Is that decent, seein' as how I'm come by special dispensation of His Excellency the Captain-General?'

'Your *business*, as you call it, could mean war,' I returned hotly. 'But you care nothing for that.'

'Jim,' says he, 'I'll tell you straight, I don't care that!' and he snapped his fingers in my face. 'Only I reckon we should part friends, Jim. Will you shake my hand?'

'I won't,' said I.

'Jim, Jim,' said he, 'you wouldn't never be tippin' old Long John the black spot would you?'

The mention of the 'black spot' was accompanied by a look from under his eyebrows that put me instantly on the alert.

'Shake my hand, Jim,' Long John repeated.

I glanced at Moreda. He was looking towards the house, tapping his foot impatiently, and Silver's bulk was forming a screen between him and me.

I extended my hand through the bars and Silver grasped it. At once I felt the hard edge of a metal object concealed in his palm.

'Friends, spite of all, Jim,' said Silver, and as I disengaged my hand from his I successfully palmed the object.

'Farewell, Dutchman,' said Silver, with a salute, and then he turned and heaved away, with Moreda, back to the house.

'Bah!' said Vanderbrecken. 'I think you will *never* learn. Always you allow that man to make the fool of you.'

At which I uncurled my fingers to show him the picklock!

So now we had the means to escape from the cage, but, as Vanderbrecken said, we still had the sentries and the troopers quartered about the house to deal with.

'We wait,' said Vanderbrecken. 'We make a plan.'

A few moments later, the sentries opened the gate and three or four wagons, loaded with produce, rumbled inside the palisade. They were accompanied by a gaggle of peasants, mostly old native women, who bore sacks of fruit and vegetables. One figure immediately claimed my attention, an old man, very bowed, who staggered under the weight of the sack he bore, which he held in such a way as to mask his face from the watchful sentries. But *I* saw his features very well – and they were those of Ben Gunn!

I watched Ben follow the others inside the kitchens and store-rooms and waited for him to come out again. Five minutes passed, and then another five, by which time the crowd of peasants had dispersed and the wagons had trundled away. Still Ben did not reappear, and I could be certain that we had a second friend within the enemy's camp.

Shortly afterwards, a smart curricle drawn by a pair of greys, and accompanied by four mounted troopers, entered the palisade and drew up by the house. A moment later Don Pedro, Silver, and Moreda appeared. Silver and Don Pedro entered the curricle and Moreda mounted upon horseback. Then the curricle and its escort jingled away through the gate. This put me in a fever of impatience to escape, but Vanderbrecken insisted that we wait for Ben and Mr Morgan to take some action. Without their assistance we would have no hope of overpowering the sentries. Of these there were five. Two stood by the gate, two more patrolled the walls, and the fifth was stationed by the house.

And so we waited.

The sun climbed into the heaven and beat down cruelly upon us, for the roof of the cage was of iron bars, like the walls, and we had no shade. In my imagination I saw Don Pedro's curricle proceeding at a brisk trot, and this put me in a greater swelter even than the heat of the sun. And then we heard, from beyond the gate, a tuneless voice raised in song.

It was an old sea-song and it was being rendered, very much off the note, in a powerful Welsh brogue.

'A ship I have got in the North Countreee,
And she goes by the name of the Golden Vaniteee—'

Mr Morgan appeared in the gate, clutching a bottle of rum. He tripped over his own feet, giggled, then resumed his song:

'Oh, I fear she will be taken by a Spanish Ga-la-leee—
As she sails by the Lowlands low!'

The gate-sentries were so astonished by the spectacle of a clerical gentleman far gone in drink that they neither challenged nor stopped him. He advanced very unsteadily into the palisade, took a swig of rum, and wagged an admonitory finger.

'Wine is a mocker,' he declaimed, 'strong drink is raging' – here he hiccuped loudly – 'Proverbs Twenty, Verse One (hic!).'

By now the other sentries were gawping at him and I

wasted no time in taking advantage of this diversion, fitting the picklock into the keyhole, and twisting it about, as Mr Morgan began to dance a jig.

I had expected the lock to yield at once but it remained fast. With the sweat running into my eyes, I tried again. Meanwhile the sentries, all except the one by the house, were advancing on Mr Morgan, roaring with laughter as he fell over. He picked himself up, dusted himself down (all this I saw out of a corner of my eye as I wrestled with the lock), and declared with great dignity, as from his pulpit: 'Ecclesiastes Three, Verse Four – There is a time to weep and a time to laugh; a time to mourn, and a time to dance.'

Here at last the lock gave way and the door of our cage swung open.

'Gentlemen,' cried Mr Morgan, in excellent Spanish, 'I propose a toast. Damnation to the King of Spain!'

Now for one vital moment those four sentries were so completely confounded by Mr Morgan's double change – of language and of tone – that they continued to stare upon him stupidly. They were thus completely unaware that Vanderbrecken and I were advancing upon them, or that Ben Gunn had stepped out behind their companion by the house and dealt him such a blow with a cudgel as toppled him instantly to the ground.

'Eternal Perdition to the King of Spain!' roared Mr Morgan. 'May he be eaten of worms!'

This latest insult to their monarch at last aroused the Spanish sentries – but too late! As they fell upon Mr Morgan, Vanderbrecken and I fell upon them!

It was an even match, four against four (for Ben ran quickly to join in the fray, and Mr Morgan whipped out a cudgel from under his coat and laid about him to remarkable effect), and we had the advantage of surprise. But the Spaniards were armed and, moreover, it would have been the ruin of all our hopes if a single musket or pistol had been fired, since the garrison would have been aroused.

It was a near-run thing, for the Spaniards were seasoned soldiers and fought doughtily, but Vanderbrecken was worth three men at least, and in a few moments all four of the Spaniards lay senseless in the dust.

On our side, Vanderbrecken and I were entirely unscathed, Mr Morgan had received some trifling cuts and contusions, but Ben Gunn had been properly laid out. Nothing that Mr Morgan could do (while Vanderbrecken and I dragged the Spaniards into our former residence and locked them up) revived his senses, so Vanderbrecken picked him up, slung him over his shoulder, and together we ran out of the palisade.

We crossed the road without a challenge, and following Mr Morgan's directions, skirted some cane-fields, and made for a patch of woodland, not a quarter of a mile distant, where, Morgan breathlessly informed us, Señorita Isabella was waiting with horses.

There was no time to stop and consider; we formed our plan as we ran and had it all cut and dried before we reached the shelter of the woods. Mr Morgan had somehow procured a map of the island; he, with Ben Gunn and Señorita Isabella, would ride directly for the long-boat and make all ready for sea. Vanderbrecken and I would take a horse each and go hell-for-leather across country to the place where I had concealed the State Papers, hoping thereby to forestall Silver and Don Pedro, whose route, by road, was more circuitous, and whose pace, in the curricle, was less than half that of a good horse.

In a little clearing in the woods we found Señorita Isabella with three horses and a pack-mule which she had obtained, in Don Pedro's name, from the commander of the garrison. While Vanderbrecken and Mr Morgan slung Ben's still senseless body over the mule's broad back, I quickly made Señorita Isabella privy to our plan.

To my astonishment, she shook her head.

'Let Mr Morgan go,' said she, 'and I would help him if I could, but I must stay here.'

'Stay?' I cried. 'Impossible! When Don Pedro discovers that you've aided us—'

'He will laugh,' she interposed quickly. 'I know him.'

Before I could protest at this she laid a hand on my arm. Her face was very white and she was fighting back tears.

'Señor Hawkins,' she said, 'I beg of you. Go! Go quickly! I am in no danger from Don Pedro. I must go to my uncle in Mexico and my best hope is to stay here and wait for a Spanish ship.'

In the same moment that I was forced to acknowlege the good sense of this argument, it came upon me as in a blinding revelation that I was body and soul in love with Señorita Isabella Zorilla!

She continued to speak, saying that she could not risk her life again in an open boat, but I hardly heard her. I was staring upon her as one does sometimes upon a familar landscape or object that suddenly, by some shift of light, takes on a whole new aspect, a beauty and a strangeness never before perceived, while yet remaining essentially the same.

I suppose my eyes told her my story, for she shrank away and the tears, so long dammed up in *her* eyes, welled forth, to tell me in my turn what was in her heart: that she loved me too.

'Isabella,' I cried, 'I'll not be parted from you.'

'Jim,' she whispered, 'for the love of Heaven, I implore you, go. You have your duty to do. Do it. Then flee. For my sake, my dear, flee away as fast as you can, for he'll kill you.'

Never before and never since have I been so torn between my inclination and my duty. To lose Isabella in the same moment almost as I had found her seemed unendurable; to let Don Pedro lay his hand upon the State Papers without making every effort to prevent it would be a betrayal that would haunt my conscience for evermore. And Isabella was right. Once I rescued the papers, instant flight would be the only means of preserving them and my own life. I did not know what to do, could not think what to say.

But she was wiser and stronger than me. Taking my hand, she breathed: 'Jim, you'll do your duty, as I'll do mine. It wasn't meant to be, my dear. Fate makes no mistake. Englishman and Spaniard – remember Moxon. Would you sire another Moxon?'

'Jim!'

Vanderbrecken suddenly stood before me.

'We haff not a moment!' he cried.

Hardly knowing what I did, I folded Isabella in my arms and kissed her, then stumbled blindly to a horse, got my foot into a stirrup, and mounted.

'Wait for us by the boat,' I heard Vanderbrecken shout to Mr Morgan.

I saw the hooves of the Dutchman's mount make the mud fly, dug in my own heels, and spurred my nag into a canter.

Just before we quit the wood, I wrenched my head round to look back down the glade. I saw Isabella weeping in Mr Morgan's arms, and Mr Morgan comforting her like a father.

Chapter XVII

Long John Redeems Himself

I will not describe our harum-scarum dash through the fields and jungles of Santa Anna for the good reason that I remember hardly anything of it. Aghast at the turn Fortune had served me, I rode as an automaton, plantation and wilderness flitting past me as in a dream, and the gaping peasants and round-eyed urchins who stopped in their work to stare at our headlong passage seemed to be characters upon some fantastic, distant stage.

I know not whether it was an hour or half a day before we drew near to the place where my gentleman of the plumed hat had sold us to Moreda's troopers, but it was well after noon that I saw Vanderbrecken rein in his horse, with an urgent gesture to me to be silent.

For the past ten minutes we had been upon steadily rising ground, climbing with much labour through almost impenetrable scrub. Vanderbrecken had dismounted and was crouched upon one knee, peering through an arras of fleshy, green leaves. Looking over his shoulder, I saw that we were upon an eminence above the very road we had taken the day before. There was Don Pedro's curricle, stationary by the side of the way, with Moreda's horse and those of the escort tethered to trees nearby, and a solitary trooper on guard. By raising my head a little I could discern the beginnings of the path that led to the clearing where I had hidden the papers.

'First, we haff to settle him,' says Vanderbrecken in a whisper, indicating the sentinel below.

'I'll settle him,' I returned, through my teeth.

The venom with which I spoke startled Vanderbrecken.

'We don't haff to *kill* him,' he said.

I nodded shortly, and before he could stop me, slipped away and started to descend the hill. Moving with the stealth and silence of a stalking cat, I gained the deep drain or ditch that ran by the side of the road. Now imitating a snake, I crawled upon my belly along this convenient conduit, disturbing the loathsome slug-like inhabitants of its bottom as I went. Selecting a smooth, round stone suitable for my purpose, I stole upon my unwitting victim, and knocked him senseless with a single blow.

I instantly felt a great deal more cheerful, and more myself, though a trifle ashamed at having cured my own distemper at the expense of another, even a Spanish soldier. However, there was no time for such niceties of feeling: my business was to relieve him of his arms and press on to the clearing. I took his pistol and his sword, and Vanderbrecken furnished himself with his musket and poniard, and pausing only to truss and gag him, we proceeded swiftly and silently into the jungle.

We were not upon the path above three minutes before we heard voices ahead. Leaving the path, and moving now with the extremest caution, we crept through the thick foliage towards the clearing.

'Here?'

Don Pedro's voice rang out so clear and close I thought he was addressing me! Vanderbrecken and I stopped dead. We had come upon the very edge of the clearing without knowing it. Parting the branches in front of me by fractions, I peered into the clearing.

Long John Silver was leaning upon his crutch near the tree where the papers were concealed. Moreda was standing close to him, and Don Pedro opposite him. The three troopers were so positioned, I thought, as to afford Silver no possible chance to escape should he attempt to play false.

'Here?' Don Pedro said again.

A smile spread slowly over Long John's features.

'Here –' he paused inimitably '– abouts.'

'My dear Captain Silver,' said Don Pedro with a flourish of his wrist, 'you cannot, surely, be anticipating a breach of faith on my part?'

'Not I, sir,' returned Silver (and it was as good as a play to see this elegant exchange of insincerities), 'but to make a sure thing certain, as the sayin' goes, there's something as it might be advantageous to you to know.'

'What a remarkable fellow you are,' said the other. 'Your conversation *never* fails to engage my most eager attention. Say on.'

'Well, sir,' says Silver, shifting on his crutch, 'them papers lays but a few paces from where I stands now, in a place I'll show you. But they ain't all as lays there, no, by Thunder.'

'No?'

'No, sir. There's a scrap o' parchment alongside what's worth a hundred, it may be so much as a thousand times more.'

He paused. There was an expectant silence. Silver let it continue, breaking it only at the moment most precisely calculated to lend greatest effect to his next words, which were: 'Flint's treasure map!'

Don Pedro's keen eyes narrowed, but Moreda growled: 'Flint's treasure was taken ten years ago.'

'So it was,' said Silver quickly. 'Some of it.'

'How much?' Don Pedro said very quietly.

'Not a half.'

'A clumsy lie,' said Moreda.

'Possibly,' retorted Don Pedro. 'We shall see.'

Turning again to Silver, he went on mildly: 'You were Flint's quartermaster, I think.'

'So I was.'

'And took part in the later affair – with the English Squire? Are you asking me to believe that the world has been deceived in its estimates of the booty, that the tales of princely fortunes and Kings' ransoms are exaggerated?'

'No, sir,' says Silver smartly, 'I ain't sayin' that. They 'ad the gold for sure, rot 'em, but' – and here there was another masterly pause, – 'they never touched the stones!'

'Stones?' Don Pedro cried. 'You mean gemstones?'

'Aye, sir,' Silver replied, heaving forward a pace, and fixing the Captain-General with his glittering eyes. 'Diamonds, rubies, sapphires, emeralds – the pick o' the Spanish Main, what Flint kept to 'imself. He'd weigh out the doubloons, to each man his share according to the Articles, for he set no store by gold; but never the stones, though each one was worth a plate-ship!'

At this, even the dour Major Moreda betrayed a certain excitement.

'It's true,' said he. 'Flint cared more for a diamond than for a woman. The great pearl of the Incas, that Admiral D'Esquilar was to have presented to Her Most Catholic Majesty, that was lost in the sack of Porto Santo: they say Flint had it!'

'That he did!' cried Long John. 'I seen it with these eyes – greater than a duck's egg, an' shinin' like the moon!'

'And you say the English never found it?' said Don Pedro, his cheek a trifle flushed, and his eyes alight, but very cool and collected all the same.

'They never knowed,' Long John returned. 'No more did

I – 'til later. I found it out, aye, and the hidden secret o' the map too, and there's the catch, see?'

He looked directly at Don Pedro.

'I'm the only man alive,' he said deliberately, 'what can read it.'

'I do see,' says the Captain-General with a smile. 'Most clearly. And I congratulate you on possessing so – so powerful a protection for your life. You're a valuable acquaintance, Captain Silver, as I've known from the first. You may *safely* show us the hiding place.'

I turned to Vanderbrecken, unable to resist whispering in his ear: 'You underestimated him!'

I turned back to observe Silver as he cast a long, shrewd, penetrating glance at the Captain-General.

'Very well,' said he at length, and then with a gesture: 'Look you in the hollow o' that tree.'

Don Pedro nodded to Moreda.

The Major stepped over to the tree and put his hand inside the hollow. I raised my pistol, and beside me Vanderbrecken took aim with his musket, for it had been agreed between us beforehand that we would strike at the moment when the documents were found. Moreda was feeling inside the hollow, his face slowly clouding. After a moment, he withdrew his arm and held up his hand. It was empty.

'There's nothing,' said he.

With a furious oath, Long John thrust himself towards the tree. Gripping his crutch with his left hand, he plunged his right arm into the hollow, and I imagined his fingers scrabbling desperately. He in his turn withdrew his arm and, empty-handed, turned to face the Captain-General.

Don Pedro was shaking his head and tut-tutting with the air of a kindly schoolmaster over a trifling misdemeanour.

'My dear Captain,' said he, 'you disappoint me.'

'I tell 'ee, they was there!' raged Silver.

'I believe you.'

'Some lubberly son of a rum puncheon's stole them!'

'Unquestionably,' returned Don Pedro pleasantly. 'But since you cannot tell us who, your usefulness is at an end.'

'Kill me, an' that map ain't worth a farthing.'

'Come, come, Captain,' said the other, 'do not under-estimate my intelligence. If the map contains a secret as you say, be sure I'll find it.' Then, turning to the nearest soldier, and in the same mild, pleasant tone, he added: 'Shoot him.'

Now there are certain actions of mine, with respect to Long John Silver, that I can neither explain nor justify, so I will only state the plain facts. As the Spanish soldier raised his musket, so I aimed my pistol at him, and before he could fire upon Silver, I shot him dead. At the same moment, Vanderbrecken's musket roared in my ear, and a second soldier measured his length. Then Vanderbrecken and I burst into the clearing.

Vanderbrecken's victim was only wounded, and lightly at that, and launched himself immediately at me. The other fired at Vanderbrecken, missed his mark, but followed through with a furious attack with his sword. Long John, meanwhile, was grappling with Moreda. Only Don Pedro was disengaged; and I am bound to record that instead of coming to the aid of his men, this despicable poltroon turned tail and took to his heels!

His cowardice was our salvation. In a moment, Vander-brecken and I had rendered our assailants insensible, and Major Moreda lay dead with his own knife in his back.

Hardly thinking what I was at, I ran off down the path in pursuit of Don Pedro. Hearing gunshots, I redoubled my pace, and arrived panting at the road to see Don Pedro, on horseback, vanishing over a rise and driving all the other horses before him, including those procured for us by Isabella. Hopeless though it was, I was determined to give chase in the curricle, which was the sole means of transport left to us, and breathlessly told Vanderbrecken so when he came up, followed a moment later by Silver. The Dutchman made no objection and together we hauled Silver into the carriage and I whipped up the greys.

My idea was in some manner to overhaul Don Pedro before he could raise the alarm and so set every soldier in Santa Anna hunting for us. As we breasted the rise this hope, always forlorn, was completely dashed. Ahead, upon the opposite side of the valley, a column of mounted troops was streaming down the road. Their commander, seeing the Captain-General, halted his men.

I hauled on the reins to stop the curricle. What had happened was plain: our escape from the plantation house had been discovered and the hunt was up!

'Around! Turn around!' cried Vanderbrecken.

As I started to do so, Long John laid a hand on my arm.

'You ha'n't the wind, mate, not in this contraption,' said he.

'He's right,' roared Vanderbrecken. 'Out, and take to the woods!'

'Good enough for you and Jim,' returned Long John, 'But as for me, I reckon I'll bide aboard an' lead 'em astray.'

I attempted to protest, for such a course meant certain capture and death for him, but he only said: 'Dutchman, haul him away!' and before I knew it, Vanderbrecken had me by the scruff of the neck and was dragging me down on to the road and into the bushes by the side of the way.

Silver turned the curricle (I remember marvelling at the skill with which he handled the greys and wondering where on earth he ever acquired it) and trundled back down the hill at a spanking pace.

Two or three minutes later the mounted column, with Don Pedro at its head, thundered over the rise. Catching sight of the curricle as it vanished round a bend, the Captain-General let out a cry, and urging his men to greater speed, led them off in hot pursuit!

Vanderbrecken and I slipped away, and after a look at the map, found the line that would bring us most directly to the cove where the long-boat lay. We set off through the jungle at a good pace and in less than two hours heard the distant booming of the surf. Five minutes more and there was the white sand and the long-boat drawn up upon it, and Mr Morgan and Ben Gunn (fully recovered) running forward to greet us.

'May the Lord be praised!' cried Mr Morgan as he wrung my hand.

'Amen!' said Ben Gunn.

Mr Morgan had nothing of any moment to report; his journey to the beach had been accomplished without incident. Briefly, we recounted our own adventures. When we came to Silver's part, and his self-sacrifice, Mr Morgan stared and shook his head.

'Gentlemen,' said he, 'I hang my head in shame and should beg Heaven's pardon for my presumption; for I confess to you that I had considered John Silver to be beyond redemption. What does the Good Book say? "Judge not, that ye be not judged." A salutary text, my friends, a salutary text.'

We now had to consider what we should do next. The others were for immediate embarkation, but I was forced to disagree. There was still the mystery of what had become of the State Papers, and the treasure map, and until I had assured myself that they could not fall into Don Pedro's hands, I did not see that I could honourably quit the island. I said as much and provoked a hearty oath from Vanderbrecken.

'Honour!' cried the Dutchman. 'Balderdash! I say to the Devil with the papers and the map. Let's save our lives or Silver sacrificed his own in vain.'

'I concur,' said Morgan, 'most decidedly. You've done your best, my boy. No man could have done more.'

'The pastor's right,' said Vanderbrecken.

All this time, Ben Gunn was tugging at my sleeve and I was never more annoyed at his attentions.

'Ben, leave me be,' said I testily.

'Jim, Jim,' the fellow persisted, 'I've a piece to say.'

'Later, Ben, if you please.'

'Later's too late,' was the firm reply. 'What I has to say pertains to them there doccyments, aye, an' Flint's map too.'

I gaped at him. Was it possible that—?

'Ben, said I, 'I beg your pardon. Now tell me straight: d'you know where they are?'

'Ah, well now,' Ben began, with a wink.

'*Straight*, Ben, I implore you.'

'Well then, I do,' said he.

'Ten thousand Devils!' exploded Vanderbrecken. '*Where are they?*'

'Why here, o' course,' says Ben, fishing inside his jerkin and pulling out my money-belt!

Half-way between absolute exasperation and overwhelming relief, I asked Ben why, in the name of Heaven, he had not spoken out earlier?

'Why did you not inform *me*?' cried Mr Morgan.

The old maroon gaped dazedly at us and I took pity on him.

'Never mind,' said I. 'Tell us how you came by them.'

Ben brightened up. ''Twere this way, d'ye see,' he said. 'I seed you post 'em' – (turning to me) – 'an' I seed that Silver'd seen what I seed, see, and—'

But there I stopped him for I saw Vanderbrecken and Mr Morgan's faces and it was only charity to give them a version in plain English.

When Ben had been congratulated all round on his mother wit, and the money-belt was once again safe under my shirt, Vanderbrecken proposed that we put to sea without further delay. Again, I was forced to oppose him; there was just a slim chance that Silver might have given Don Pedro the slip and would fetch up at the beach, and since dusk was coming fast upon us, I proposed that we wait until sundown, in case Silver should come, and the better to make our escape, for Don Pedro might have posted look-outs along the coast.

Vanderbrecken grudgingly agreed, and we spent a profitable hour, gathering fresh fruits and berries in the forest to supplement our supplies, before darkness fell.

There was no sign of Silver, and since to delay our departure any longer would have been folly, we determined to embark; but it was with a heavy heart that I put my shoulder to the long-boat's prow to launch her. All Silver's unspeakable treacheries were forgotten, as in my imagination I saw his capture and miserable death. While Vanderbrecken busied himself with the jury-sail, Mr Morgan, Ben and I unshipped the oars, and we pulled steadily away from the Island of the Damned. Never in my life was I more grateful to be quit of a place – save Treasure Island itself!

We were rounding the point, and a breeze was just springing up to fill our little sail, when I saw Vanderbrecken, at the tiller, give a great start and pick up his musket. I screwed round my head to see a light, out at sea, bobbing between us and the extremity of the point.

'Saints protect us,' Ben Gunn muttered, 'a ghost ship!'

'A Spanish cutter more like,' growled Vanderbrecken. 'Jim, your pistol.'

I took up my pistol, primed and loaded it. While I did so, the mysterious light grew rapidly larger and, of a sudden, the shape of the approaching craft was revealed. It was only a native piragua, and contained but two beings. The first, who was dipping the paddle, could be plainly seen, for his companion, who sat behind him, was holding up a torch over his head: it was none other than my gentleman of the plumed hat!

With a guttural oath, Vanderbrecken put his musket to his shoulder.

'No!' I cried, 'hold!' for I suddenly had an inkling of who the second figure in the piragua might be.

'Ahoy! Silver!' I shouted.

The torch moved – to reveal the grinning face of Long John Silver!

Part IV
Jamaica

Chapter XVIII

Ben Gunn Drops a Brick

The explanation of Silver's escape, which seemed supernatural, was simple enough; I recount it as a tribute to his resource and cunning, and because I cannot resist describing how Don Pedro d'Aquilar y Montilla got his just deserts.

As I had feared, the Captain-General and his riders gained very rapidly on the curricle; Silver knew that he was doomed unless he could contrive some means of checking them. Though he had trod that road only twice before, he remembered it well enough to recall that, not far ahead, lay a bend of particular severity, where the way turned almost completely back upon itself. He arrived at this spot just sufficiently ahead of his pursuers to enable him, without being observed, to halt the curricle, jump down, and conceal himself in the jungle that pressed densely upon both sides of the road. A moment later, Don Pedro galloped round the bend at the head of his men to find the stationary curricle blocking the way and no time to rein in! Don Pedro's horse reared up and its rider took the toss of a lifetime.

The other riders, streaming round the bend, encountered the double obstacle of the curricle and Don Pedro's plunging charger and in a second all was a horrible confusion of flying hoofs and cursing men.

Long John did not stay to enjoy the spectacle. He had

gained some time by his stratagem and must now profit by it. He had a rough idea of the direction in which the long-boat lay and set off through the jungle. It was not long before he became aware that he was followed, and guessed the identity of his tracker – the gentleman of the plumed hat who had once before been the cause of his capture. But instead of attempting to evade him, or to kill him, as no doubt I would have done, Long John, when he came to a clearing, stopped in the centre of it, threw away his cutlass and knife, and jingling some gold coins in his hand (where he obtained them he would not say) called out to him to show himself.

'Indian, white man, or Hottentot, a bounty hunter's a bounty hunter, an' what he hunts is gold,' said Long John at this point in his narrative.

So it proved.

The Indian appeared at the edge of the clearing, and when Long John threw him a doubloon or two, approached without hostility. Since Long John had more than a smattering of Spanish, they soon came to terms, with what result we know.

All this Silver told us during the first night of our voyage away from Santa Anna.

The following morning, when we were upon the high seas, we held a conference. Vanderbrecken proposed that we should set our course directly for Jamaica. He calculated that, if the winds were favourable, four or five weeks would see us there and he pointed out certain islands, mostly uninhabited, where we could replenish our supplies of food and water. To my surprise, we had not a murmur of dissent from Long John, though it was obvious that once he set foot on British soil he would stand in jeopardy from the law. I soon saw the reason for his compliance, however: the treasure map. So long as it was in my possession, he would stick to me like a barnacle. I had no fear that he would attempt to steal it during the voyage, for he was one against four, and had no desire to be marooned, which would have been Vanderbrecken's sentence on him, had he made an attempt.

I will not dwell upon our voyage, which was extremely prosperous. The breezes were steady and strong, Vanderbrecken was a prince of navigators, our water and provisions held out well, we never had so much as a hint of foul weather, and in short it was quite one of the pleasantest cruises I ever enjoyed. Four weeks to the day after we quit Santa Anna, we sighted the peaks of the Blue Mountains, and within a few hours were beating up towards Kingston, Jamaica.

It was time for Long John to declare his position, and so he did, as follows:

'It may be,' says he, 'as there's a deppytation in wigs an' lace, and a pipe band, awaitin' for *you* in Kingston Harbour, but, sure as a gun, there's a *rope* awaitin' for John Silver; and I'll make so bold as to remind you that there's some aboard what owes their lives to me.'

This was undeniable and it was agreed that we should put in to a little-frequented cove, not far from Kingston, where Long John could step ashore. Should we be questioned about him, we were to say that he had been left behind on Santa Anna. What Silver planned to do ashore he would not reveal; only he bade me remember 'that the map weren't worth a brass dollar without him to read it.'

How wise he was to make himself scarce was shown when we were hailed by a Government lugger as we tacked past the ruins of Port Royal, and upon berthing at the quay in Kingston Harbour, were immediately surrounded by Militiamen.

We told our story to the Captain of the Militia, a dour, soldierly fellow called Williams, but it did not satisfy him. He said that he had instructions to convey us to the Governor himself, Lord Charles Devereux, and in spite of the most vigorous protest from Vanderbrecken, to Government House we went, under escort, as if we were under arrest. Upon being shown into a large, elegantly furnished library, the first person we saw was Captain Parker!

I think we all stood stock still in sheer amazement, and

then the Captain stode forward with a 'Hawkins! Hurrah!' to clap me on the shoulder and shake hands with the others.

Seated at an ornate desk, in the French style, and observing our reunion with an air of superior boredom, was a lean elderly man with a monstrous hook of a nose, who I took to be the Governor. He was perfectly powdered and very finely dressed in a coat of brocaded silk.

'Hawkins,' says Parker very confidentially to me, 'the State Papers, man—?'

'Safe,' I replied. 'I have them with me.'

'Heaven be praised!' he said; then, turning to the Governor: 'Splendid news, sir! All is well as I predicted. You're acquainted with Mr Morgan and Mr Vanderbrecken, of course, but may I present the hero of the hour – Mr Hawkins.'

I was bursting to know how Parker had escaped from the Spaniards but was forced to make my bow to Lord Charles. He returned the courtesy frigidly and said in a languid, sneering drawl: 'It would appear that one of your party is missing.'

'If it's to John Silver you refer, sir,' said I, 'then you are perfectly correct. I have already informed your officer, Captain Williams, of the circumstances.'

'Indeed,' returned Lord Charles, very smelfungus-mundungus. 'I am asked to believe that an arrant scoundrel like Silver sacrificed himself in order that you should escape.' He gave an affected laugh. 'My dear young man, credit me with a modicum of intelligence.'

He turned to Mr Morgan, and looking at him directly, asked him for corroboration. Mr Morgan shifted his feet, cleared his throat, and mumbled something about 'owing a debt to Silver.'

I, meanwhile, had taken the State Papers from my money-belt, and now slapped them down upon the desk.

'Lord Charles,' said I, 'you owe the preservation of these documents entirely to me and my friends. I think we have deserved better than to be subjected to an inquisition upon a matter of which you have had a full account.'

'That's right,' grunted Vanderbrecken.

Lord Charles was at first too astonished to reply, but recovering his composure, he said with a supercilious smile: 'I see that you adhere to the principle that the best means of defence is attack, Mr Hawkins.'

Before I could retort to this, he turned suddenly and fixed Ben Gunn with his eye.

'You,' said he sharply. 'What's your name?'

'Me, sir?' croaked Ben, thoroughly rattled, and looking desperately about him.

'You, sirrah! Your name!'

'Benjamin Gunn, Your Worship, at your service.'

'Gunn? Benjamin Gunn? I know that name.'

'Oh no, sir!'

'Oh yes, sir!' said Lord Charles triumphantly. 'You sailed with Flint and Silver. D'you deny it?'

'Ah, well now, as to that,' says Ben, twisting his hands, 'in a manner o' speakin' – but that were an age ago, Your Honour.'

'Perhaps,' says Devereux, 'but you belonged to the Brotherhood, and as like as not you're lying now to protect an old shipmate.'

'Not I, sir!' cried Ben.

'If you are, I'll see your neck stretched, Benjamin Gunn. Come now – where's Silver?'

To my utter horror Ben replied: 'Well, sir, I'll tell ye, sir.'

Before I could stop him, Ben continued: 'John Silver, 'e won't trouble you no more, sir, nor anybody else neither. Slipped his cable he has, sir, for good an' all. And there' – crossing himself – 'is Ben Gunn's oath on it.'

The Governor raised an eyebrow and a thin smile of triumph flickered upon his lips.

'*Slipped his cable*, eh?' he drawled. 'Not "captured" or "dead" but – *slipped his cable*.'

It was time for me to step into the breach.

'Lord Charles!' said I very sharply.

He turned his head at once and eyed me as if I was a footman who had dropped his salver.

'Is it your intention to lay a charge against my servant?'

'A charge?'

'Or against me, or my friends?'

'I merely wish—'

'Yes or no, sir?'

'For the moment,' he replied, 'no.'

'Then I have the honour to bid you good day, sir. Come, Ben.'

And with that, I walked out of the room.

Vanderbrecken, Mr Morgan, and Ben Gunn followed. In the vestibule we were soon joined by Captain Parker, upon whom we pounced for an account of his adventures since we last saw him. But the Captain shook his head with a worried frown.

'The Governor don't believe your tale, Jim,' he said. 'He swears Silver's in Jamaica and that you're hiding him. You're not, are you, Jim? It'd go hard with you if you are.'

'Captain,' I cried, 'To the devil with the Governor – I beg of you, I implore you to relieve us from the torture of curiosity.'

Parker laughed and told us briskly how the *Saracen* had been wellnigh sunk by the same storm that we encountered. Half crippled, she had, by great good fortune, encountered the Jamaica Fleet. Moxon's men had hauled down the Spanish flag, and surrendered.

'And Moxon himself?' I asked.

'Shot by his own men,' said Parker laconically.

'And Mistress McPhail?'

'Returned to Scotland to take out a lawsuit!'

On the way to the dock-yard, where the *Saracen* was undergoing repairs, and where we retrieved our baggage, we gave Parker an account of our own adventures. I engaged rooms in a nearby tavern, and after a bath and a change of clothing, began to think about my business in Jamaica. I dispatched a note addressed to Joshua Hallows Esq. at the Trelawney Plantation, announcing my arrival.

Next morning, while I was breakfasting with Vanderbrecken and Mr Morgan, the reply came, brought by a young Negro, about sixteen or seventeen years old, whom Mr Morgan instantly greeted.

'Why, Abed!' he cried, springing to his feet. 'Abed Jones!'

The boy saluted Mr Morgan joyfully.

'Massah Hallows tell us the Spaniards kill you, Reverend,' he said.

'Then Mr Hallows is in for a disappointment,' said Morgan. 'Bless my soul, how you've grown! What's that? A note for Mr Hawkins?'

Turning to me, he said: 'Jim, this is Abed Jones, one of Trelawney's people.'

Without thinking, I offered the boy my hand. He made no attempt to take it, but stared at me for a moment as if I was mad, then thrust the note at me. To relieve the awkwardness, I immediately opened the note, which contained compliments from Mr Hallows, apologies that he was prevented by business from coming to meet me in Kingston in person, and a suggestion that, if I was in a hurry to visit the plantation, I might avail myself of the farm cart that had come to fetch supplies. I thought that Hallows could have done better than a farm cart for the owner's Agent, but I was not one to stand on ceremony.

As Abed Jones went away to fetch the cart, Vanderbrecken drew me aside.

'A word of advice, my friend,' said he quietly. 'In Jamaica, a white man don't give his hand to a black man, especially not a *slave*.'

You will think I must have been a great blockhead to be surprised that Abed Jones was a slave, but you must remember that I was new to the West Indies.

And here, at the risk of offending the reader, I may as well state my true colours on the issue of slavery. I utterly abominate and oppose the trade, and would see it abolished tomorrow. There are a hundred arguments – moral, religious, and even economic – that I could advance against it; but of its evils let my tale speak for itself.

Abed Jones returned to the tavern with the cart and I

climbed up beside him, while Ben Gunn scrambled into the back with our baggage.

We rattled off down King Street, past the churchyard where Admiral Benbow is buried, then through neat plantations of banana, coco-palm, orange and mango trees. I was full of questions to Abed, but he seemed disinclined for conversation, and I left him to his sulks.

We entered wilder country – forest and jungle. Giant silk-cotton trees reared against the deep azure of the sky, and the blooms of the datura and yucca plants, crimson and white, made a brilliant display. The soft, temperate air was heavy with the spice of pimento and alive with the songs of a myriad exotic birds. My senses were lulled, and my spirits soothed by the contemplation of such beauty, and I was about to make a new overture to Abed when a perfect fusillade of musket-shots thundered suddenly from the forest!

Chapter XIX

Mr Hallows Theorises

The horses bolted at once.

Before I could think, the maddened beasts were careering away, the old rattle-trap cart was bucketing about like a bark in a hurricane, and my arms were being torn from my body as I hauled desperately upon the reins.

I'd rather fight a dozen Spaniards single-handed than stop a pair of stampeding cart-horses! Alone, I could never have done it, and even with Abed's strength added to mine, it was a close thing, and we were very nearly dashed to flinders against a rock before a sudden steep rise came to our aid, and we were able to pull the horses up.

'Mr Jones,' said I, when I'd caught my breath, 'you'll not

refuse to shake my hand now, I hope, for we owe each other our lives.'

Abed dashed the sweat from his eyes; with a frank, unaffected smile, he shook my hand.

'Amen to that!' said a trembling voice from behind, and we turned to see Ben Gunn crossing himself energetically.

It seemed best to proceed with our journey, but I loaded two pistols, one for me, and one for Ben. No further incident occurred, however, and within an hour we were passing between handsome gates, with the Trelawney arms above them, and drawing up before a large, modern plantation house, in the severest Classical style.

Mr Hallows, the manager of the plantation, received me in the hall, and expressed the utmost horror at my account of our misadventure.

'I confess, my dear sir,' said he as he ushered me into a dining-room, where refreshments were laid out upon a buffet, 'that I have sometimes despaired altogether of your safe arrival here. First a mutiny at sea! Now this! Such adventures!'

He was a man of some forty summers, plainly but elegantly dressed, with features coarsened and roughened by long sojourn in tropical climates. His manners were polished and gentlemanly, but I noticed that the smiles that formed so frequently upon his lips were not reflected in his eyes, which were cold, grey, and calculating.

Since my arrival must have been the very *last* thing he desired, his professions of concern rang very hollow and I was glad when he handed me over to his clerk, a little, weaselly fellow called Sharpe, excusing himself on the ground that he was a Magistrate and must report the attack upon me to the authorities.

I had a better opportunity to form a judgement of Hallows in the evening, when we dined alone together. That he was given to display and rich living was clear; I was quite startled by the profusion of silver upon the table, the number and excellence of the dishes, and, in particular, the very superior quality of the wine. I complimented him upon it.

'You're very charitable,' he returned with a smile, 'but it's a feeble enough vintage, I fear.'

Lighting a cheroot, he asked me whether he was not correct in supposing I had been at New College? I confirmed that I had been.

'I too,' said he. 'Was old Warden Heatherington still alive in your day?'

'Very much so.'

'Ah,' said Hallows, with a wistful sigh, 'he had the finest cellar in Oxford. I often dream of his Burgundies and Clarets. *He* was a judge of wine, indeed.'

Taking a pull at his cheroot, he suddenly went off on a new tack.

'Mr Hawkins,' said he, 'I have been making enquiries about the attack upon you. I have pondered a little, and formed a theory.'

'Indeed?'

'I am almost certain that it was the work of the Maroons. I see I puzzle you. The Maroons are a gang of desperadoes, descendants of the Spanish slaves, who live wild up in the mountains, which they claim as their own State! Their true business, however, is murder and pillage. We've suffered six or seven raids ourselves in the past year – they've contributed considerably to our losses.'

'I see,' said I very cool. 'You blame the losses on these Maroons?'

'In part, certainly.'

'There are other causes?'

He smiled and affected to yawn.

'Mr Hawkins,' says he, 'it is getting late and I make it a rule never to discuss business at the table. If you've no objection, we'll defer the matter to the morrow.'

I went to my bed that night with a theory of my own forming: that Hallows himself was most probably responsible for the attempt upon my life. I decided to tread warily, bide my time, and treat Hallows with all the appearance of friendliness.

But the very next day we had the first of our clashes.

Mr Morgan arrived soon after breakfast with a letter in Squire Trelawney's own hand authorising a grant of a certain piece of land for the building of his church.

Hallows read the letter.

'As ever,' said he, 'Mr Trelawney expresses himself with admirable, one might almost say Boeotian simplicity.'

Handing the letter back to Mr Morgan, he declared coolly that he would write to the Squire with all possible dispatch.

'Write to him?' cried Morgan, astonished. 'I do not follow you at all, sir. His instructions are clear enough, surely?'

'Perfectly clear,' returned Hallows with a shrug. 'But I would be failing in my duty if I did not advise Mr Trelawney most strenuously to withdraw them.'

'Withdraw them?'

'Certainly,' was the unabashed reply. 'A degree of folly must always be permitted to the rich. If Mr Trelawney wishes to give away valuable land, that's his affair.'

'Indeed it is!' said Morgan hotly.

'But since he wishes to give the land to *you*,' Hallows continued, 'so that you may build a church, it becomes my affair.'

'How so?' I asked quietly.

Hallows turned to me.

'Let me appropriate some of my employer's bluntness,' he said. 'Because I won't have Mr Morgan preaching to my slaves and filling their heads with nonsense.'

'You call the teachings of the Church nonsense?' cried Mr Morgan, outraged.

'Dangerous nonsense,' replied Hallows steadily, 'for you'll turn them not towards religion but towards rebellion, and so I shall advise Mr Trelawney.'

'You may save yourself the trouble,' said I. 'As the Squire's Agent, I have full powers of decision.'

'Undoubtedly,' said Hallows, eyeing me narrowly. 'However—'

I did not let him finish.

'I'd be obliged if you'd make the necessary arrangements without delay,' I said shortly.

For a moment it seemed that Hallows would challenge me openly, but he thought better of it.

'As you wish,' he said, with a slight bow – adding that he would like a word with me in private.

'Mr Hawkins,' said he smoothly when we were alone, 'our esteemed employer no doubt places great faith in your abilities; but, if you'll permit me to say so, I have a wealth of experience in managing a plantation, whereas you have – none.'

'If you'll permit *me* to say so, Mr Hallows,' I replied, 'your wealth of experience appears to have contributed very little towards making *this* plantation profitable.'

He flushed with anger at this, but controlled his temper.

'Well, well,' said he, 'on your head be it.'

I went outside to see Mr Morgan and told him that he could start to clear the land as soon as he liked.

'God bless you, Jim,' he said. Then, drawing me aside: 'But Jim, don't cross Hallows for my sake, I beg you. He has an evil reputation.'

'I think I have the measure of him,' I replied.

Mr Morgan's was only the first warning about the Manager I had that day. In the afternoon, Hallows showed me the factories where the raw sugar-cane was brought in from the fields to be boiled down into molasses, the storehouses where the molasses were kept in barrels, and the office where Mr Sharpe wrote up the books. Making an excuse, he left me there, to begin my examination of the accounts, promising me a more extensive tour of the property in a day or two. Towards dusk, sore-eyed from poring over the account-books, and needing to stretch my legs, I took stroll in the gardens. I was stopped by a low, urgent voice hissing my name from a shrubbery.

It was Abed Jones. He was standing in the shadows, beckoning to me, with a look of fear in his eyes.

'Massah Hawkins,' he whispered as I stepped closer to

130

him, 'you got to get away from here. I hear talk. They gon'
kill you – Massah Hallows an' –'

There he stopped with a gulp of terror and shrank further
back into the shadows. Footsteps were approaching, and I
turned to see Gaynes, the overseer of the slaves, to whom
Hallows had introduced me earlier in the day. He was a
huge brute of a man, like a pugilist, and he was glaring at
me suspiciously.

'Good evening, Mr Gaynes,' I said as nonchalantly as I
could. He continued to glower at me, but I stood my
ground, and he grunted out a very uncivil 'Good evening,'
and walked away. I waited until he was out of earshot, then
stepped back into the shrubbery.

But Abed Jones had vanished.

It was only the beginning of the mysteries of that night. I
dined alone. Hallows, no doubt wishing to avoid my company, had gone to Kingston. After dinner, I continued my
scrutiny of the account-books in my room. It was after
midnight, and I was just thinking of turning in, when I
heard a scratching at my door. Taking up the candle, I
opened the door and before I could blink an eye Ben Gunn
darted inside.

'Jim, mate,' he whispered hoarsely, his eyes as round as
marbles, 'there's things afoot.'

Tapping his nose, and winking importantly, he added: 'I
seen 'em, the devils!'

'Devils?' I asked, setting down the candle.

'That's it!' said Ben.

'That's what?' I cried.

'Hush!' said Ben, finger to lip. 'Dirty work, mate – a
whole crew o' blackamoors mustered an' carryin' off the
grog. I *seen* 'em, I tell ye.'

That was enough for me. I had no idea in the world what
Ben meant, but he had proved his value as a spy so often
before that I was prepared to act. Seizing a brace of pistols, I
followed Ben out of the house and through the gardens.

There was a full moon and we had to move with great
caution, slipping from shadow to shadow. When we were

near to the store-houses, Ben motioned me to stop. The regular tramping of feet, like a platoon of soldiers on the march, was clearly audible above the incessant chirping of the cicadas. Peering round the trunk of a silk-cotton tree, I saw a dozen or more Negroes, each with a barrel of molasses upon his shoulder, moving in a file out of the storehouse, past the factory buildings, and into the jungle. A lantern was burning in the open doorway of the store-house, shedding a strong radiance. Into this light suddenly stepped Overseer Gaynes.

I drew back my head quickly, and motioning Ben to follow, made my way back to the house.

'Jim, mate,' says Ben, when we were safely inside, 'it's a do – that's Ben Gunn's opinion.'

'Mine too,' said I. 'And first thing in the morning we'll find out what sort of a do it is.'

Chapter XX

A Footprint in the Sand

At first light, while the house still slept, Ben and I crept out. It was a glorious morning, clear, fresh, and sparkling; every bush and tree seemed to be clothed in diamonds as the first rays of the sun lit up the dew-drops upon their leaves. We made our way directly to the store-houses.

The doors were closed and barred and there was no sign of any watchman. All was silent and deserted. Determined to use the utmost caution, however, we took a circuitous route to gain the jungle. Almost at once we came upon the path that the Negroes must have taken, for the dew-drenched soil still bore the prints of their bare feet. We followed the path, which began to descend quite steeply, twisting and turning. A salty tang in the air, and the cries of sea-birds told me that we were approaching the coast, which was evidently much nearer to the plantation house than I had imagined.

Sure enough, in a few minutes, we emerged from the jungle on to a rocky bluff to see below us a little, sandy cove, shaped like a horseshoe, and fringed all around by palm trees. A series of broad steps, cut into the rock, led down directly to the beach.

There we had only to use our eyes to know the whole story of last night's work. A boat had been in the cove – a big lugger I judged from the mark of its keel still visible in the sand on to which it had plainly been drawn; scuffs upon the bark of the nearest palm-tree showed where the painter had been made fast. All around, the beach was completely churned up, and it required no very great intelligence to deduce that the barrels transported from the store-house had been loaded on to the lugger. I was examining the keel-mark more closely when a cry from Ben brought me to my feet.

He was crouching upon the sand twenty or thirty paces away, and as I strode towards him, I could see that his face was white, and his eyes bolting. When I asked him what was up, he merely pointed a trembling finger at the ground.

I looked, and instantly saw what had excited him. There in the sand, plain as print, was the mark of a heavy sea-boot – but only of the right foot. Where the left foot should have been there was an indentation that could have been made by nothing other than a crutch!

'Silver,' breathed Ben. 'As God'll judge me, Silver's been 'ere!'

'Impossible!' I cried.

'Jim,' says Ben, clutching at my sleeve, 'that's Silver's mark! I knows it!'

He gripped my arm tighter. 'What if he ain't gone?' he said. 'What if 'e's 'ere now, a-spyin' on us?' And he looked up towards the jungle, his cheek twitching.

I thought it most unlikely that Silver, for all his aptitude for villainy, could have become embroiled in Mr Hallows's conspiracy (or whatever it was) so soon upon arrival in Jamaica, and said as much to Ben.

But Ben would have none of it. All the way back to the plantation house he kept insisting that he could sense Silver's presence, and very near jumped out of his skin at every bird that flew from a tree, and every animal that rustled in the underbrush! And no sooner had I returned to the house than I was given a further reminder of Silver.

As I entered the hall I encountered Captain Williams, who gave me a hard stare and a gruff 'Good morning,' as he went out.

I walked into the dining-room to find Hallows, returned from Kingston, sitting at table over a dish of coffee, and I immediately enquired about Captain Williams's business.

'Oh, it's no very great matter,' said Hallows. 'He merely suspects you of harbouring a notorious felon, that's all!'

If he had expected to throw me off balance, he was disappointed.

'How very singular,' I said coolly, drawing up a chair to the table.

'It seems there is a great hue and cry after John Silver,' Hallows continued. 'A reward of fifty guineas! Half the Militia turned out of barracks, and I don't know what!'

He looked at me quizzically as I sat down at the table.

'Treasure Island!' says he after a moment. 'Jamaica's been agog at the tale these ten years. They say you still have Flint's map?'

'I keep it as a curiosity,' I replied. 'It has no value.'

'Quite so,' he returned. 'You must show it to me some day.'

A short bow was my only reply.

'You have been taking the morning air, Mr Hawkins, so I'm informed,' said he suddenly.

I merely nodded.

'I'm *well* informed, you see,' he continued with a mocking smile, as if to say: 'I know what you've been about and it troubles me not at all.'

Such cocksureness from a man who was no better than a common thief sorely tried my patience and I longed to wipe the superior smirk from his face; but I still had to find out the exact nature of the conspiracy, and to prove Hallows's complicity. Patience and restraint were my best weapons, but I did not think it would be long before matters came to a head.

I was right.

Directly after breakfast, I inspected the store-houses and made a rough tally of the stock. Having compared my findings with the entries in Saul Sharpe's ledgers, I went to the office to speak to that gentleman himself.

He gave a start when I entered and favoured me with a sickly smile as I placed the account-books upon his desk.

'A most meticulously kept account, Mr Sharpe,' said I.

He looked heartily relieved, bobbed his head, and thanked me for the compliment in his whining little voice.

'However,' I went on, 'they tell a story that I find hard to credit.'

'Sir?' said he, with a gulp.

'Your expenditures,' I continued crisply, 'wages, slave-rations, seed, repairs, and so on, bear no relation to your receipts.'

'Sir—?'

'It's possible, I suppose, that the discrepancy could be due to an exceptionally low yield—'

'That's it, sir,' cried Sharpe eagerly.

'But,' I went on firmly, 'I happen to know that the Trelawney land is some of the best in Jamaica.'

'Very true, sir, very true,' said Sharpe rather desperately, 'but, if I may make so bold, you 'ave to take into account what you might call natural 'azards, sir. 'Urricanes, sir, something terrible they are, an' the blight, and the Mar-oons. Good land is one thing, sir, if you'll permit my sayin' so, but good luck's another.'

'Juggle it how you will, Mr Sharpe,' said I, 'your books don't balance.'

'Mr Hawkins!'

Hallows's voice rang out from the doorway. I turned my head as he advanced into the room, and I could see that he was in a rage. The bland self-assurance of an hour ago was gone.

'Do I understand that you accuse my clerk of falsifying the accounts?' he said.

'The accounts speak for themselves,' I replied with a shrug.

'Do they indeed?' returned Hallows with cold fury. 'I trust you can prove that to the satisfaction of a court!'

'A court, Mr Hallows?'

'A court, sir! The law of defamation, sir,' he said furiously. 'I've about done with your pryings and insinuations. I'm tired of being told my business by a jumped-up innkeeper's son.'

I smiled, for I felt that I was getting the better of Mr Hallows at last, and replied: 'One thing you learn in the innkeeping trade is – *how to count barrels.*'

And I turned upon my heel and walked away.

I went directly to the stables, and told them to saddle me a horse, for I had arranged with Mr Morgan to view the site of his church, and thought it no bad policy to let Hallows stew for a few hours, while I kept the appointment.

With a plan of the plantation to guide me, I rode at a leisurely pace up through the lush fields of sugar-cane, then into a belt of jungle, where the land was too steep for cultivation, but where a rough road had been made for hauling timber. The church was to be built upon the high ground on the far side of the jungle, a mile or so from the sea, near a great cliff known as Lugger Point.

I found Mr Morgan, in his shirt-sleeves, standing in the midst of a veritable wilderness of cactus plants and creeping weeds, and laying about him zealously with a scythe.

'Mr Morgan!' I cried, jumping down from my horse. 'Spare yourself, I beg you.'

'Jim, my boy!'

He threw down his scythe and puffed towards me in a torrent of sweat.

'I know that faith is supposed to be able to move mountains, sir,' said I, 'but—'

'But they that wait upon the Lord shall renew their strength,' said he. 'Isaiah Forty-one!'

'Isaiah notwithstanding, I'm sure we can spare some hands from the plantation to clear this ground for you.'

'Very generous of you, my boy,' he said awkwardly, avoiding my eye, 'but, d'you see, I couldn't, ah, avail myself—'

'I'm certain the Squire would wish it.'

'The fact is, Jim,' he said, suddenly solemn, 'that I'll not have my church built by slave labour. Slavery is an abomination in the sight of God, and I'll not condone it.'

'Bravo, sir!' said I. 'But you'll not refuse a contribution of money from the estate, I'm sure, so that labour may be hired. I know I speak for Mr Trelawney.'

'For Mr Trelawney, perhaps,' he replied, with a shrewd look, 'but what of Mr Hallows?'

'You may take it from me, sir,' I replied, 'that the days of Mr Hallows's authority are numbered.'

'I'm glad to hear it,' said he, shaking his head, 'but tread carefully, Jim – that's all I'll say.'

When I had extracted a promise from him, that he would attempt no more land-clearance on his own, I bade him goodbye and set off back to the plantation house. I was proceeding cautiously down the jungle road, for the ground was treacherous, and turning over in my mind a plan to frighten Saul Sharpe into giving evidence against Hallows, when my horse stumbled so violently that I was thrown from my saddle.

I fell heavily to the ground and lay supine on my back for a moment, with the breath quite knocked out of me, sick and dizzy. The horse was plunging about, whinnying with fright, its hoofs ensnared in a sort of shallow pit in the road. I swear that as I attempted to rise, to go to the nag's aid, I thought I had been the victim of a simple accident. Even when a man – a Negro – melted out of the shadows and stepped to the horse's head to quiet the beast, I took no alarm, assuming that he was attached to the plantation and had merely happened providentially by.

But when a second Negro appeared, with a pistol in each hand, I knew that I had to do, not with an accident, but with murder.

The second fellow advanced towards me. He was a giant in stature and wore the tatters of military dress – a cocked hat, scarlet coat, white breeches, bandoleer. His ugly face was cracked into a snarling grin, and death stared out of his eyes. I did the only possible thing to save my life – flung myself forward at him.

He fired off both pistols and the burning powder scorched my cheek as I fell upon him. I was unhurt – but in a poor condition to grapple with an assailant of his strength. He parried my first blows with consummate ease and dealt me a counter-blow, like the kick of a mule, that knocked me off my feet. Through a haze I saw him draw a cutlass. Then I heard a pistol's roar and my attacker crashed down like a felled oak and lay still at my feet.

The other fellow ran forward. Again a pistol barked; he clapped a hand to his breast with a shriek of pain, and took to his heels.

I picked myself up and turned, for the pistol shots had come from behind me. There was a sound of movement in the shadows of the jungle, a rustling and stirring of foliage, and then out into the light stepped Long John Silver!

Chapter XXI

I Enter a Partnership

'Steady, Jim,' says Long John, 'bide still a moment, mate.'

He heaved past me quickly and stooped over the body of the man he had shot. His grunt of satisfaction told me that my former assailant was dead. Silver fumbled inside the dead man's coat and fished out a purse. Turning towards me, he weighed the purse in his hand, causing the coins to jingle.

'Twenty guineas, I'd reckon,' he said.

He threw the purse to me and I caught it.

'But you count it out, mate,' he continued, 'for a man has a right to know the price another sets on his hide.'

I did not accept this invitation but threw the purse on to the ground.

'I know *your* price, Long John,' said I. 'It's fifty guineas, so I hear.'

'Aye,' says he, with a sly grin, 'fifty for John Silver, accordin' to the Governor o' Jamaicy; twenty for Jim Hawkins, accordin' to—'

He stopped there, and sniffed, and scratched his head. 'Well now,' he resumed, 'I reckon I might know who that would be.'

'Mr Joshua Hallows, I imagine,' said I.

Long John's eyes shifted under his brows, and he chuckled. 'Jim, you're smart,' says he. 'Smart as paint – didn't I always say so? Here's I, riskin' all to bring you a warning, and you has the whole business figured out from stem to stern.'

'Not quite.'

'Ah,' says he very shrewdly, 'then it may be as I can supply the ballast.'

'I believe you may,' I replied, 'for I know you were a party to last night's affair.'

'You knows that, do ye? Well, well – and what else d'ye know?'

'That the Squire is being systematically robbed and the account-books falsified to conceal the crime.'

'Robbed?' says Silver, with a rich chuckle. 'Fleeced to the bare bone, more like, by Hallows an' Lewis.'

'Lewis?'

'Caleb Lewis,' said he, 'citizen and merchant o' Kingston, Jamaica.'

He leaned upon his crutch and took out his pipe and tinder-box.

'I'll make it short, and I'll make it straight,' he said, when his pipe was fairly alight. 'I had but the one purpose in Jamaica – to get what's mine: the map. How was I to do it, says you – one man alone, and he wi' a price on his head? I'll tell you. I've followed the sea for forty years, Jim, and there ain't a port 'twixt Havana and the China Sea but you'll find an old shipmate o' Long John's ready to pipe 'im aboard.'

A broad wink accompanied this latter statement.

'Well then,' he continued, 'in Kingston, Jamaica there's Caleb Lewis, a gentleman o' substance, Jim, and proper filled out amidships since he sailed wi' Captain Flint. A lean young shaver 'e were then, and Caleb *Powell* were 'is name, and he'd ha' keelhauled his own mother for half a doubloon.'

He tapped the dottle from his pipe and began to refill it with plug.

'He's changed his name, has Caleb,' he went on, 'but not his ways, as I very soon found out when I hauled up alongside. Three years he's been in league wi' Hallows, and a rare old game it is, and money in it too, I reckon.'

'A small fortune, I should think,' said I.

'Mebbe,' said Long John, 'but groats by comparison wi' what I could put 'im in the way of. You see, I don't dissemble wi' you, Jim: Caleb was to get a ship an' a crew, an' I was to get the map.'

'An excellent plan from your point of view,' said I. 'What happened to upset it?'

'Not what, Jim,' he returned, 'but *who*. Hallows, that's who, for Caleb peached to 'im. "'Ere's luck," says Hallows, "'ere's how to kill two birds wi' a single stone. I'll scupper Hawkins and have the map, and you'll scupper Silver." '

'I see,' said I, regarding him thoughtfully. 'And now you have a fresh proposal, I assume?'

'Well,' says he, 'I looks at it this way, Jim. What's your business? To sink Hallows. What'll sink 'im? Proof o' the

crime. That's sense – but where's the proof? Well – sup-
posin' there was a book, a book of account, we'll say, what
Caleb Lewis keeps for 'is dealings wi' Hallows. That'd sink
'em for sure.'

'Without doubt.'

'And there's your business done, and John Silver to
thank for it, and for your life too, though I don't insist on
that.'

'And in return?'

'We're partners, Jim.'

'Partners?'

'That's it, mate. *You've* the map, *I've* the secret o' how
to read it. You fit out a ship an' muster a crew – your own
crew, Jim, mark that well – an' it's Treasure Island an'
equal shares o' the stones. What d'you say?'

'Just this,' I replied cheerfully. 'I trust you no better
than a rattlesnake and I don't give a fig for Flint's stones.'

He flushed angrily and his eyes narrowed.

'However,' I continued, 'I have a great desire to settle
Mr Hallows's hash for him and so I'll take you up on your
proposal.'

His face cleared at once, and cracked into a grin.

'Jim,' says he, 'you're plank and caulking, so you are,
and I ain't intendin' to diddle you, my hand on it.'

We shook hands solemnly.

Long John then described Caleb Lewis's place of business, a large warehouse upon the quay at Kingston, and
told me to meet him there that night.

'It's no trouble to me,' I said, 'but there's a regiment of
militia out looking for *you*.'

'Aye,' says he with a wink, 'but so long as they don't
look out to sea, I'll come and go as I please, I reckon.'

I left Silver in the forest, and remounting the horse,
which was uninjured, returned to the house. There was no
sign of Hallows in the dining-room or the library, and a
servant informed me that he had gone off to Kingston. I
went to my own room, and was about to open the door,
when I detected a slight sound from within. I had no pistol

with me, but I loosened my sword, and then flung open the door.

Saul Sharpe was crouched near the bedstead with his back to the door. The room had been thoroughly ransacked. At my sudden entrance he let out a shriek of fright and nearly jumped out of his skin.

He twisted round, and when he saw me, the blood drained out of his face and he stared at me with a mixture of awe and abject terror, as if I was a supernatural being. The explanation struck me at once: he was privy to his master's plans, and had thought me dead. He cowered away and fell on his knees as I advanced towards him.

'Well, Mr Sharpe,' said I, 'I'm thoroughly alive as you see – and you may search this room for a month if you like, but you'll not find the map.'

At this the miserable creature mewed and gibbered, begging for mercy while protesting his utter innocence. Without troubling to mask my disgust, I ordered him to his feet.

'Mr Sharpe,' said I, 'you've but the one chance to save your wretched neck, and that's to make a full confession.'

'I dare not,' he cried, trembling from head to foot, 'indeed, sir, I dare not. Mr Hallows would—'

'You've nothing to fear from Hallows,' said I. 'His race is run – and so is yours unless you do as I say.'

It took me some time to persuade him, for he had a mortal dread of Hallows, but at length I hauled him away to his office, sat him down, put a quill in his hand, and made him write down what he knew.

It took a deal of time because he interrupted every line with protestations of innocence, how at every turn he had been forced to act against his will by Hallows, how, but for fear of Hallows, he would have exposed it all to the Squire long since, and so on and so forth. But at last it was done, and I had in my hand written testimony that Hallows had plotted my death and had paid the Maroons to murder me. Warning Sharpe that if he attempted to run away, or to communicate with Hallows, a warrant would be issued for his arrest, I left him and went to Ben Gunn's quarters.

Sharpe had confessed that, on Hallows's instructions, he had plied Ben with rum until he was dead drunk, with the intention, no doubt, though Sharpe denied it, of killing him later. I found Ben still half in a stupor, lying on his bed. I sluiced a bucket of cold water over him, but experience told me that it would be two hours at least before he would be fit to ride with me into Kingston.

Leaving Ben to his moans and groans, I sought out Abed Jones. I found him in the gardens, where he was chiefly employed, raking one of the walks. Taking care that I was not observed, I drew him away and asked him if he was willing to help me.

'I reckon I am,' says he. 'I reckon you a good friend to me.'

I gave him a brief account of what had happened and then took the map out of my money-belt.

'I want you to keep this safe for me,' said I, 'until I return from Kingston.'

He readily agreed, but warned me on no account to trust Sharpe.

'When I return,' said I, 'you'll have no more to fear from Sharpe, or Hallows, or Gaynes, or any of them.'

I returned to Ben's quarters to find him just about on his feet, and as full of innocence and excuses as Sharpe himself. I apprised him of all that had happened and bid him saddle up the two best horses in the stables.

We set off together half an hour later, each armed with a brace of pistols and ready to use them. I was uneasy at leaving Sharpe at large, but I did not think he could do much harm, and short of putting an end to the villain's life myself, there was not much to be done with him. Very soon, night fell and we redoubled our vigilance, riding at a slow trot. Nothing untoward happened, however, but by the time we entered Kingston it was late and the town was asleep.

We found Lewis's warehouse without difficulty and I bade Ben stay with the horses and keep his eyes and ears open.

There was not a soul abroad on the quayside, all was very

quiet and peaceful as I approached the warehouse, yet my 'sixth sense' warned me of danger. I knocked three times very softly on the door, according to Silver's instructions, and a moment later it opened a crack, and Silver himself pulled me quickly inside.

It was very dark and there was a pungent reek of tar, molasses, and spices. As my eyes grew accustomed to the light I saw that I was in a great cavern of a place, open to the rafters like a barn, with a gallery of sorts under the eaves. Sitting upon the ground, with his back to a heap of barrels, and trussed up like one of his own bales of cloth, was the proprietor, Caleb Lewis. He was a plump, grizzled old fellow, and in the light of the single lamp, his eyes burned with rage and hatred.

Without a word, Long John handed me a thick ledger, bound in well-worn leather. I took it near to the lamp and opened it. A cursory examination of a few pages was enough to show me that it was exactly what I required to prosecute Hallows: it was an account, in detail, of all his transactions with Lewis.

'Well then, Jim,' says Long John, 'what d'you reckon to it? Will it cook 'em?

I nodded.

'But what you requires,' Silver went on, 'is to make a sure thing certain, as they say; to which end Caleb here is ready an' willin' to sing like a bird – ain't that right, Caleb?'

Lewis's reply was to spit vigorously and curse Silver in terms I dare not set down. Silver merely chuckled.

'That's you, Caleb,' he said cheerily, 'never at a loss for an oath. But it's sing or swing, mate. Sing, and I'll undertake you'll find Squire Trelawney a liberal man wi' a reward. Stay mum, an' a Court o' Law'll learn the name you was baptized with – not forgettin' as there's a *rope* awaitin' for Caleb *Powell*.'

Lewis's smouldering eyes turned to me and then back to Silver, and after a moment he nodded shortly.

144

'But I'll find you, Silver,' he added between his teeth. 'I'll spill your tripe if it's the last thing I do.'

'The finding,' returned Silver mildly, 'that'd be the last thing, Caleb.'

He heaved closer to me. 'Now, Jim,' he breathed, 'the map.'

'It's safe enough,' said I coolly.

Fury blazed for a second in his eyes, but he mastered himself, and smiled slowly.

'That's the way of it, eh?' he said. 'You've learned caution, Jim.'

'Yes,' said I. 'In a hard school.'

'You has a proposition, I takes it.'

'I have,' I replied. 'I'll hide you at the plantation house for as long as it takes to settle with Hallows. Then I'll fit out a ship and we'll sail together to Treasure Island.'

He considered this for a long time, his lids drooping over his eyes, then he nodded.

'So be it then,' he said.

We both turned in astonishment as Lewis let out a wheezing laugh.

'Well,' he croaked, shaking all over, 'if that ain't rich. John Silver bluffed and bubbled by a boy not dry behind the ears.'

With a roar of rage, Silver whipped out his knife, and hopping like a monstrous bird, fell upon Lewis, and pressed the blade to his throat.

'That's right, mate,' cackled Lewis. 'You spoil Mr Hawkins's witness for him. Then you take 'is word and let 'im lead you up to Execution Dock.'

'You misbegotten mongrel dog,' says Silver, with murder in his voice, 'I'd take 'is word if it led me down to Hell itself.'

'Long John,' said I, laying a restraining hand on him, 'let it be.'

'That's it,' says Lewis tauntingly. 'Let it be, mate.'

Long John released Lewis, and stepped away, tucking his knife back into his belt.

'Come, Mr Lewis,' said I, 'we have an engagement with the Governor.'

I gave him a hand to help him to his feet and at that moment a musket cracked from the gallery above us, the lead whistled past my ear, and Lewis crashed to the ground. I flung myself to one side as a second shot roared, struggling to draw my pistol. I looked up to the gallery and saw Gaynes, the overseer, raising a musket, and aiming directly at me.

Long John's pistols barked, and Gaynes ducked down, then ran off towards the far end of the building. Sweating and cursing, Long John heaved away in pursuit, and I was about to follow when I was stopped by Lewis's tortured voice.

'Rum – for the love of God,' he gasped. 'Rum! Fetch me rum, curse you.'

I knelt beside him and opened up his coat. The great bloodstain on his breast told me that all was up with him.

'Rum, damn your soul,' he croaked, even as the light dimmed in his eyes, 'fetch me rum or I'll haunt you.'

These were his last words, for a terrible rush of blood from his mouth choked him, and a moment later he died.

As I closed his eyes, I was dimly aware of the tread of boots. I turned my head and saw that militiamen were swarming into the warehouse. Captain Williams was striding towards me. I rose. Williams looked at the dead man, and then at me.

'Mr Hawkins,' he said, 'I arrest you in the King's name.'

Chapter XXII

His Excellency The Governor

They clapped me in irons and marched me out.

As we passed along the quayside I saw Ben Gunn out of the tail of my eye, watching from the shadows of an alleyway. I derived no little comfort from it. This is not to say that I anticipated remaining under arrest for very long. I had Lewis's ledger and Saul Sharpe's testimony in my pocket and I was confident that, when they were placed before the Governor, he would acquit me of any responsibility for Lewis's death, and would issue warrants for the arrest of Hallows and Gaynes.

However, nothing in this world is certain and I soon learned the truth of that dictum. Lord Charles expressed only the most formal interest in my accusation against Hallows, and none at all in the Captain's accusation against me, that I had killed Lewis. He was concerned with nothing but Silver, and my connexion with him, which I neither confirmed nor denied, but challenged him to prove.

'Explain to Mr Hawkins why you set a watch on Lewis's establishment,' Devereux said to Williams.

(The three of us were alone in the library.)

'I always had my suspicions of Lewis,' the Captain replied stolidly. 'I know an old buccaneer when I see one.'

'Quite so,' was the supercilious reply.

'My supposition is that Silver had a hold over Lewis,' Williams went on. 'Lewis no doubt informed Hawkins where he could see his friend.'

'Well, Mr Hawkins?' said Devereux.

'The Captain's suppositions do not amount to evidence,' said I.

'So,' said Devereux, pursing his thin lips, 'you persist in denying your tryst with Silver tonight?'

'It's for you to prove, sir,' I replied, 'whereas the proofs of my accusation against Mr Hallows lie upon your desk and I demand that you examine them.'

'*Demand*, sir?' says Devereux with an unpleasing sort of archness. 'You're in a fine position to make demands, I should think. If Mr Hallows is implicated in any way you may be sure he'll be brought to book; but you have yet to explain your own position to my satisfaction. Come now, sir. Don't trifle with me. You went to meet Silver. Why deny it?'

'I repeat – there is not a shred of evidence.'

Devereux turned to Williams and said very peremptorily: 'I assume your search of the building revealed Silver's hiding-place?'

Captain Williams looked absolutely startled at this and could not reply.

'D'you mean to tell me there's been no search?' cried Devereux furiously.

'In, in all the confusion, sir—' stammered Williams.

'Confusion be damned,' roared Devereux, pale with rage. 'Duty, you blockhead! Duty!'

It was the Captain's turn to flush with anger.

'Sir, I protest—'

'Protest? Damme, I should break you! Well, don't stand there like a cretin! Do it, man! Do it now!'

Containing his anger with difficulty, Williams saluted and quit the room, leaving me alone with the Governor.

Devereux picked up my money-belt, which had been discovered during the thorough search I had been subjected to, and weighed it in his hand. Casting a shrewd look in my direction, and in a completely new tone of voice, he said: 'Where is it?'

For a moment, I swear I did not comprehend him.

'Don't play the bumpkin with me, boy,' he went on. 'The treasure map – where have you hidden it?'

I was so utterly taken aback by the implications of his question that I could make no reply, but simply stared at him.

He smiled at me.

'You appear to be tongue-tied, Mr Hawkins,' he said.

'Forgive me,' I replied, 'but His Majesty's Governor of Jamaica enquiring about a pirate's treasure map – it's somewhat surprising.'

'Life,' said a voice, 'is full of surprises.'

I turned my head to see Hallows entering the room. 'That,' he said as he strolled nonchalantly towards Devereux, 'is what makes it worth living.'

Hallows had a document in his hand, which he passed to Devereux.

'This,' said Devereux, holding up the paper, 'is a sworn testimony from one Saul Sharpe that you have been seen in the company of the convicted felon John Silver. On this evidence I may hold you in custody for as long as it pleases me.'

He moved closer to me and shrugged. 'On the other hand,' he continued, 'if you tell me where you have concealed the map—'

'And withdraw your absurd allegations against me,' Hallows put in smoothly.

'—Then the affair can be closed without further *inconvenience* to you,' Devereux concluded.

I looked Devereux squarely in the eye.

'Treasure,' said I, 'the great leveller. It turns the Governor of Jamaica into a common criminal.'

Rage leaped into Devereux's eyes.

'If the circumstances were otherwise,' he said in a voice that trembled, 'I'd prescribe the rack. However, a diet of plain water is a great loosener of tongues.'

He strode to the door and summoned the guard. Two militiamen appeared, and without addressing another word to me, Devereux ordered them to take me away and lock me up in close confinement.

I fancy it was Shakespeare who wrote somewhere that 'the sight of means to do ill deeds, makes ill deeds done.' As the two militiamen, one upon either side, marched me along the passageway that led towards the cells, I saw ahead of me an open window.

Without stopping to think about the false position that an attempt to escape would place me in, or about the unlikelihood of its succeeding, I put out a foot and tripped up the first of my guards, while simultaneously swinging round my arms so that the heavy irons that encased my wrists caught the second guard full in the face. Then I hurled myself through the open window!

Though I broke my fall by rolling head over heels, I was badly winded. Desperation lent me strength, however, and I scrambled to my feet and took to my heels. Muskets roared behind me, but I was untouched and redoubled my pace.

I was in the garden of the Governor's residence. In front of me was a considerable shrubbery that would afford me temporary shelter. But as I made for it, I heard the alarum bells ringing, and saw three or four militiamen running to head me off. I thought I was done for, but in the next instant pistol shots belched from the shrubbery and one of the militiamen was hit, while the others scrambled for cover.

Ben Gunn – God bless him! – ran out of the shrubbery.

'Jim! Jim, mate! This way!' cried Ben, but as I closed on him, a musket spoke, and Ben took the ball in his shoulder.

'On my back! For your life!' I gasped.

Ben scrambled somehow upon my back and together we crashed and stumbled into the shrubbery. I plunged forward blindly. Ben's weight was nothing and I think I could have carried Vanderbrecken himself so urgent was I to get away. We came to the high wall that enclosed the garden. I scaled it in a trice, hampered though I was by my irons, and reached down to haul Ben up – a feat that would have tested a stronger man whose arms were free, but I was desperate!

We dropped down upon the other side of the wall, and Ben gasping that he was fit to run, we pelted away into the quiet streets of Kingston.

Ten minutes later, having encountered not a soul on the way, I was knocking furiously upon the door of Mr Morgan's parsonage. The door creaked open and there was Mr Morgan's honest, blinking face, crowned with a night-cap. Before he could utter a word, I slipped past him, pulling Ben with me, and slammed the door shut.

'Lord bless my soul!' said Morgan, wiping the sleep from his eyes. 'Jim! Ben! Whatever's to do?'

Breathlessly, I told him my story, but he could hardly comprehend it, and I had to repeat it more slowly. When I came to the revelation of the Governor's part, and his complicity in Hallows's plot to get the map, I thought Mr Morgan would swoon away with shock.

'May the Lord God of Heaven forgive us all, I never heard of such wickedness in my life!'

When I had finished my recital he cried: 'Vanderbrecken! We must seek out Vanderbrecken! He'll know what to do! Yes, yes, we must have Vanderbrecken's advice at all costs.'

Mr Morgan dressed himself hurriedly and went out to fetch the Dutchman, who was aboard his boat, which he had been fitting out and provisioning ready for his departure to Mexico. While we waited for Mr Morgan to return, I looked at Ben's wound. It was not dangerous, but serious enough, I thought, to confine him to bed for a day or two. Ben consoled himself with a bottle of rum, which we found in Mr Morgan's cupboard. I tried to think what to do. My position was wellnigh hopeless. Devereux would issue a warrant in the morning and a full-blooded manhunt would ensue, which I would have little hope of eluding. Once caught, I was doomed. I could expect no sort of justice from Devereux. I would be condemned for the murder of Lewis, and no doubt offered my life in exchange for the map, and then, likely as not, be disposed of anyway! Worse, Hallows might easily find the map on his own. If he assumed, as he reasonably could, that I had concealed it at the plantation house, and if I had been observed talking to Abed Jones, then he would have the solution in his hands, and Abed's ruin would follow my own.

And what of Silver?

These gloomy reflections quite cast me down, and by the time Mr Morgan returned with Vanderbrecken, my spirits were at a low ebb. But the sight of the Dutchman, steady-eyed, cheerful, full of confidence and vigour, revived me at once. He shook his head at me, and sighed, but there was a twinkle in his blue eyes.

'*Never*, you learn,' he said. '*Never*. Always trouble, trouble, trouble.'

He sat down at the table and slapped his hand upon the board.

'Our good friend haff told me everything,' said he. 'So. Now we make a plan. It is very simple. I was to leave the day after tomorrow; I leave tonight, and you come with me.'

'Impossible,' said I. 'Until I have recovered the map—'

'Bah! The map!' he cried explosively. 'All I hear is the map, the map, the map! The devil with it!'

I explained the predicament in which I had left Abed Jones, and the danger in which the boy stood from Hallows.

'I'll not quit Jamaica until I'm sure that Abed's safe,' I maintained, and Mr Morgan backed me up.

'Very well then,' said Vanderbrecken. 'We go first to the plantation. But we must go quickly, before first light, before they turn out the soldiers.'

So it was agreed by all – save Ben Gunn. He would not be left behind, and swore by all the Saints that he was 'fit as a flea on a dog's back'; but both Mr Morgan and Vanderbrecken were adamant that he lie up and rest his arm. Poor Ben was forced to give way, at last, but he wept like a child when I bade him farewell.

Vanderbrecken and I slipped out of the house and under cover of darkness gained the quay where his vessel was berthed.

The boat, named *Amsterdam*, was the trimmest little yacht I ever saw, ketch-rigged, with a neat cabin amidships, and so fitted out that a single man could sail her with no great difficulty, and two men with the greatest of ease.

We had a sail hoisted and were tacking out towards Port Royal into a stiff breeze within twenty minutes, and reached open sea without any challenge. As dawn came up, crimson and gold, we were skimming along the coast before the wind. Vanderbrecken, who was sitting at the tiller, drew in a great breath of the wonderful air, and exhaled in a long sigh of satisfaction and pleasure.

'The sea,' said he, 'it is good. A man can breathe. He is free.'

I nodded and took up the telescope to see if I could spy Lugger Point. Vanderbrecken jogged my arm.

'Look at the *sea*, my friend,' he said. 'Look at the sky, at the sun as it rises.'

I could not conceal a smile, for I had never expected to find a streak of poetry in my bluff Dutch friend.

'Bah!' he said. 'You make mock of me! You are clever young man, Jim, but also you a fool. You chase after a map! You are a man of affairs!'

'As are you,' I replied.

'Affairs! Yes! A forest in Mexico. That is a great affair!'

'You search for rare woods, others search for gold,' said I. 'In the New World every man seeks wealth in his own way.'

'And they are blind,' cried the Dutchman. '*This* is the wealth of the New World, my good friend. The freedom of the high seas. People look at it and they don't see it.'

'Is the New World so very different from the Old?' I asked. 'I haven't found it so in Santa Anna or Jamaica!'

'Bah!' he returned. 'Two islands out of ten thousand – and a hundred thousand more no man has ever seen. Great forests – empty, virgin! Mountains upon which no human foot has ever trod! And always the sea – limitless.' He shrugged his massive shoulders. 'I come from a little country,' he said. 'A man trips over his neighbour's boots. I cannot breathe in a place like that.'

Perhaps an hour later, we rounded Lugger Point and reduced sail under the lee of its towering cliff, then steered for the cove below the plantation house. Very soon I could make out the familiar horseshoe shape, and the strip of white sand upon which Ben had found Silver's print, and something else besides – a jolly-boat drawn up upon the beach!

I turned my head to catch Vanderbrecken's eye.

'Silver?' said he.

'*Silver*,' I replied.

Chapter XXIII

I Laugh Until I Cry

We secured the *Amsterdam* and took the path up through the jungle, keeping our eyes skinned for any sign of Silver. We reached the factories and store-houses without any incident, and proceeding very cautiously, stole towards the rude, thatched huts where the slaves were confined at night.

All was very quiet and still, no smoke was rising from the chimney of the plantation house, no sound came from the slave quarters. We were creeping towards the first of the huts when we were brought up all-standing by a scream of agony that rent the silence so brutally that it was like a physical blow.

For a moment Vanderbrecken and I stood like two statues, staring at each other, then, as a second tortured cry howled in the air, we abandoned all caution and ran full tilt towards the source of the appalling sounds.

Vanderbrecken outpaced me. Coming to the last hut he suddenly halted and put out an arm to stop me. We peered round the corner of the hut to see, ten paces away, a whipping-triangle to which Abed Jones was strapped. His bare back was towards us and it was running with blood. Gaynes, a monstrous oxhide whip in his hand, was standing behind Abed. Hallows was facing him, and beside Hallows stood Sharpe.

Sharpe was speaking.

''E was seen with 'Awkins, I tell you,' the vile creature said, 'not half an hour 'fore 'Awkins set off for Kingston. 'E *knows*, all right.'

'If he does,' Hallows replied, 'then he'll spill. No doubt of that. Lay on, Mr Gaynes.'

I was pelting forward, drawing my sword, before Gaynes had started to raise his whip. By the time he did so I was close enough to strike, and my blade severed the whip as a scythe cuts grass. Then I let the villain have the hilt in his face with all the force I possessed, and he fell to the ground and lay still.

Vanderbrecken, meanwhile, had dealt with Hallows – who was face down in the dust – and was striding after Sharpe, who, attempting to flee, had tripped over his own feet and was struggling to rise. It did my heart good to see the giant Dutchman pick up Sharpe by the scruff of his neck, shake him as a dog shakes a rat, until his teeth rattled in his head, turn him upside down, and drop him on to the hard ground, which met the top of his skull with a most satisfactory thump.

We cut Abed down and would have carried him into the shade, but he stopped us.

'I hide the map for you, Massah Hawkins,' he panted. 'I hide it good. I no tell. I take you. Come.'

I begged him to rest but he would come with me, so leaving Vanderbrecken to truss up Hallows and the other two, I accompanied Abed to the house.

'I ask myself where Massah Hallows never gon' look,' he said as we went. 'Why, where he look already. In Massah Hawkins's room!'

We entered the house and hurried into my room. The first thing I did was to give Abed one of my shirts, telling him to put it on to protect his raw back. Then I knelt down and felt under the bed, where the faithful fellow had concealed the map. I found it almost at once, grasped it, and was about to rise when a voice behind me fairly rooted me to the spot.

'Steady Jim!'

I had entirely forgotten Silver!

I turned to see the rogue standing behind Abed, pressing a pistol to the boy's head.

'I ain't bluffin', Jim,' Silver said. 'You may lay to that.'

Slowly I got to my feet.

'Now then,' says Silver, 'I'll trouble you for that map.'

I looked at him coolly enough, I think, though inwardly I was in a fearful wax.

'I thought we had a partnership,' said I.

'Dissolved, mate,' he replied, utterly unabashed, 'by mutual consent of all parties, as you might say.'

Pressing the pistol harder into Abed's neck, he went on: 'I'll tell 'ee what ye'll do. You'll step up – slow and sober – and you'll place that map in the right-hand pocket o' my coat – and then you'll step back a pace or two and I'll tell 'ee some more.'

What could I do but obey? I took a step towards Silver, then another, and then, from outside, a bugle call rang out high and clear. Silver's head whipped towards the window and I hurled myself at him.

But Abed was quicker than me. He twisted and wrenched himself free, and Silver's pistol went off – harmlessly.

I fell on Silver but he threw me back with a blow that sent me reeling towards the window. Picking myself up, I saw Silver vanishing through the door, then looked out of the window. Captain Williams was leading a troop of mounted militia. Attracted by the pistol shot, they were pounding towards the house. Shouting to Abed to come with me, I ran out of the room and would have made for the hall and into the arms of Captain Williams, like as not, had not Abed grabbed my arm and led me another way.

We quit the house by a door at the rear and made straight for the jungle path. I had no idea what had befallen Vanderbrecken, but if he was still at liberty, he would make for the *Amsterdam* for certain.

So it proved. We were not half-way to the cove when we saw the Dutchman ahead, stepping out from behind a tree.

He held up a hand to stop us.

'No good,' he said. 'Soldiers!'

'By the beach?' I cried.

He nodded.

'I'll draw them off,' I gasped. 'You and Abed launch the boat – go round past Lugger Point. Lay to and wait for me.'

Before Vanderbrecken could protest I was off and pelting down the path. It was up to me to do my best to secure the Dutchman's and Abed's escape if I could; better that I should perish, who had embroiled them in my troubles, than that they should suffer on my account.

Three militiamen were patrolling the beach.

For a moment, I observed them from above. Then, stepping out into the open upon the rock above the cove, I fired my pistol. They took the bait, all three of them, starting to clamber up the path, while I plunged back into the jungle, taking care to make as much noise about it as I could! After three or four minutes I stopped, first to ease a pain in my side like a sword-thrust, second, to make sure that my pursuers were still about their business – which my ears confirmed to me. My plan was now simply to outstrip them and leave them floundering in the jungle, while I found the road I had taken once before, that would lead me up to Lugger Point.

All went well: in less than twenty minutes I came upon my road and half an hour later I was striding across the springy turf towards the edge of the cliff at Lugger Point. I stopped about a foot from the edge and looked out to sea, shading my eyes with my hands, and scouring the waves for a sight of the *Amsterdam*. And then a blow upon my head knocked me senseless to the ground.

When I regained my senses I was lying flat on my back, looking up into the blue sky, where the sea-birds were wheeling and crying. My hand flew instantly to my money-belt. It was gone! Struggling upright, I saw Captain Williams standing a few paces away. In his right hand he held a pistol, in his left, the map.

I got shakily to my feet and looked around, expecting to see militiamen – but there were none.

'We are quite alone, Mr Hawkins,' said the Captain steadily.

'*You*, at least, I took for an honest man,' I replied.

'So I am, I hope,' said he after a moment, 'and not the fool His Excellency the Governor takes me for. I want the truth, Mr Hawkins. Did you kill Caleb Lewis?

'I did not.'

'It was Silver, then.'

'It was Gaynes,' said I.

Williams nodded thoughtfully.

'But still, you *did* have an assignation with Silver?'

'Yes. It was Silver who gave me Lewis's account-book, which proves Hallows's guilt.'

'But it's for *this,* I imagine,' said Williams, holding up the map, 'that Hallows requires your capture so urgently.'

'Hallows,' said I, 'and his confederate.'

Williams eyed me hungrily. 'Yes?' he said.

'Lord Charles Devereux, Governor of Jamaica.'

'I knew it,' Williams breathed. 'I knew it. Will you swear to that in a court?'

'Willingly,' said I. 'But to what purpose?'

'To expose that arrogant popinjay for the blackguard he is!'

'My word, the word of an accused murderer, against Lord Charles Devereux?' His face clouded. 'I must clear my own name before I can blacken his,' I went on, for I had begun to see a way out of my trouble. 'To do that I must return to England and lay the facts before the Secretary of State.'

Williams looked at me hard.

'I have powerful friends in England,' I said. 'There is no other way. Will you help me?'

He never had a chance to reply – for at that moment we were both startled by the sudden approach of two horsemen. Since they were Hallows and Gaynes, however, I thought I should soon discover whether or not Williams would take my part, and was greatly encouraged to see him hastily conceal the map in his coat.

'You've had good hunting, I see,' said Hallows, as he and Gaynes dismounted. While Gaynes remained with the horses, Hallows strolled towards us.

'What news of Silver?' he asked, halting a few paces away.

Williams shrugged. 'Hawkins is my business,' said he. 'There's a dozen good men who'll settle with Silver, I've no doubt.'

'You underestimate yourself, my dear Captain,' said Hallows smoothly. 'I rather think that without their gallant commander your excellent fellows will allow Silver to give them the slip – and what Lord Charles would say to that, I dare not imagine! So I should be off if I were you.' He added: 'Have no fear that this young murderer will give *me* the slip. I'll answer for his hide.'

'My thanks, sir,' returned Williams evenly, 'but I regard Hawkins's recapture as my peculiar responsibility – and will take him back to Kingston myself.'

'You must, of course, be the best judge of your own duty,' said Hallows, 'but heed my advice, I beg you – if Silver should escape again, it would go very hard with you.'

Williams bowed stiffly. 'I am indebted to you, sir, but my clear duty is to see Hawkins safe back to Kingston.'

I am certain that Williams never intended to give the word 'safe' any particular inflexion, but all the same it seemed to contain an implication, and Hallows sensed it.

'I am, as you know well, a Magistrate,' he said. 'I could *order* you to hand Hawkins over to me.'

'With respect, sir,' returned Williams, 'I doubt if the powers of a Magistrate extend so far.'

'You refuse to hand him over, then?'

'I think I have made my position plain,' was the steady, courteous reply.

'I wonder,' said Hallows. 'It occurs to me now, that Hawkins may have been, shall we say, talking to you – and, worse, that you may have listened to him.'

'I am answerable only to the Governor,' returned Williams shortly. 'Stand aside, if you please.'

'As you wish,' said Hallows, moving away.

I let out a shout of warning as he did so for I saw that Gaynes was raising his musket to his shoulder.

It was useless. The overseer fired, Captain Williams spun on his heels and fell dead to the ground. With his pistol pointed at me, Hallows stooped by the body and felt inside the dead man's coat.

'I thought as much,' said he, plucking out the map, and

rising. Gaynes, meanwhile, had advanced nearer, and I was glad to see that his face was all swollen from the blow I had dealt him, and that half his teeth were gone.

'Well, well, Mr Hawkins,' says Hallows. 'It's a merry dance you've led us indeed. However, *sed haec prius fuere*, "it is all over now" as the poet says. You were a dead man from the moment you set foot in Jamaica.'

I made no reply. I was watching Gaynes and at the same time calculating the distance from where I was standing to the edge of the cliff, for I had formed a desperate plan to save my life.

'I had hoped,' Hallows continued, 'to have the pleasure of killing you myself – but I would be churlish indeed if I denied my friend Gaynes.'

'*Williams – no!*' I cried.

A pretty feeble bluff, you'll say – but it was good enough to make both Hallows and Gaynes take their eyes off me for a fraction of a second. And that was all I required to fling myself backwards over the precipice!

I have since learned that the cliff at Lugger Point is three hundred feet high, which is something I suppose, but all I can say is that it seemed hardly a moment between launching myself into the abyss and plunging into the sea. But what is stranger still is that, as I plummeted down, I was able to consider quite calmly what I should do when I entered the water: stay under for as long as possible, and when it became absolutely necessary to breathe, do so in a manner that would least expose me to Hallows and Gaynes on the cliff-top above.

Now, though I say it as should not, I am an excellent swimmer, and it was no trouble to me to carry out my policy. For a long time I kept myself floating just below the surface of the waves, breathing mostly through my nose, and though I swallowed a great deal of sea-water, I did very well.

At last, when I thought that Hallows and Gaynes must have given up watching and assumed me drowned, I put my head out of the water to see that the current had taken me well past the point. When I turned to looked out to sea I saw the *Amsterdam*, close-reefed, not a quarter of a mile away.

I struck out strongly and was soon within hailing distance. Vanderbrecken spotted me at once, and put the yacht about, and a few moments later his powerful arms were hauling me aboard. I was very much exhausted, and was glad to lie down on the little stern-deck, while Abed plied me with fresh water and Vanderbrecken told me how they had effected their escape from the cove.

I was just about to ask him if he knew what had befallen Silver, when the voice of the villain himself brought me bolt upright!

He was standing in the hatchway of the cabin, levelling a pistol at us and from the expression on the Dutchman's face it was plain that Silver had stowed away without his knowledge.

'I'll take that map now, if you please,' said Silver.

The world, I know, takes me for a solemn sort of fellow, not much given to laughter. But I think I have as keen a sense of what is absurd or ironical as the next man, and the sight of Silver thrusting his pistol at us, his eyes narrowed to slits, all grim purpose, and ready to do murder for something that was now hopelessly beyond his reach, struck me as irresistibly comic. I laughed and laughed and laughed until I cried, and the more that Silver gaped at me, the more uncontrollable did my laughter become.

At last–

'Hallows,' I gasped, '*Hallows* has it!'

At that even Vanderbrecken broke down, and his deep bellows of laughter were added to mine. Abed, too, caught the infection, though he could hardly appreciate the full delectable irony, and anybody looking on would have taken us for a crew of madmen. And all the time Silver stared upon us, his face puckered up like that of a baby about to cry.

Chapter XXIV

A Broadside!

For the rest of that day Silver was very silent and subdued and sat with his back to the foremast, brooding, while Abed and I crammed on all sail, and Vanderbrecken pored over his charts, plotting our course for Mexico. But towards dusk, when the outline of Jamaica had long since disappeared over the horizon, he rallied, and was ready as ever with a proposition.

'Hallows is in possession o' the map,' said he as we ate our evening meal, 'but that ain't the end of it – not by a long sea-mile.'

'For me it is – and a good riddance,' was Vanderbrecken's gruff reply.

'We knows where Treasure Island lays,' said Silver, undeterred. 'We has the bearings.'

'I tell you again,' said Vanderbrecken firmly, 'I sail to Mexico, to my forest. I haff been away too long.'

'That's it!' cried Silver. '*Time!* That's the nub o' the business, don't ye see? Hallows must find a ship, fit her out, muster a crew. It'll cost 'im time – time enough for us to haul along o' Treasure Island' – here he looked particularly at me – 'set up snug in the old stockade, and wait. Hallows'll step ashore alone, you may lay to that' – his voice grew more and more excited – 'and we'll take him, *and* the map, and we'll have Flint's stones within the hour. And wi' your share, Dutchman, you can buy every last twig and leaf in Mexico, if you has a mind.'

He sat back, apparently satisfied that he had made out an excellent case.

'If I want money,' said Vanderbrecken, 'I earn it – with this,' and he flexed his brawny arm.

Long John regarded him shrewdly. 'I've the run o' you, I reckon, Dutchman,' says he. 'You ain't a man to chase after gold. No. Freedom, that'd be your creed, I should think.'

He slapped his fist into his hand and went on, with a sudden passion: 'Mine too, by the Powers! But unless he has a heap o' gold to buy it, there ain't no freedom in this world for any man.'

'You understand nothing of me,' returned Vanderbrecken quietly. 'But I know *you*, and I know your kind.' He snapped his fingers. 'That to you and your buccaneer gold!'

'Jim,' says Long John, 'will you stand by and see Hallows take the prize? Him what's robbed you and blackened your name?'

'Not I,' I said. 'Which is why I'm for England by the swiftest passage – to *clear* my name.'

'Is that your answer?' says Long John. 'Is that your gratitude? To put John Silver ashore on Spanish soil and see 'im swing on the Dons' gallows?'

'Ah,' said Vanderbrecken. 'So that's it, is it? The Spaniards too have a price on your head.'

'I ain't denyin' it,' returned Silver coolly. 'Well, Jim?'

'This is Vanderbrecken's vessel,' said I. 'He's Captain here.'

'But you ain't cabin-boy no more, Jim,' Silver replied quickly. 'If you won't go to Treasure Island, so be it – I'll abide by that. But there's debts you owe me, Jim, and I'll see them honoured, by Thunder!'

'What do you want, Silver?' said Vanderbrecken shortly.

'Not much, Dutchman,' he replied. 'Just fer you to alter your course a point or two to westward, that's all.'

'Ah,' says Vanderbrecken, nodding, 'I understand. Machado Island.'

'Aye, Machado,' says Silver. 'I've friends there, old shipmates.' Turning to me – 'You owes me that much, Jim.'

'Vanderbrecken must decide,' I said.

I looked towards the Dutchman and so did Silver. Vanderbrecken considered a moment and then shrugged his shoulders.

'I want to be rid of you, Silver,' he said.

'I ain't blamin' you for that!' said Silver with a sly smile.

'So I agree,' Vanderbrecken continued. 'I take you to Machado.'

'Then that's settled,' says Silver, rising. 'I reckon I'll take a turn in the galley.'

As he hauled himself down into the cabin, Vanderbrecken turned to me.

'I am a great fool,' he said. 'I should throw that man to the sharks. But I haff pity on the poor sharks.'

After this, all Silver's old cheerfulness returned and he became what he could always be – the finest shipmate you could hope for, with his sea-songs, and yarns, and his marvellous skill in the galley. Even Vanderbrecken was forced to admit that he was a handy man to have aboard. He was also the means to raise Abed Jones's spirits, for Abed had relapsed into that sullen, taciturn state in which I had first known him.

One night, two or three weeks after we had quit Jamaica, I awoke in the small hours. Silver was at the tiller, and Abed was keeping watch and handling the sails, while Vanderbrecken and I were supposed to be taking our rest. I was about to turn over and go back to sleep when I heard Silver address Abed thus: 'Well now, you're a singular young fellow you are to be sure. Here's you, wi' your freedom won, an' a face like a tombstone.'

'I ain't gon' to have no cause to smile when we reach land,' Abed replied sulkily.

'I reckon you can count on Jim Hawkins to see you right,' says Silver.

'So then I be Massah *Hawkins's* slave.'

'You won't never be that, boy,' Silver returned very sharply. 'An' freedom don't mean licence to blackguard a true man.'

'I ain't sayin' no bad things 'bout Massah Hawkins,' said Abed. 'But you tell me what I'm gon' do, where I gon' go? Ain't no place in the world for a black man.'

'Well now, that ain't exactly the case,' says Silver. 'Not in my cognizance, leastways. A black skin ain't no help to a man, but it ain't no absolute hindrance neither. Why, there was a tar-black Negress once kept a tavern in Bristol.'

'In England?' cried Abed, greatly astonished.

'In England, aye,' returned Long John. 'Ashanti, she were, an' took by the slavers when she were no more'n a chit of a girl.'

'She run away?' Abed asked, fascinated.

'There weren't an owner in all the West Indies could hold her, boy, the spirit she had in her.'

His voice took on a quality I had never heard in it before – a sad softness, almost a gentleness.

'Aye,' said he, 'and she were hostess o' the Spy-glass Inn, and held to be a lady by one an' all – and her name were Mrs John Silver.'

'You took a black woman to wife?' gasped Abed.

'I did,' said Silver in a voice more like his own. 'In a church too, wi' a parson and a choir all proper.' His tone now vibrant, he went on: 'She had her place in the world, boy, for she *built* it, aye, out of her own wit and fortitude, she built it.'

There was a long silence and then Abed asked, almost in a whisper: 'She dead now, Massah Silver?'

'She is, boy,' came the reply at length. 'And I hope there be a Heaven, for if there is, she's there.'

It was not long after, that fresh trouble broke out between Silver and Vanderbrecken. At first light one morning, we sighted a sail on the western horizon. All through the early hours, Vanderbrecken kept track of the vessel through his telescope, at length reporting that he thought she was a Spanish warship. Throughout the forenoon we watched her anxiously to see if she would alter course in our direction, and were heartily relieved when she held to her way and finally disappeared. Vanderbrecken, however, having consulted his charts, declared that he had changed his ideas about Machado; there were certain islands in the vicinity, Spanish possessions, that he now thought it prudent to avoid. He had lived and worked among Spaniards long enough to know their temper.

'I haff no fear of your shore-going Don,' said he, 'for he's bound by the law like any other man, and I haff my charter from the Viceroy of Mexico himself. But send a Spaniard to sea and you make a pirate of him, and though you haff a hundred charters he will rob you and kill you just the same. So I say we must change our plan.'

'Is that right, Dutchman?' says Silver. 'That's your notion, is it, o' respect for the Articles?'

Vanderbrecken shrugged. 'I will not risk three lives,' said he, 'to humour *you*, Silver. But do not be concerned for yourself – I take you to Port Louis. You'll find buccaneers enough there, I think, to give you sanctuary.'

Silver spat upon the deck. 'So much for the word of a Dutchman,' he said, then, turning to me: 'Jim, will you stand by and see him break his bond?'

Vanderbrecken laughed. 'He's seen you break *yours* many times I think.'

'Mebbe he has,' returned Silver quickly, 'but he's seen me save his life as often, I reckon. Well, Jim?'

Vanderbrecken grunted. 'Why so eager to come to Machado, Silver?' he said. 'It's a poor place, and a dangerous one, too. You haff a plan?'

'I looks to you, Jim,' says Silver, ignoring the Dutchman. 'You've a debt to settle.'

'What's the true risk?' I asked Vanderbrecken.

He shrugged again. 'With Spain,' said he, 'always there is a risk.'

'If we make for Port Louis we lose what – two weeks more? Whereas Machado is less than three days. I leave it to you to decide.'

Vanderbrecken smiled. 'You haff a powerful argument, I think.' He pondered a moment, then – 'very well, we hold our course; but' – turning to Silver – 'if you were looking to berth in Machado harbour, think again, my friend.'

'Berth where you will, Dutchy,' returned Silver shortly, 'just so long as you abides by the Articles.'

Vanderbrecken was faithful to his instinct; three days later, when towards the middle of the afternoon we sighted

Machado Island, he put the helm over in order to approach from the east; the main settlement lay upon the western shore. Silver said nothing but he looked pretty black and I was more than half certain that the Dutchman had frustrated some plot to seize the *Amsterdam*.

We made for a headland at the eastern extremity of the island, and an hour later dropped anchor in a sheltered bay, where a great swamp of mangrove trees pressed down to the water's edge.

I had volunteered to row Silver ashore in the gig, but before he would let us go Vanderbrecken raked every inch of the shoreline through his telescope, and even when he was satisfied that there was no danger, he insisted that I take a brace of pistols with me.

I rowed Silver across the bay to a narrow spit of sand – the only place where he could get ashore. I beached the gig, jumped out, and gave him a hand out.

'Well, Jim,' says he, 'I reckon the cruise ends here for you and Long John.'

'I reckon it does,' said I. 'And I'll shake your hand.'

'You're throwing away a fortune, Jim,' he said as he took my hand.

'I've a fortune already,' said I.

'Ah,' says he, 'that's true. I was forgettin' that Jim,' he said after a moment, 'will you wish me luck and – give me your blessing?'

'*Blessing*, Long John?'

'Well now,' he returned with a smile, 'I reckon you'd rather see John Silver rollin' in a carriage an' dressed in fine linen than Joshua Hallows.'

'That I would,' said I heartily. 'And here's my blessing for what it's worth.'

'I'll tell you what, Jim,' he replied in a strange voice, 'it's worth a heap an' more to Long John Silver.'

Then he turned abruptly, and sketching a sort of salute, heaved rapidly away and soon vanished into the mangrove forest.

Ten minutes later I was back aboard the *Amsterdam* and

Vanderbrecken was hauling up the anchor as fast as he could.

'I'll not breathe easy 'til we're on the high seas,' he said.

'Come,' I replied. 'We're shot of Silver for good this time.'

But Vanderbrecken only shook his head and muttered darkly about 'a feeling in his bones.' I laughed and called him a superstitious old Calvinist.

I vow that I'll never make such a jest again, nor disregard the instinct of a sound and sober man. As we scudded out of the bay and rounded the point we saw a man-o'-war bearing down upon us under a full press of canvas, with the flag of Spain flying at her masthead, and her gun-ports open along her starboard side.

With a terrible oath, Vanderbrecken put over the helm.

'Can we outrun her?' I cried.

'Pray to God we can!'

As I sprang for'ard to hoist more sail, I saw to my utter horror that the Spanish ship was paying off to larboard, bringing her guns to bear upon us.

My cry of warning was drowned in the monstrous thunder of the broadside.

I was plucked into the air as if by the invisible hand of a giant while the *Amsterdam* was pounded into flinders about me, and then I knew no more.

The first of my five senses to return to me was that of hearing. I was floating in a black void but I was aware of a sound which at first I thought was the distant roar of surf on a beach. Then I knew that it was cannon-fire and instantly remembered who I was and what had happened. I tried to move but found my limbs were powerless. I tried to open my eyes but had not the strength even for that. Gradually I became aware of pain, a dull throbbing ache in my head, and keener, stabbing pains in my legs and arms. I was grateful – it proved that I was alive. Again I tried to open my eyes, and this time I succeeded, though at first I could see nothing but a faint blur. Slowly the blur formed into a shape, and the shape into the semblance of a face, and at last I recognized the features of Vanderbrecken.

The knowledge that my friend was alive was evidently the

medicine that my body required: almost at once I felt some of my strength return and I attempted to speak.

'Lie still,' Vanderbrecken said softly.

'Abed—?'

'He's here – by my side.'

'Where are we?'

'In good time. You've taken a knock that would haff done for most men.'

By now I had become aware of the creak of timber and the lap of the sea, and realized that we were aboard a ship – the Spanish warship, most likely.

'Prisoners?' I asked Vanderbrecken. He nodded and again bade me conserve my strength.

'For the love of God,' said I in a stronger voice, 'tell me what's happened.'

He shrugged. 'We're prisoners of the Spanish, that's all.'

'But the gunfire—?'

'The Spanish fleet reducing Machado town to rubble,' was the laconic reply. 'Our luck ran out, my friend. We sailed into a war!'

Part V
Spanish Gold

Chapter XXV

Narrative continued by Dr Livesey: The Return of Ben Gunn

My friend Jim having requested me, as once before, to fill in a gap in the story here and there, I cast my mind back to a blustery Autumn night, some six or seven months after he set sail for Jamaica on the Squire's business. I had taken out a dog and a gun and had just returned home, and was pulling off my boots, when a servant brought me a note from Trelawney – a line of his scrawl summoning me urgently to meet him at the Admiral Benbow inn. Supposing that Mrs Hawkins must be taken ill, I set off on horseback at once, with a groom to carry my medical chest.

It was dark by the time I reached the inn. Leaving the groom to see to the horses, I went straight inside and was about to enter the parlour, when I was stopped by the following remarkable dialogue:

'I don't believe a word of it, ma'am!'

It was the Squire's boom, very loud and angry.

'Do you not, sir?' came Mrs Hawkins's voice, low and miserable, in reply.

'Not a word!'

'I knew how it would be,' moaned Mrs Hawkins. 'I knew it in my heart.'

'Nonsense ma'am!'

Then, to my utter astonishment Mrs Hawkins, by nature so mild-mannered and respectful, burst out: 'It was you

171

first gave him his taste for seafaring! You and your cursed treasure!'

I thought it was about time for me to interfere so I opened the parlour door and strode in.

'Livesey!' cried Trelawney with heartfelt relief. 'Thank heaven!'

Mrs Hawkins was standing by the fire, twisting a handkerchief in her hands, fresh tears glistening upon her cheek. To my amazement, the good lady came at me like a fury.

'And you!' she cried. 'You're no better! A plague on the both of you!'

'Whatever's to do?' I asked Trelawney.

'I'll tell you what's to do,' said Mrs Hawkins, perfectly hysterical. 'My son is dead, thanks to him.'

'Madam—' protested Trelawney helplessly.

'Who sent him to Jamaica?' shrieked Mrs Hawkins.

'Control yourself, ma'am,' said I, quite sharply.

She ignored me entirely.

'And why?' she ranted on. 'To guard your profits. Profits! Haven't you gold enough, curse you?'

Such words were too unseemly to be borne. 'Mrs Hawkins,' I said, taking her arm. 'You forget yourself, ma'am. This is no way to address your betters.'

At that the poor lady burst into tears. I put an arm round her and guided her to a chair. She put her face into her hands, sobbing and moaning, and I turned to Trelawney, who was gaping in the most stupid manner, and demanded to be told what the Devil had happened.

'It's this confounded letter!' said he, thrusting a paper into my hand.

I read it through while Trelawney paced up and down, huffing and puffing, and Mrs Hawkins wept and wailed. It was a copy of a report to the Secretary of State from the Governor of Jamaica, and I swiftly grasped the essence of it – in short, that Jim Hawkins was dead, and was moreover branded a murderer.

I will not weary the reader with a description of my emotions upon reading this, except to say that I felt at once that it was a pack of lies, and said as much to Trelawney.

'Scandalous falsehoods!' said he. 'That blackguard Hallows is at the back of it, I'll stake my wig upon it!'

I was about to concur when a fearful scream from Mrs Hawkins made me jump out of my skin. She had risen from her chair and was staring in the direction of the door, her eyes bolting. I turned.

Standing in the door was a figure like a lunatic escaped from a Bedlam, a wild-haired, wild-eyed, gibbering scarecrow of a man, dressed in rags and tatters.

'Jim Hawkins is alive,' croaked this apparition, and only then did I recognize him.

'Alive!' he said again, crossing himself. 'And there's Ben Gunn's Christian oath on it!' At which he swooned away and fell to the floor with a crash that shook the room.

I pass over the next hour, during which I was kept pretty busy reviving Ben with a strong negus, and calming Mrs Hawkins down with a tincture of laudanum, while the Squire stumped up and down in a perfect fury of impatience.

I will not repeat Ben Gunn's account of the events in Jamaica, which he gave in an almost incomprehensible manner, driving Trelawney into a frenzy; the reader is already acquainted with the facts. I will, however, recount as briefly as possible, how Ben came to be in England.

The report of Jim Hawkins's death had been in general circulation in Kingston within a few hours. He had shot an officer of the Militia, so rumour ran, and in attempting to escape had fallen over a precipitous cliff and drowned. This was conveyed to Ben by his friend Mr Morgan, the Parson, but Ben would not believe it. The fact that the Dutchman – Vanderbrecken – had never returned convinced him that Jim had survived his fall, had got aboard Vanderbrecken's vessel ('for Jim 'Awkins swims trimmer than a seal') and was even then making his way back to his native country.

The next intelligence that came to Mr Morgan's ears was that the Governor and Hallows were scouring the island for Ben Gunn himself, and offering a substantial reward for his capture, which was not surprising, since he could testify to their crimes.

With Mr Morgan's aid, Ben succeeded in stowing away on the *Saracen* – the very ship in which he had made his outward voyage – which was about to return to England.

After a week at sea, during which he had hid himself away in one of the holds, he was discovered and taken before the Captain – Parker – who recognized him and, having heard his tale, let him work his passage home. Arrived in Bristol, Ben jumped ship, with the intention of getting home to the Admiral Benbow as swiftly as possible. In this he was frustrated by a series of misfortunes and accidents (his narrative became extremely obscure at this point, and I suspect that most of his troubles stemmed from a visit to a tavern) and the journey took him a fortnight.

Captain Parker, meanwhile, had accompanied the Mail (which included Governor Devereux's report) to London, and it had been through his good offices that Trelawney had been apprised of the news from Jamaica.

The day after Ben's reappearance, Trelawney posted to London. His mission was nothing less than to see the Secretary of State himself – who happened to be related to him on his mother's side. He returned a week later, and summoned me to dine at the Hall.

'Well, Livesey,' says he, flinging his wig on to a chair and rubbing his hands, 'it's all set and done. I've a Commission in my pocket signed by the Secretary of State himself to examine the whole circumstance of Jim Hawkins's disappearance. My excellent cousin was shocked, Livesey, absolutely shocked at what I had to say of that villain of a Governor. Good Mr Blandly's lookin' out for a schooner at this moment and I've dug old Smollett out of his sett. It's the ship's company of the *Hispaniola* come to life again! We'll sail before the month is out, or Blandly'll have socks from me! What d'you say, Livesey?'

'I say it's a fool's errand, if ever I heard of one.'

Trelawney gaped at me, and then looked so crushed and disappointed that I took pity on him.

'But there again,' said I, 'since you're determined to embark upon it, I'd better come along to keep you steady!'

'Bravo, Doctor!' cried Trelawney. 'Spoken like an Englishman!'

Chapter XXVI

Narrative resumed by Jim Hawkins: The Pit of the Damned

I have earlier stated my views upon the slavery question, and pretty strongly too. Now is the time to reveal the true reason behind my passionate conviction – *I have been a slave.*

It was to perpetual slavery that Vanderbrecken, Abed, and I were condemned, along with the other prisoners aboard the Spanish man-o'-war, by the Captain-General in command of the small port upon the coast of Mexico to which we were taken some weeks after our capture.

We had already suffered all the tortures of close confinement and perpetual hunger and thirst aboard that accursed ship. But our treatment at the hands of the Spanish marines was mild by comparison with the barbarities practised by our new gaolers.

In sacking Machado, the Spaniards had intended a double purpose: to destroy the stronghold of the buccaneers, but also to capture slaves for their gold-mines. In vain did Vanderbrecken attempt to put our case, to plead that we were wholly innocent, and had no connexion with the Machado pirates – it was useless. To the Spaniards we were but the booty of war, to be treated like beasts of burden, and worked until we dropped.

The Spaniards were building a new road, to connect the chief town of the Province, near to which a gold-mine had been discovered, with the coast. It was a distance of some fifty miles, and three prisons had been erected at intervals along the way, in which the slaves were confined, and from which they were driven out each day to break stone in the broiling heat.

It was to the second of these man-made hells that we were sent and I will not dwell upon the agonies we endured during the first two months of our servitude, or, what was worse in a way, the atrocious cruelties we saw inflicted upon others.

Though, God knows, it is saying little enough, we fared better than most of our fellows, for we were three strong men and could just about endure the back-breaking toil to which we were forced by the whips and cudgels of the overseers. For the weak there was no mercy; they were beaten and tortured and starved until they went mad or died.

After two months, a Commission arrived to select the strongest slaves to be marched inland to the third of the prisons, near the capital, and we were accorded the dubious honour of being included in the party.

We arrived at our new place of confinement at night. Half-dead with exhaustion, we were kicked and cursed through the gates, across a broad compound, and into a big stone-built cell.

We were instantly set upon by a jabbering, scavenging swarm of our fellow prisoners, demanding food and plucking at our clothes. One fellow in particular, an ugly brute of a half-breed, singled me out. He pinned me against the wall and fingered the stuff of my coat, and I was too weakened to throw him off.

'Well, well, what have we here?' he crowed. 'A pretty little *gentleman*, we have, brothers.'

I struggled to escape his grip and he laughed in my face.

'He don't fancy our company, it seems,' he said.

Vanderbrecken was attempting to come to my aid but three or four of the others fell on him and held him back. There was general laughter now, and I did not like the look of things, for believe it if you can, it was a common thing for the slaves to single out a victim from among their own company to taunt and bully and sometimes kill for their amusement.

And then from the dim, shadowy reaches of the cell a voice bellowed out like the roar of a lion.

'Belay that!'

It was Silver's voice – yet I could hardly believe it.

Silver? Here?

More utterly amazed than I have often been in my life, I saw Silver heaving towards me, and the crowd of prisoners, now silent, standing aside to clear a path for him. He halted a few paces away and fixed my tormentor with his eye.

'You'll oblige me,' said he quietly, 'you'll greatly oblige me, Señor Lopez, by takin' your mongrel dog's paws off that man.'

For a moment Lopez hesitated. 'I meant no harm,' he said.

'That's lucky for you,' returned Silver. 'So step aside lively, mate, or by the Powers I'll spill your tripe at your feet.'

Lopez released me at once and shuffled away, his eyes cast down. Silver took three steps towards me and halted again. He shook his head and a slow smile spread over his face.

'Well, Jim,' says he, 'as I've remarked before – there ain't nothin' so mutable as Fortune.'

Summoning Vanderbrecken and Abed, he led us to a corner of the cell that he seemed to keep as his private preserve and – wonder upon wonder – produced fresh bread, and fruit, and water for us. We asked no question but fell upon the provender like the starving creatures that we were, while Silver told us his story.

It was simple enough. He had escaped the massacre of the Machado pirates only to be caught a few days later while attempting to steal a boat to get away. Like us, he had been condemned to slavery.

'There's a fever abroad, ye see,' said he, 'rampagin' from

Vera Cruz to Santiago – gold fever. The King o' Spain's in low water, so they says, an' the orders be all hands to the gold-mines – not exceptin' John Silver. But 'ere's the catch. It's a case o' cheatin' the gallows to skip on the gibbet, as the sayin' is. For this place ain't no better than a scaffold, only they kills you by inches. I seen some human hell-holes in my time, but I tell you, *this* be the nethermost pit o' the damned.'

'We know that,' growled Vanderbrecken. 'We haff had two months to learn it.'

'Aye, so you may,' said Silver, 'but I warrant you'll learn worse in this place. There's one 'ere, Garcia by name, Superintendente they calls him, what could be Flint come to life again – I tell you I'm afeared o' him myself, and Silver don't scare easy.'

I remarked that he seemed to have fared none so badly.

'By the Thunders!' said Vanderbrecken. 'I believe you're cook here!'

'Not quite, Dutchman,' Silver returned with a grin, 'only cookhouse scullion – but near enough.'

I began to understand Silver's power over the other prisoners. In the country of the blind, they say, the one-eyed man is King; in the realm of the hungry, the cook-house scullion was Emperor.

'By God,' said Vanderbrecken, 'I believe you'd find yourself a soft berth in hell itself.'

'I ain't complainin' ' said Silver. 'This be no pleasure cruise, as I've said, but still, there's opportunities for an enterprisin' man.'

Fingering his chin, he looked at us one after the other very shrewdly.

'Aye,' says he after a moment, 'I reckon you've been sent by Providence. Three old shipmates I can trust – it's Fate all right.'

I could not for the life of me comprehend what he was driving at, and nor could Vanderbrecken.

'What you mean – opportunities?' the Dutchman asked.

'Well now,' Silver replied, 'a slave's life ain't exactly

congenial to you, I'll hazard. If someone were to offer you a means to escape, well, I don't reckon you'd spit in 'is eye.'

'Escape?' said Vanderbrecken. 'Impossible!'

'Says you,' was the reply, 'but I calculate as how I can slip my cable when I chooses.'

And at that, very covertly, he felt in his pocket and brought out his picklock!

'By the Thunders!' breathed Vanderbrecken.

'Any time I chooses,' Silver repeated.

'You *waitin'* for something?' said Abed sarcastically.

'Mebbe I am, boy,' Silver replied.

'Waiting for what?' said the Dutchman.

'You forget,' said I. 'There's a gold-mine hereabouts.'

'So there be, Jim,' said Silver softly, looking at me sidelong.

'I think at last you go mad,' said Vanderbrecken. 'You are *prisoner* here.'

'So I be,' returned Silver. 'I'm inside where it'd take a siege army to place me otherwise. They keeps their gold *here*, you see, in a strong-room within the prison wall.'

'I say if we can escape, we escape, and be damned to any gold,' said Vanderbrecken.

'And *I* says there's no escape without Silver, and Silver ain't quitting this pit o' hell empty-handed, by the Powers!'

Intimately acquainted though I was with Silver's cunning, I was aghast at his audacity. To escape would be a miracle in itself, but to steal their gold from under the very noses of the Spaniards! Apart from any other considerations, where was the boat to get away in?

I might have known that Silver would have the answer.

'As to that,' says he, 'well I ain't alone in the business – that would stand to reason. There's others in it too, on the other side o' the wall, waitin' on my word.'

'Silver,' says Vanderbrecken, 'you're a great blackguard, but I swear you're a great man!'

'Well, Dutchman,' said Silver, smiling, 'I take that kindly.'

Chapter XXVII

A Reunion

Next morning, I saw for the first time the man of whom Silver had spoken with such uncharacteristic awe – Superintendente Garcia.

We were waiting in line for our breakfast – a thin, noisome gruel – which was served from a table out in the open compound by the cook and his scullion, when Garcia stalked out of his quarters and walked towards the gate. He was very tall, and thin to the point of gauntness. He was dressed all in black, and with his dark hair, and sharp beak of a nose, had the look of a carrion bird. He stopped for a moment, to survey the slaves, and as I observed him more closely, I began to grasp why even Silver went in dread of him.

He had the cruellest eyes I have ever seen in a human face: two black orbs that seemed to be flecked with red, and which burned with a mixture of hatred and fever. The fever was real. Garcia was a sick man; the skin on his face was a greyish yellow, and his breath whistled and gurgled in his lungs.

I felt that he noticed me staring at him and quickly cast down my eyes. I had no wish to attract the attention of such a man. As he went away, the prisoner standing next to me spat and growled: 'There goes a 'uman Devil if you like.'

The speaker was an Englishman, a survivor of the Machado pirates, named Boakes. He was a grizzled old fellow, with a scar, shaped like a sickle, that ran from his chin to his forehead. He was very thick with Long John, and was destined to play a part in future events.

Our breakfast done, such as it was, we were marched out to the stone-quarry a mile from the prison. The quarry was cut into the spur of a considerable hill, and in the course of being worked, had formed a precipice some ninety or a hundred feet in height. The slaves were divided into three parties. The first, in which I worked, was set to hewing fresh stone at the base of the precipice; the second, in which Vanderbrecken and Abed toiled, had the task of carrying the newly won stone on litters to the road, where those in the third party broke it up with hammers and crowbars. We all laboured under the watchful eyes of the overseer, Madero, and his men, who were ready to punish any faltering in our work with the whip.

It was at about midday that every man in the quarry, the overseers included, were startled by a gunshot. It came from above, from the top of the hill, and a moment later was followed by a cry of mortal terror.

A shower of stones cascaded down into the quarry and then, with a shriek that echoed and re-echoed, the body of a man plummeted from the summit and landed not three feet from where I stood. Out of sheer instinct I ran to his side and knelt by him.

He was dead – but in his hand was clutched a paper. Again, from pure instinct, I quickly snatched the paper and hid it in my shirt. I was only just in time, for Madero and his men were running towards me. They dragged me away from the dead man, throwing me to the ground, and laid on with their whips.

Suddenly they stopped.

A man on horseback was entering the quarry. It was Garcia. He dismounted rapidly and strode over to where the dead man lay. He knelt beside him, just as I had done, and felt through his clothing. Having failed to find what he was looking for, he rose and turned his terrible eyes towards me. He asked Madero a question in Spanish and Madero nodded, pointing at me. Garcia advanced slowly towards me. I found that I could not take my eyes from his – and the paper I had seized from the dead man seemed to scorch my skin under my shirt. Garcia suddenly stopped and turned. A second rider was entering the quarry.

It was a girl, a slim young girl dressed in an elegant riding habit. She was veiled against the heat and dust but I would have recognized the proud lift of her head had she been masked with iron. It was Señorita Isabella Zorilla.

She reined in her horse and lifted her veil. Her chalk-white face and staring eyes told me at once that she had seen me. For a moment she could not find her voice, then –

'Superintendente Garcia,' she said. 'Release that man immediately.'

Garcia made her a bow. 'My dear Señorita Isabella, what an unexpected pleasure,' he said.

'Do you hear me?' said Isabella.

'This man?' replied Garcia smoothly.

'I know him. He is to be released. At once, if you please.'

'My dear madam,' said Garcia, with another bow, 'I think you must be mistaken. This fellow is a slave – a common pirate, taken at Machado.'

'I am not mistaken,' retorted Isabella sharply, 'nor do I care what he is. Release him. I make myself responsible.'

'Madam, I regret to say that it is not within my power to do as you ask without an order signed by His Excellency.'

'Very well,' said Isabella, 'I will obtain an order. In the meantime, if he is ill-treated, you will answer to my uncle for it.'

'As you wish, dear lady,' Garcia replied with yet another bow.

Isabella touched her horse's flank with her heel and rode away. Garcia watched her go through narrowed eyes, then turned to Madero and barked an order to him. Madero strode over to me, gripped me by my arm and marched me out of the quarry.

My feelings may as well be imagined as described. Foremost among them was hope – a real hope of deliverance. A benign Providence had brought me to the very Province of which Isabella's uncle was Governor! I was so stunned by the turn in my fortunes, so dazzled by the emotions that had been reawakened within me by seeing Isabella, that it was not until I was back inside the prison compound that I thought of the mysterious paper I had taken from the dead man. Somehow I must contrive to put it in safe-keeping – but how?

It was then that I spotted Long John. He was in the cookhouse, bending over a steaming pot.

'Señorita Isabella does not like her friends to go thirsty,' I said to Madero.

He looked at me hard for a moment, then with a grunt pushed me towards the cookhouse. Long John glanced up as we approached and could not conceal his surprise at seeing me.

'Jim?' he said.

'A mug of water,' said I.

Long John looked to Madero for permission and the overseer nodded curtly. During this exchange I managed to slip the paper from my shirt into my hand. Madero saw nothing – but the slight movement did not escape Long John's sharp eye. He took a mug and poured water from a pitcher. He passed the brimming mug to me and I took it in my left hand – the paper was in my right. I drank the water quickly and when I passed the empty mug back to Long John I did so with my right hand. Long John's dextrous fingers twitched the paper from my palm as he took the mug, and not for the first time I thanked God for his quick wits.

Madero took me straight away to Garcia's quarters where he left me, under close guard. Garcia came in about twenty minutes later and ordered the guards to search me thoroughly. He watched while they did so and sighed wearily when they found nothing.

'Well, well,' said he, seating himself upon the edge of his desk, 'have you destroyed it or hidden it?'

'I know not what you mean,' said I.

He sighed again, the breath rattling in his lungs. 'You may have observed,' he said, 'that I am a sick man. I am indeed a *dying* man, though I've some time yet – time enough to get the truth from you at any rate.' I felt his fiery gaze upon me and kept looking at the ground.

'My – infirmity,' he went on, 'naturally affects the value I place upon the health – and indeed the lives – of others. Do I make myself plain?'

I thought it was time for a little defiance and answered boldly: 'Señorita Isabella made herself equally plain, I think.'

He laughed. 'My poor young man,' said he, 'you utterly delude yourself if you place any reliance upon help from that quarter.'

'I think not,' I replied. 'Her uncle is Governor of this Province after all.'

'Are you *acquainted* with His Excellency?'

'Only with the niece.'

'Ah,' was the reply, 'then you know nothing of Don Jaime's character?'

'No – but a great deal about Señorita Isabella's.'

He rose and came towards me. He put out his hand and his long, cold fingers, like talons, closed upon my chin, forcing my head upwards so that I could no longer avoid his eyes. I despair of describing how dreadful they were when seen close to.

'Listen to me,' he said softly. 'I am a high priest of pain. I know how to endure it and I know how to inflict it. I know how to torture a man without leaving a mark upon his body – not a trace.' Pressing his claws into my flesh, he continued: 'I require the return of the paper you took. I require it urgently. It is nothing to you, but a great deal to me. Tell me where it is and I will not oppose your release – on the contrary, I will recommend it. Continue to thwart me and I promise you I will teach you the meaning of the word suffering and it will be a lesson that will leave you a ghost of yourself, young and strong as you are.'

The stoutest-hearted man, if he is honest, will admit that there are times when his courage utterly fails him. I confess it here, that Garcia had reduced me to such a state of terror that I think I would have betrayed my country and even my friends to escape him. Since it was only a matter of some scrap of paper, of whose significance I knew nothing, I was prepared to tell him all.

I was spared that shame by the opening of the door, and the entry of a foppish young Spaniard of about my own age.

Garcia released me immediately and took a step backwards, bowing to the newcomer.

'My dear Don Felipe,' he said.

'Superintendente,' said the other, returning his bow faintly, 'I have here an order from His Excellency.'

Garcia took the order and glanced at it. 'Very well,' said he, without apparent emotion, 'this man is released into your custody. Will you have the goodness to inform His Excellency that I will do myself the honour of waiting upon him later in the day?'

Don Felipe bowed again, and gestured to me to accompany him. He escorted me outside where there was a carriage waiting. 'Get in,' said he, and those were the only words he condescended to address to me during the whole of the twenty minutes or so it took to drive into the town.

We drew up in front of a substantial stone building, which I took to be the Governor's residence. With a wildly beating heart I followed Don Felipe into the house, past sentries who presented arms smartly. He took me across a vast hall, paved with marble, and ushered me into a handsomely furnished withdrawing room. With the very slightest of bows, he left me, closing the door behind him.

Isabella was standing in a window, her back towards me. She turned to face me.

'So,' said she, 'once again I rescue you from a Spanish prison.'

I tried to speak, but could not find my voice.

'Oh, Jim,' she cried, and running towards me, flung herself into my arms.

Chapter XXVIII

Don Jaime de Pachero

I forbear to describe the first transports of our joy at being reunited. To those of you who have known what it is to love it would be a familiar story, I dare say, and to those who have not, a dull one. I will proceed, instead, directly to the matter most pertinent to my narrative, namely the explanation of the paper that Garcia was so anxious to recover, and the identity of the man from whom I had taken it. His name was Montez, and he had been the manager of the gold-mine. For some time, the yield from the mine had been falling short of expectation, to such an extent that the Viceroy of Mexico himself had begun to make enquiries, to the alarm of Isabella's uncle, the Governor.

Isabella had made it her business to look into the matter and soon grew suspicious of Garcia, who must, she thought, be falsifying the returns. To prove her case she had approached Montez secretly and he, being an honest man and fearful for his own position, had agreed to furnish her with a copy of his own returns. She had, indeed, been on her way to see him when he met his death – at Garcia's hand, it was now certain.

I told her how I had entrusted the paper to Silver, and when she had recovered from the shock of learning that her old enemy was at hand, she said that we must go at once to her uncle. I protested that I was not fit to be seen by a servant, let alone a Governor, all filthy and ragged as I was, but, brushing my objections aside, she led me out of the room by a different door, through a vestibule, to her uncle's room. She was about to knock upon the door when we heard the voice of Garcia himself addressing the Governor.

'Forgive me, Excellency,' he was saying, 'but I must make my position perfectly plain. I cannot sanction

Hawkins's release under any circumstances.'

Isabella put a finger to her lip and both of us placed our ears to the door.

'Superintendente Garcia,' replied the Governor, in weak, quavering voice, 'I would beg you to consider that, for me, and for my niece, it is a question of the honour of our family. We are under a considerable obligation to this young man.'

'And I,' replied Garcia, 'am under an obligation to finish my road – for which purpose I am unable to spare a single hand. I must further remind you, Excellency, that in all matters concerning the prison and the mine I am empowered to act upon my own responsibility. I am answerable only to the Viceroy.'

'I don't deny it,' replied the other. 'For that very reason you will observe that I have not ordered the young man's release, but merely that he should be placed in my custody until such time as the Viceroy shall review his case. I have written to the Viceroy upon the subject and can expect his reply within a very few days.'

A silence followed this statement, and I could well imagine Garcia's chagrin, for the very last thing he would want was the Viceroy of Mexico to investigate the affair.

'Are you then determined to act counter to my wishes in this matter?' he said at last.

'I very much regret the necessity,' replied the Governor.

'You *will* regret it, Excellency,' said Garcia shortly and angrily. 'I bid you good-day.'

We heard the slam of a door, and, taking my hand, Isabella introduced me immediately into her uncle's room.

Don Jaime de Pachero was seated at his desk, a very worried expression upon his face. He was an elderly man, with more the air of a gentle, unworldly scholar than of a Governor of a Province.

He greeted me kindly, though in a very distracted manner, and made a little formal speech, thanking me for 'the great services I had rendered to his dear niece'.

'Señor Hawkins is in the way of rendering yet greater service, Uncle,' said Isabella quickly, and told him about the death of Montez and the paper which had so providentially come into my hands. As she spoke, Don Jaime appeared to become ever more nervous and fussed, shaking his head and tut-tutting.

'My dear,' he said when Isabella had finished her recital, 'we cannot act precipitately in this affair. I – I must not provoke Garcia.'

'Provoke him!' cried Isabella impatiently, 'You can break him, Uncle.'

'My dear, you are too hasty and rash. You do not understand what manner of man we have to deal with.'

'A thief!' she said. 'A common robber – who will lay all the blame at your door if you do not take care.'

'Garcia has the ear of the Viceroy,' said Don Jaime with more spirit, 'and besides, he has command of troops who will obey him before they obey me.'

'Uncle, your shilly-shallying will be the ruin of us all,' cried Isabella with a stamp of her foot.

'You uncle is right,' said I, for I was beginning to understand the Governor's character. Ignoring the look of angry astonishment she cast at me, I went on: 'We must take it step by step.' Turning to Don Jaime: 'If I may be permitted to make a suggestion, Excellency, the first thing is to recover the document. Only when we have ascertained its contents can we know how best to proceed.'

Don Jaime looked heartily relieved.

'I must recover it myself,' I continued, 'for Silver will give it to nobody else. If, therefore, I could be provided with an escort, I will return to the prison.'

Don Jaime readily agreed and summoned a servant to fetch his secretary, Don Felipe.

'May I beg a further favour, Excellency?' said I, as we waited.

'Anything, my dear boy, anything at all.'

'I am sorely in need of a bath and a change of clothing.'

'Of course, of course,' said he, 'I should have thought of it myself,' and, Don Felipe now entering, he consigned me to his care.

It was a very different creature to the dirty, half-naked slave that had been released from the prison who set out, an hour later, to return to it. I had bathed luxuriously and shaved off my beard, and was dressed in a fine suit of Don Felipe's. This young fellow continued to treat me with frigid disdain, lending his clothes with a very ill grace, and not troubling to dissemble his dislike of me. I began to suspect that he was in love with Isabella and that jealousy of me was the explanation of his ill manners.

We entered the carriage and set off at a brisk clip. We were passing through the town, near the market-place, when to my astonishment I saw Silver himself heaving along the road! He was pushing a hand-barrow, to which he was shackled by a short chain, and he was in the company of the prison cook, and two of Garcia's soldiers. Bidding Don Felipe stop the carriage, and telling him to wait for me, I jumped out and followed Silver and his escort into the market.

They were standing by a fruit-seller's stall. Approaching nearer to them, and concealing myself behind a pile of baskets, I watched and listened. Silver was feeling a melon with a professional air.

'Passing ripe,' said he, 'ripe enough,' and the old crone who kept the stall beamed upon him.

Then he took from his pocket two or three gold coins (yet *again* I wondered where in Heaven he obtained his supply of money) and favoured the cook and the two soldiers with a broad wink.

'Fetch me a bottle o' grog from the tavern, eh, mates?' said he. 'I'll bide 'ere and see the old gammer don't diddle us.'

The cook took the gold with glistening eyes and he and the soldiers went away to spend it. No sooner had they disappeared than a man stepped out of the crowd and up to Silver. He was a big, hairy fellow, raffishly dressed, and a Spaniard by his looks. While the stall-keeper and her helper loaded fruit and vegetables on to the hand-cart, Silver and his friend (Sanchez was his name, I found out later) fell into low, urgent conversation. Remembering what Silver had said about having friends 'on the other side of the wall', I concluded that this was the leader of the gang with whom he was in league.

I waited until their conference was over and Sanchez had vanished into the crowd, then I walked over to Long John, whose back was towards me.

'Well, Long John,' said I.

He gave a great start and for a moment stared at me, completely dumbfounded.

'By the Powers,' he said at last. 'Jim! An' dressed like a Lord to boot!'

As briefly as I could I explained the circumstances of my release and he shook his head, and spat, and said: 'Well if this don't beat it. Here's John Silver riskin' all to save our hides, and there's you wi' the Governor hisself in your pocket!'

'Yes,' said I, 'but we're not out of the wood on that account,' and told him about Garcia. 'So you see,' I concluded, 'that I need that paper.'

'Aye,' said he, with a look of indescribable cunning, 'that would be a valuable doccyment, now, I reckon.'

I looked him coolly up and down. 'If it's of the value to yourself that you're thinking,' I said, 'it lies in giving it back to me.'

He made no reply but fingered his chin and half closed his eyes in a way that at once revived all my old exasperation at his self-seeking wiles.

'It'll be the saving of us all,' said I. 'It sinks Garcia, and until that's done we're none of us safe.'

I knew what he was thinking: his sole concern was whether, by producing the document, he would spoil his chance of stealing the gold.

'Your friends will be returning from the tavern soon,' said I, 'so make up your mind quickly.'

'Not them,' said he, 'for they never spends less than an hour in drinking Silver's health.'

'Well, *I* am pressed for time. The Governor will wish to know your decision.'

He cocked an eye at that and sniffed. 'I takes it,' said he, 'that there's a pardon in it for John Silver.'

'You have my solemn word.'

He thought a moment longer, then dipped his hand inside his coat and brought out the paper.

Returned to the Governor's Residence, I laid it directly on Don Jaime's desk. I had looked at it during the journey back, but had made nothing of it – it consisted of a series of dates and figures. Isabella and her uncle, however, were greatly excited by its contents and straightway sent a summons, by Don Felipe, to Garcia to attend upon the Governor forthwith.

Garcia did not obey the summons until just before dusk. From an upper window I saw him descend from his carriage. He was bristling with pent-up fury and his eyes burned as never before.

With Don Jaime's permission, Isabella and I listened to his interview with the Superintendente from the same post we had used before. In a manner less diffident than hitherto, Don Jaime asked Garcia for an explanation of Montez's death and of the paper that had been found upon him.

'I advise you to consider carefully before you accuse *me*,' Garcia replied, adding, with calculated insolence, 'Excellency.'

'Here,' said the Governor, 'is a precise record, by Montez himself, of the amount of gold obtained from the mine. *Here* is your own account – *with your official seal upon it*. They do not tally, Superintendente. They do not tally at all. There is a – vast discrepancy. How do you explain it?'

'I am not required to explain it,' Garcia returned confidently. 'As you point out, Excellency, *my* account bears an official seal. The other is a mere piece of paper. It means nothing.'

'It is in Montez's hand – that can be proved.'

'Perhaps – but between that and the substantiation of your absurd suspicions of me there is a great gulf fixed.'

'An explanation will nevertheless be required,' said Don Jaime. 'By the Viceroy.'

'Then it is to the Viceroy that I shall answer,' replied Garcia. 'I have the honour to bid you goodnight.'

Isabella flung into the room almost before Garcia had quit it. 'Uncle, you should have arrested him,' she cried.

'Quite unnecessary, my dear,' he returned, rising from his chair. 'The man is finished and he knows it.' He placed a hand reassuringly on her arm.

'I have dealt with such cases before,' he said. 'I've no doubt at all that he'll bolt for it with his ill-gotten gains – they invariably do. I shall report the matter to the Viceroy, and the Viceroy will spare *me* the trouble of hunting Garcia down and bringing him to justice. And now – shall we dine?'

He took my arm as we went into the dining-room. 'The moment I hear that Garcia has fled,' said he, 'your friends shall be released – first thing tomorrow morning, if I know aught about it.'

But I was by no means so sanguine that Garcia would allow himself to be so easily beaten, nor was Isabella. After dinner, we walked together in the garden, while Don Jaime went to his room to write his report to the Viceroy, and Isabella determined to make a fresh attempt to persuade her uncle that Garcia should be arrested. But before she could execute this resolve, Don Felipe approached with a message from his master, who desired to see me alone and at once in his room.

Wondering what Don Jaime could want me for, I accompanied the Secretary into the house. He knocked upon the door of the Governor's room, opened it, announced, 'Señor Hawkins, Your Excellency,' and stood aside to let me pass.

The Governor was as usual seated at his desk, bending low over his papers. I heard Don Felipe close the door behind me as I stepped towards the desk. I should explain that there was but a single candle burning upon the desk, and but one lamp on a table nearby, and so the light was very dim.

'Excellency?' I said.

He did not reply, nor did he look up from his papers.

'Excellency?' I said again.

Still, he neither moved nor spoke.

A sudden fear gripping me, I ran forward, took up the candle, and to my unspeakable horror saw the hilt of a poniard projecting from the small of his back.

Chapter XXVIX

Garcia's Riposte

Don Jaime de Pachero was dead.

For a moment I stood over his body utterly unable to move or even to think, so confounded was I by the ruthless boldness of Garcia's riposte – for there could be no doubt at all who had been responsible for the murder. At last I got my wits into some semblance of order and was about to run to Isabella when the door was flung open and my lady herself appeared.

She took in the situation at a glance and could not suppress a scream. This aroused the house immediately and before I could escape (for that was our only hope now) Don Felipe and two sentries rushed into the room.

In vain did I make a dash for the second floor – 'Seize him!' cried Don Felipe, and the two sentries fell upon me.

If I had been armed I might have done something. I put up the best fight I could but Don Felipe summoned more sentries and in a moment I was overpowered, and in spite of Isabella's protests, carried away to a cellar. They clapped me in irons and locked me into a sort of cupboard, and there, in a perfect frenzy of impotent apprehension, I waited.

Half an hour later – but it seemed like an age – a key rattled in the lock and the door was flung open. A couple of sentries gripped me and marched me upstairs and into the late Governor's room. His body had been removed from his chair, which was now occupied by Garcia himself.

Ordering the sentries out, Garcia raised his dreadful eyes to me and said: 'Behold the Acting Governor.'

Don Felipe was standing by the desk and I turned at once to him.

'Where is Señorita Isabella?'

Garcia answered for him. 'The lady is in a state of considerable distress,' said he. 'It is hardly to be wondered at. Her uncle murdered by her own lover! A tragedy worthy of the stage!'

'If you harm a hair of her head—'

'My dear young man,' said Garcia. 'Harm her? My own physician is attending her this very moment, and my own men are standing without her room to see that no further mischief occurs.'

I was half choked with rage at his mocking tone but I knew that if there was any hope at all it lay in remaining as cool-headed and calculating as Garcia himself.

'This gentleman,' said I, indicating Don Felipe, 'will testify that I can have had nothing to do with murdering the Governor.'

Garcia looked at Don Felipe. The secretary cleared his throat.

'I can testify,' said he, 'that the Governor was alive when I took Hawkins in, for he spoke to me. When I next entered this room he was dead.'

You will think me a fool, but until I heard that lie tripping off Don Felipe's tongue I had not even considered the possibility that the villain had turned his coat. I laughed shortly.

'Yes,' said I, 'dead – and all my hopes with him. That would sound well in a court of law I should think – but I assume there will be no trial.'

'On the contrary,' said Garcia. 'Owing to Don Jaime's untimely and tragic demise I have, as I am empowered to do, taken over his responsibilities, the first of which must be to bring his murderer to justice in the proper form. I have great hopes, you see, of being appointed his successor by the Viceroy. And the Viceroy' – here he took up a sheaf of papers from the desk, one of which was Montez's account – 'is a stickler for proper forms and procedures.' Saying this, he rose, carried the papers to the fire and threw them into the flames.

I will not dwell upon the next hour. The reader may well imagine the utter despair and mortification that gripped my soul as I was taken back in chains to the prison and locked away in a cell. What drove me half mad was the thought that Isabella was now completely in Garcia's power. That he would somehow contrive to take her life was certain, for she was more dangerous to him than anybody. He would do it, moreover, before I was brought to trial – and I was utterly helpless to save her.

For what remained of the night, I paced my cell, and saw dawn come up through the bars of its one, small window. I heard reveille sounded for the garrison, and the slaves mustered and driven out for the day's work, but not a soul came near me.

The hours crawled by.

The sun beat down upon the roof of the cell, turning the interior into a kiln, so that to all my mental torture was added the physical one of thirst. It was towards evening that I heard the key turn in the door at last and one of Garcia's troopers entered, levelling a musket at me, and standing aside to make way for – *Silver*!

It was Silver indeed, bearing a pitcher of water and a hunch of stale bread. He placed these delicacies on the stone ledge that served as a table and as he did so he winked at me and mouthed one word – '*Tonight*!'

It is, I suppose, an indication of the state I was in, that not until Silver's broad back had disappeared through the door, and the trooper had slammed it shut and locked it, did I fully comprehend the import of his message. My anguish over Isabella's horrid predicament had banished Silver and his schemes completely from my mind. Now, as I remembered his secret conference with Sanchez, it dawned on me that they had been settling the date for their attempt upon the gold – which was to be tonight.

My hopes, which had been dead, soared; I vowed to myself that if Silver should succeed in liberating me, thus saving not only my life but my darling's as well, he should have the whole of Flint's treasure to himself, and I'd help him to it.

Since the reader should know how Silver carried out his plan to steal the gold, but since I was not myself a witness to his actions, let me tell the story here as I later pieced it together from the accounts I received from Vanderbrecken, Abed, and Long John himself.

Sanchez was an old acquaintance of Silver's whom he had seen by chance a month before while making one of his regular excursions to the market – a privilege he had obtained by bribery. He was a Spaniard and had been a buccaneer in his time and Silver's first thought had been to use him to effect his own escape. But Sanchez had proposed a better plan – to steal the gold kept within the prison – and had a band of six or seven men ready to assist in the venture. All that was required was a boat and Sanchez had procured one – an old ketch – which he had concealed in a cove upon a wild part of the coast, some twenty miles from the town.

All being in readiness, and the date and time agreed, Silver apprised Vanderbrecken, Abed, Boakes, and two others he trusted, and secured their participation. They waited until well after midnight, by which time all the other prisoners, utterly exhausted from their day's labour, were fast asleep. Then they crept to the door of the cell and Silver opened it with his picklock. They slipped out and Silver made the door fast again behind them.

They waited in the lee of the cell for the sentry, who regularly patrolled that part of the prison, to appear. When he did, Vanderbrecken quickly and silently settled him, and took his musket, pistol, knife, and sword. The next part of the plan was to silence the sentries who kept the gate, of whom there were two, and those upon the ramparts above the main compound – six in number. This would be no mean feat, for absolute secrecy and silence were essential if the garrison was not to be aroused. Ten minutes later it was done, and Silver and Vanderbrecken were opening the gate to let Sanchez and his men in, and a cart, drawn by a pair of greys, to carry away the gold.

Concealed in the cart were arms and powder – the latter to be used to force the door of the strong-room, which lay in Garcia's quarters. These rooms were occupied by four or five of the officers and Sanchez and his men had the task of disposing of them – which they successfully accomplished. Silver, meanwhile, had brought up the cart, and unloaded the arms and powder.

The time for silence and stealth was now over, and Silver armed his men and placed them about the barrack-house ready to shoot down the troops when the powder exploded. As an added measure – and it proved the masterstroke – he planned to arm and liberate the slaves at the moment the power was ignited.

The first I knew of all this was the explosion itself. A moment later the door of the cell swung open and there was Vanderbrecken, the picklock in his hand, and Abed behind him. They hurried me out into the main compound where I saw Silver roaring commands at the top of his voice as Sanchez and Boakes and two others carried bars of gold to the cart. Around the barrack block it was a perfect inferno of gunfire and I saw that Silver's men were being forced back by the superior numbers of the Spaniards. There was no time for me to linger, however, and I dashed immediately to the stables to saddle up a horse.

Vanderbrecken followed me and I breathlessly told him my mission – to ride forthwith to the Governor's Residence to rescue Isabella.

He called it madness and tried to dissuade me – but an army could not have stopped me. All I wanted to know was where the ketch lay; promising to see him there, I mounted my horse and spurred it out into the compound.

I was just in time to see the slaves pouring out of the

cell, yelling like fiends, and plunging into the fray by the barrack block, to turn the tide of the battle; then I was through the gate and going like the Devil for the town.

Chapter XXX

Poetic Justice

Nearing the Governor's residence, I reined in my mount and proceeded more circumspectly. All was very quiet and still – no news of the affray at the prison could have yet reached Garcia. I took a narrow lane that ran beside the residence and was bounded upon one side by the high wall of the garden. Tethering the horse, I scaled the wall and dropped down into some bushes upon the other side.

Lights were shining in three or four of the windows which meant that all the household was not yet abed. I crept forward very cautiously and ducked down quickly when I saw a figure come out of the house and stand upon the terrace. The man was smoking a cheroot – I could see the glow of its red-hot end like a firefly in the darkness. I was about to steal forward when the man moved – towards me – coming down the steps and strolling into the walk where I was concealed. As he approached, humming to himself, I saw who it was – Don Felipe.

I slipped my knife out of my belt (I had taken a knife and a pistol from Vanderbrecken) and waited for him. As he came abreast of me, I pounced. In a second I had knocked him to the ground and my knife was at his throat.

'*Not a sound!*' I hissed.

He stared up at me, stark terror in his eyes.

'Tell me where she is – whisper it or you're a dead man.'

His mouth was dry from shock and fear and his tongue worked desperately to moisten it. After a moment – 'At table – with Garcia,' he croaked.

With my free hand I took out my pistol, reversed it, and with as much relish as I have ever done anything, cracked it hard upon his skull. His eyes rolled up and he went limp under me. Crouching low, I ran towards the house, on to the terrace, and into the withdrawing-room.

I opened the door a crack and peered into the hall. It was in darkness – and deserted. Light, however, was streaming from under the door opposite, that of the dining-room. I crossed the hall on tip-toe and put my ear to the door. At once, I heard Garcia's voice.

'My dear young lady,' he was saying, '*somebody* has to hang for your uncle's murder.'

'Very well,' I heard Isabella reply in a calm, strong voice, 'but it does not have to be Señor Hawkins.'

'I fear it does,' was the reply. 'The young man's death solves so many riddles for me.'

This exchange was enough to prove to me that Garcia and Isabella were alone, for he would never have talked so freely before a third party. Without further ado I drew my pistol and opened the door.

They were at table – decanters and the remains of a dinner were upon the board. Garcia sprang to his feet with a cry as I entered.

'And your death solves *my* riddle, I'd remind you, Superintendente,' said I, levelling my pistol at him.

He sat down very slowly, his breath wheezing and gurgling in his lungs. Isabella had gone white at my entrance and I thought she would swoon away. She rallied however, and with a gasp of 'Jim!' rose and came to my side. Garcia, too, recovered his poise.

'How do you intend to kill me?' he asked coolly. 'With that? You'll rouse the household.'

I took a step towards him.

'Señor Hawkins,' said he, with less assurance, 'consider well before you commit any irrevocable action. You may kill me – but what then? The whole of Mexico will be stirred up against you. You will have no possibility of escape.'

'I have no intention of taking your life,' said I, stepping

yet nearer to him. 'Your Maker will do that – and pretty soon too, I should judge.'

He flushed at that and bared his teeth. 'You damnable puppy-dog,' he snarled, and that was all, for I served him as I had done Don Felipe, bringing the butt of my pistol down upon his head with all the force I could command. He slumped forward in his chair and his head hit the top of the table. Taking Isabella by the hand, I said: 'Come, my lady, we have a journey ahead of us.'

We flitted through the hall and out into the garden. Don Felipe lay as I had left him, and as we stepped past him Isabella whispered: 'Bravo, Jim!' I helped her up and over the wall and we both mounted the horse.

When we were well clear of the town, we halted, for although I knew in general the direction we must take, I was not sure of the precise line. In this, Isabella's knowledge of the country proved to be invaluable. By her direction, we first took the new road – and a curious experience it was for me, who had contributed so much of my own sweat and muscle to its building, and seen so many wretched creatures donate their lives to it, to be cantering over its smooth surface, a free man. After several miles, Isabella showed me a track that led up into the hills, and we followed this for an hour or more.

I cannot overstate how perfectly wonderful she was that night. She had taken that way only once before – in a hunting party – it was pitch dark, and she must have been almost completely exhausted, but she never once faltered in the directions she gave, nor complained at the discomfort of sharing a saddle with me. When at last dawn came, we found ourselves descending through thick forest towards a plain. Beyond the plain lay a range of considerable hills barring the way to the coast which lay beyond them. At the edge of the forest we stopped by a rill to drink and make what toilet we could.

The five minutes we spent by that sweet, tumbling water stand out clear in my memory to this day. The sun had just risen, and its first rays were gilding each branch and leaf, each stone and ripple of water with a magical light. Kneeling by the stream upon a sward of green grass, her simple white dress clinging softly to her form, her curling tresses loose about her shoulders, Isabella made the most bewitching picture – a nymph escaped from Arcadia, a goddess of the dawn. Looking upon her, I felt suddenly very rich, but also humble; I could scarce believe that I had earned the right to be loved by such a creature.

Twenty minutes later we emerged from the forest to see a distant plume of dust rising from the plain below us.

'Silver and his party,' said I, and spurred our mount forward.

It took us the better part of an hour to catch up with the cart and its escort of riders. Of these there were but six – Vanderbrecken, Abed, Boakes, and three of Sanchez's men. Sanchez himself, and Silver, were driving the cart. Vanderbrecken was overwhelmed with relief to see us and Silver, greeting Isabella with his most charming smile and a handsome, flowery speech of welcome, made room for her beside him, and invited her to travel in the cart.

As our cavalcade set off once more towards the hills, I rode alongside Vanderbrecken, and he told me their story, which was short enough. The Spanish troopers had proved to be both more numerous and more determined than had been anticipated, had broken through Silver's line and very near brought the whole enterprise to disaster. Had it not been for the release of the slaves they would all have been taken and killed; as it was, there had been a pitched battle, through which they hacked their way to the gate, with the loss of most of Sanchez's men, and all Silver's save Boakes.

We came to the first hills and the track began to ascend steeply, twisting and turning, and slowing down the heavy-laden cart to a snail's pace. Several times we had to dismount and put our shoulders to it, and on one of these occasions I happened to look back.

We were upon a spur, or shoulder, from which the whole of the plain we had traversed was clearly visible. In the centre of the plain was a veritable cloud of dust, such as could be raised only by a large troop of cavalry! Vanderbrecken whipped his head round at my cry of alarm and let out a thunderous oath.

'We must abandon the gold,' he said as the others stopped and turned their heads.

'Abandon the blunt, ye Dutch booby?' roared Silver, taking out his pistol. 'Here's lead for you if you does.'

'It's a millstone,' growled Vanderbrecken.

I backed him up, but Silver blustered and threatened and Sanchez and the others supported him. I think that Silver might have hesitated to fire upon us but Sanchez and his henchmen would have no such scruples, so there was nothing for it but to press on as fast as we could.

It was a dreadful business. The road grew ever steeper as we mounted higher and we could keep the cart in motion only by exerting all our strength on the spokes of the wheels. We sweated and grunted while Silver cursed and lashed on the horses and Abed, who had been made lookout, reported that the Spaniards were gaining upon us rapidly.

Again, Vanderbrecken begged Silver to let the cart go and save our lives but Silver raged and cocked his pistol and would have shot the Dutchman dead, such was his lust to preserve the gold.

'There's the summit, blast your soul,' he bellowed, 'lay on or I'll send you to hell!'

The summit was indeed in sight, not a quarter of a mile ahead. At this point the road was cut into the side of the hill, which rose sheer to the left of it and dropped sharp to the right into a precipice so deep that it appeared bottomless. As I bent to the wheel-spokes and Silver's whip cracked on the horses' flanks I thought we might just about do it; but at that moment a fusillade of musket-shots rattled out *from ahead of us*, and Sanchez fell to the ground, blood streaming from his throat.

The Spaniards had outflanked us! The main body of their cavalry was in sight, thundering up the hill towards us, while we were pinned down by the musketeers above us, who must have been sent ahead on foot and had so out-stripped us. We were caught in a trap, and Garcia himself was leading his troops up the road to complete our doom.

Silver was down on the ground bellowing at Boakes and Sanchez's men to take to the rocks above and settle the musketeers, who were loosing off a second salvo.

'Jim,' roared Vanderbrecken, 'help me cut the traces! Quickly man, for your life!'

'No!' cried Silver, bringing up his pistol.

But the Dutchman was ready for him and knocked him to the ground with a single blow.

Garcia and his men were but fifty paces away; Boakes and his companions were scrambling up the rocks above us; Vanderbrecken and I were hacking desperately at the traces; Isabella, who had jumped down from the cart at the first shots, had got a knife somehow, and was aiding us. The traces parted; Isabella and I urged the terrified horses out of the shafts and Vanderbrecken put his mighty shoulder to the cart.

Slowly the cart began to roll backwards. Gathering momentum, it bounced and juddered down the slope towards Garcia and his men. I heard Garcia shriek some order, saw him attempt to turn his horse's head.

Too late!

The cart struck him, swept him and his mount clean off the road, ploughed into the knot of cavalry behind and overturned. With a shriek, Garcia plunged down into the precipice; and the gold, for which he had twice committed murder, fell into oblivion with him.

Vanderbrecken picked up Silver bodily and slung him, with his crutch, over the saddle of a horse. Boakes scrambled down into the road, blood pouring from a gash across his forehead and gasped: 'All clear ahead!' We mounted up – Vanderbrecken leading Silver's horse – rapidly gained the summit and went hell-for-leather down towards the sea. I kept twisting my head round as we rode, certain that I should soon see Garcia's troopers in pursuit; but when, after twenty minutes, they had not appeared, I began to breathe more easy, and to believe that we could get clean away.

At length we gained the belt of forest that lay between us and the coast, and here the track petered out and we were forced to abandon the horses, so impenetrably thick was the vegetation. Luckily, Silver had by this time recovered his senses, for we should never have been able to carry him through that jungle. We had to cut our path with cutlasses and knives as we went, and so slow was our progress that my fear of being overtaken returned. Vanderbrecken, however, was more sanguine.

'They've richer fish to trawl,' said he, as we paused for five minutes to rest. 'They'll be scouring that valley for the gold!' at which Silver looked very black and muttered into his beard.

The sun had been our sole guide since entering the jungle, but soon after our rest we heard the distant roar of the sea and it was not long before we were descending through more open woodland towards the shore. We now had to cast about for the cove where Silver's late confederates had concealed their craft and Silver turned out to have a most imperfect recollection of where it lay. We set out to follow the line of the shore eastwards, and as luck would have it, we had not been searching above an hour when Abed's keen eye spied the masts of a ketch rising above the mangrove trees which, thereabouts, grew most luxuriantly. We made our way down to the cove, half-expecting to be hailed from the vessel by some friend of Sanchez; but there was not a soul aboard.

We took possession immediately and Vanderbrecken pronounced the ketch seaworthy enough. When it came to stores, however, we had a surprise, for the provisions were hardly enough to sustain a score of men during a considerable voyage, as Sanchez had promised.

'Methinks your Spanish friend would have betrayed you,' Vanderbrecken told Silver with a chuckle.

'There's vittles enough for us, so I reckon,' said Silver, with a shrug, 'so unless you has a mind to tarry here for the

Dons, I say let's slip our cable and be gone.'

'Gone?' growled Boakes suddenly. 'Where to? That's the first matter what 'as to be decided.' So saying he placed a hand upon his pistol.

'Hold hard, Sam,' says Silver quickly. 'Powder and shot won't settle it – ain't that right, Dutchman? You're Cap'n by election, I'm supposing, and though I'll say my mind, as I'm entitled, in my turn, it's for you to speak first.'

Vanderbrecken regarded him narrowly for a moment, then turned to me. By a gesture I indicated that I would abide by his decision.

'We haff little choice, I think,' said he with a shrug. 'We have compass, sextant, charts – so – give me the bearings of Treasure Island.'

I cast a glance towards Silver. His eyes were glittering and a smile flickered upon his lips. 'Well then,' said he, 'that's settled. Treasure Island!'

Chapter XXXI

Narrative continued by Dr Livesey:
The Mighty Fallen

Of our voyage to Jamaica there is little enough to say. Old Blandly procured a very weatherly schooner for Trelawney – at a pretty steep price I should have said, but I am no great judge – and Smollett mustered a handy crew. Our passage was completely prosperous. Trelawney, or 'Admiral' as he delighted to style himself, was like a boy let out of school, and the most generous, free-handed owner who ever put to sea. Living well himself, he loved to see others content.

It was upon the evening of our thirty-first day at sea that Smollett came into the Great Cabin, where Trelawney and I were at table.

'Breeze has freshened, gentlemen,' said he, sitting down and taking wine. 'If it holds, we'll see Kingston Harbour before tomorrow's out.'

'Hurrah!' cried Trelawney, raising his glass. 'I drink to you, Smollett, the finest Master upon the high seas I should think, and to the damnation of Lord Charles Devereux and that blackguard Hallows.'

'Desire is one thing, Trelawney,' said I, 'performance another. Suppose Devereux objects to being damned? He *is* Governor.'

'Pah!' returned Trelawney. 'If I didn't know you for the soundest fellow in England, Doctor, I'd grow weary of your crimping and carping.'

'Nevertheless, sir,' said Smollett, 'Livesey has a point. As I understand it, your Commission from the Secretary of State empowers you to investigate, but—'

Trelawney cut him short. 'You understand nothing at all of the matter!' he cried. 'What the devil's the use of investigatin' if you can't *act*, eh?'

'None whatsoever,' I put in. 'Therefore it seems to me that you must be withholding something from us.

Trelawney attempted to look sly. 'Only this, sir,' said he. 'That if I prove Devereux a villain then I'm appointed Acting Governor in his place. What think you of *that*, Doctor?'

'I think you might have informed us of it before.'

'Sealed orders, my dear sir, sealed orders,' said Trelawney very importantly. 'And here's something more: the Commander of the Jamaica Militia has been instructed – in strictest secrecy, mind – to obey me to the letter!'

It was indeed the Militia Commander, Colonel Fenton, who met us on the quay when we berthed in Kingston Harbour next day. He saluted Trelawney very respectfully and in a confidential tone confirmed that he had received dispatches from the Secretary of State.

'I consider myself under your command, sir,' said he.

'Capital, capital,' cried Trelawney, and then in a very slightly lower voice: 'But mum's the word, what?'

We were strolling along the quayside towards the carriage that Trelawney had ordered, when a short, dishevelled figure in clerical garb puffed towards us.

'Morgan,' Trelawney breathed in my ear. 'Local parson. Sound fellow, though he *is* a Welshman.' Then, striding forward to greet Mr Morgan: 'My dear sir, how d'ye do, how d'ye do?'

'The Lord be praised,' cried Morgan. 'Mr Trelawney, sir, you are the answer to a prayer.'

Then he caught sight of Ben Gunn and fell upon him with delight and pumped his hand.

'How d'ye do, how d'ye do,' croaked the old maroon. ' "Well enough", says you!'

We took our leave of Fenton and repaired at once to the best inn in the place, where Trelawney had taken rooms. Over an excellent dinner, we questioned Mr Morgan closely, and gained much valuable information. Hallows was gone. He had quit the island four or five weeks before our arrival in a ship, so rumour had it, paid for by the Governor. Rumour also had it that it was a treasure cruise he was embarked upon. The affairs of the plantation had been left in the hands of the clerk, Saul Sharpe, and it was in this person, so Mr Morgan advised, that the means to bring the Governor to justice might be found, for he had been hand-in-glove with Hallows.

'If he could be induced to turn his coat,' said Mr Morgan, 'then perhaps we would have the makings of a case against Lord Charles.'

'Turn his coat!' roared Trelawney. 'I'll have it inside out before the sun goes down or my name's not John Trelawney!'

Nothing would satisfy him but to set out forthwith for the plantation. 'What's the use of pigging it at an inn,' said he, 'when I own the finest house in Jamaica?'

Accordingly the carriage was ordered and Trelawney, Smollett, and I set forth. Trelawney grew very excited when the road began to run through his own estate, pointing out landmarks, and extolling the richness of the soil, the first-rate aspects enjoyed by certain fields, and so forth, with all the pride of a proprietor, while fulminating against Hallows for his villainous mismanagement of it all.

We came at last to the plantation house itself, just as the sun was setting, and I had to admit that it was very handsome, though I could not quite share in its owner's transports. We were met by an overseer of sorts, a white man, who looked very frightened upon learning the identity of his visitor. Commanding this man to summon Saul Sharpe immediately, Trelawney entered the house, amid the bowings and scrapings of a small army of black servants, and ushered us into a large dining-room, shouting for food and wine at the top of his voice.

A few moments later, Saul Sharpe came in.

The fellow was in a most complete state of panic and terror, and I thought that my medical skills might be called upon, for he seemed about to swoon away. I had anticipated some difficulty in inducing this man to turn evidence against the Governor, but one look at his twitching, snivelling face was enough to convince me that he was ours to use if we liked. So it proved.

In a very few moments he was pouring out a full confession, interlarded with many tearful pleas for mercy, but since the reader is already acquainted with all he had to tell, I will not reproduce his statement. It seemed to me to contain but one fact that we could turn into a weapon to defeat the Governor, and so I told Trelawney when Sharpe had been dismissed with a promise, conditional only, that if he testified against Lord Charles it would be taken in mitigation for his own crimes.

'*One*, sir?' cried Trelawney, greatly put out. 'One? We've learned enough tonight to hang the blackguard a thousand times!'

I insisted on my point, however, and Smollett backed me. Together we prevailed upon Trelawney to let us arrange matters in our own way.

Next morning, we returned to Kingston.

Colonel Fenton met us at the inn and told us that Lord Charles had learned of our arrival, and was in an angry, defiant mood.

'Defiant, is he?' thundered Trelawney. 'We'll see where his defiance leads him!'

Smollett and I took Fenton aside and questioned him further. He was convinced that Lord Charles had got wind of Trelawney's Commission and was preparing to defend himself with all the means at his disposal. When we told him what line we intended to take he whistled and raised an eyebrow.

'Well, sirs,' said he, 'it may sink him or it may not – we can but try.'

We waited upon the Governor that very same afternoon.

He received us in his library in a very cool and stately manner which masked, so I thought, a considerable apprehension. Colonel Fenton accompanied us, and, unknown to Devereux, we had Ben Gunn, Mr Morgan, and Saul Sharpe waiting in the next room. Trelawney produced his Commission with a flourish and placed it upon Devereux's desk.

'You'll oblige me by reading that through, sir,' said he. 'And observe the seal at the foot of the page.'

Devereux took up the parchment with a very supercilious expression on his face, which did not alter at all as he perused it, though its contents cannot have pleased him. At length he threw it down and looked up at Trelawney.

'Well, sir,' said the latter, 'the Secretary of State writes plain enough, I think.'

'Very plain,' returned Devereux, with a shrug. 'May I enquire what are these crimes I am accused of?'

Trelawney told him – with a great deal of bluster and a distressing lack of coherence.

Devereux laughed affectedly. 'I see,' he said. Taking up the Commission again, he continued: 'Well, as you say, the Secretary of State is perfectly unambiguous. Until you are able to *prove* these preposterous accusations you have no standing here. You may therefore go to the devil.'

I thought Trelawney would fall down in an apoplexy. His face grew purple with rage, and he was quite speechless. I thought it was time for me to say my piece.

'If I may be permitted a word,' said I.

Devereux turned towards me and favoured me with a cold, contemptuous stare.

'The charge,' I continued, 'that you conspired with Hallows in his criminal traffic with Caleb Lewis can be straitly substantiated.'

'So you are to play prosecutor are you, Doctor?' said Devereux sneeringly, but with a trifle less confidence. 'You take a great deal upon yourself, by Heaven.'

I nodded to Fenton, who stepped to the door and admitted Ben Gunn.

'Benjamin Gunn, for one,' said I, 'will witness to it.'

'So 'e will,' says Ben, crossing himself as was his way.

Devereux laughed out loud. 'This babbling idiot? He'll make you a fine witness indeed.'

'There is another,' I replied, and Mr Morgan stepped into the room.

'A canting priest and a half-witted buccaneer?' said Devereux. 'You'll need to do better than that, Doctor.'

'And so we will, confound your impudence!' roared Trelawney, whose temper had been simmering dangerously throughout my exchanges with Devereux, and now boiled over. He strode to the door, flung it open, and fairly dragged Saul Sharpe into the room by the scruff of his neck.

Devereux turned pale and his eyes narrowed.

'I believe you are acquainted with Mr Sharpe, Lord Charles?' said I.

'All Jamaica is acquainted with him,' said Devereux, his voice now trembling a little. 'And knows him for the lying vermin he is.'

'Sharpe had been privy to *all* your transactions,' said I. 'Your connection with Lewis; your false accusations against Jim Hawkins, which you made in order to obtain the map of Treasure Island.'

'I trust,' said Devereux, rising, 'that you are a better doctor than you are a lawyer, sir. Hearsay is not evidence.' He gestured imperiously to Fenton.

'Colonel,' said he, 'remove these gentlemen. They weary me.'

Fenton did not move a muscle. His lip quivering with rage, Devereux repeated the order.

'Evidence *does* exist,' said I quietly. 'In the form of a ledger kept by Lewis to record his dealings with Hallows. That ledger is, I believe, in your possession.'

Devereux absolutely started, and put out a hand to steady himself.

''E keeps it locked away in 'is desk,' Sharpe said, 'so as to 'ave an 'old over 'Allows – so 'Allows won't diddle 'im over the treasure.'

Devereux stared at us, one after another, like an animal at bay. 'Lies!' he hissed. 'All lies! Get out! All of you! Out!'

Colonel Fenton cleared his throat and stepped forward. 'The key, sir,' said he very solemn and steady. 'I must request that you give me the key of your drawer.'

'Stand aside!' cried Devereux. 'Stand aside, I say, or I'll break you!'

Fenton stood his ground. 'The key, sir,' he repeated. 'I am instructed to employ force if necessary.'

Devereux gaped at him as if he had suddenly broken into Chinese. As a man in a dream, he felt in a pocket and brought out a small key. Fenton took it, unlocked a drawer in the desk, and brought out a fat ledger, bound in leather. He examined it briefly and then turned again to Devereux.

'And now your sword, sir, if you please,' said he.

Devereux stood for a moment as if turned to stone. Then his shoulders bowed and he staggered blindly to his chair.

There is little more to tell. Smollett and I, and the others, went into the next room, leaving Trelawney and Fenton alone with Devereux. Five minutes later, Trelawney came out, his eyes gleaming and his cheeks flushed.

'Blackguard's broke,' he announced shortly. 'Full confession! He resigns, we hush up the scandal.'

He strode over to Smollett and clapped him heartily upon the shoulder. 'Smollett, my man,' he cried, 'prepare to weigh! At first light tomorrow we sail for Treasure Island!'

Part VI
Treasure Island

Chapter XXXI

Narrative Resumed by Jim Hawkins: History Repeats Itself

About seven weeks after quitting the coast of Mexico we sighted Treasure Island. It was an hour after dawn when the sea-mist lifted and Abed, who was on look-out, shouted 'Land-ho!' We rushed to the side and there, to the south, were the three conical hills of that accursed place rising out of the ocean in stark relief against the rose-pink of the sky.

Vanderbrecken laid the ketch three points nearer the wind and set a course that would bring us round towards the south side. Within the hour we had come close enough to bring a telescope to bear upon the islet that masked the entrance to the haven – Captain Kidd's Anchorage, as it was called by the buccaneers. And there, as plain as print on a page, the telescope revealed the masts and spars of a ship lying at anchor behind the islet.

We had already determined that the element of surprise would be our most useful weapon against Hallows, and so Vanderbrecken immediately put the helm over and we headed out to sea again in order to approach from the north – our plan being to beach the ketch in the North Inlet, the very place, you remember, where I ran the *Hispaniola* aground and had my final brush with Israel Hands.

We were fairly upon our new tack and were gathered in the stern when Long John spoke up.

'There's a matter,' said he, 'what has to be determined.'

213

Removing his pipe from his mouth and tapping the bowl, he continued: 'There's a king's fortune in precious stones buried on this island and we must agree Articles as to a just division. Jim? What's your notion?'

'My business here is with Hallows,' said I.

'Dutchman?' said Long John. '*You're* in low water I should think. And you, lady?' – turning to Isabella.

Isabella shrugged her shoulders. 'The time has long since past,' said she, with a smile to me, 'when I pretended to anything else. With my uncle dead, I'm in a worse case than before. So I'll take my share, if you please, and work for it too.'

'What's *your* notion, Silver?' growled Vanderbrecken, who continued to entertain the liveliest suspicions of him.

'Well now,' returned Long John, scratching his chin, 'the first consideration is this – 'tis only I can read that map. And the second is that them stones is mostly mine by rights, seeing as how I was Flint's quartermaster. But, there,' he went on with a great air of magnanimity, 'I ain't standing on neither. Equal shares for all, that's my idea.'

'Boakes?' said Vanderbrecken. 'What do you say?'

The old ruffian shook his head and rolled his quid. 'I reckons as Long John 'as the right of it,' said he. 'Equal shares is good enough for me.'

'Then we're agreed,' said Long John.

'Yes,' Vanderbrecken replied, looking at him very hard. 'We have a bargain that *I* will enforce.'

Perhaps two hours after this conversation, we beached the ketch in the North Inlet. So far, I have said nothing of the emotions aroused in me at beholding again the dismal grey woods and brooding hills of Treasure Island, or at hearing the eternal thunder of the surf that had echoed so often through my youthful nightmares, or scenting the fetid vapours of its pestilential swamps. A flood of bitter memories oppressed me as I recalled the vow I had made to myself ten years before, that oxen and wainropes should never drag me back to that place. The shades of old

Redruth, and Joyce, and Hunter, and the other honest fellows who had lost their lives in our first adventure there seemed to rise up before me in sad reproach. As I watched Silver hobbling ashore through the shallows, I could not but recall his part in the affair, the mutiny, the murders, the rum-sodden savagery of the villains he had commanded.

But perhaps because my recent misadventures, dreadful enough in all conscience, had hardened me, or because my man's estate demanded that the ghosts of childhood be laid, I was the first to volunteer to scout out Hallows and his party, and proposed taking Abed with me.

Vanderbrecken readily agreed but Long John demurred. 'I reckons it's Boakes and I should do it,' said he.

Vanderbrecken grunted. 'Why so eager, my friend? You won't see *Jim* break the Articles. Besides, I think it is a task for youth and stealth, no?'

Long John muttered and cursed under his breath but even Boakes, who was wont to side with him in everything, was against him in this, and he had to give way.

Abed and I, therefore, set out, each armed with a brace of pistols and a cutlass. Our first objective was to get a sight of Hallows's ship and so we made directly across country for the anchorage, moving always with the greatest caution through the woods, and taking care never to expose ourselves. It was as we rounded the lower, eastern spur of Spy-glass Hill that we had our first evidence of Hallows and his party. I caught a glint of bright light, as of the sun on burnished steel.

It came from the plateau that lay below the southern flank of Spy-glass and commanded the anchorage itself; the very same plateau, in a word, upon which Flint had buried his gold. It struck me at once – and should have occurred to me before – that, of course, this would be the place to find Hallows at work; for he must assume that Flint had concealed the stones very near to his other cache.

Crouching low, and without making a sound, Abed and I crept forward through clumps of azalea and nutmeg towards the forest of pines, and the giant – the 'tall tree' of Flint's map – that towered over its fellows and marked the spot where the treasure had lain hid. Now, guided by the sounds of pick on stone, the rasp of shovels, and the grunts and curses of men hard at work, we crawled like snakes upon our bellies until we had the diggings in sight.

Above a dozen men were labouring in a prodigious excavation that extended in a circle round the tall tree. To judge from the colossal breadth and depth of the pit they had made, and the corresponding ramparts of earth they had raised up about it, they must have toiled for many weeks.

Hallows was taking his ease, seated upon an upturned cask, fanning himself with his broad hat, and slapping with his hand at the biting insects that assaulted his neck.

Of a sudden, one of the diggers let out a choking cry, swayed on his feet, and then swooned away. At once the others paused in their work, and Hallows rose from his seat. One of the diggers, a rascally-looking fellow with a yellow-spotted bandanna kerchief knotted round his forehead, threw down his shovel and knelt beside his comrade.

He examined him briefly and then rose and walked truculently towards Hallows.

'Jack's done,' said he. 'The fever's on 'im.'

Hallows gave a slight shrug of his shoulders. 'Then let him be carried to the stockade, Mr Boatswain,' said he with cool indifference.

'Hold hard,' growled the boatswain angrily.

'What's this, Mr Adams?' returned Hallows. 'More of your crabbing?'

'We wants a sight o' your map,' said Adams, and there was a low murmur of approval from the men.

'Do you indeed?' says Hallows.

Half-turning towards the others, Adams spat and said: 'We've shifted dirt for days an' nothin' to show for it but a row of graves.' Sullen grunts of agreement came from half a dozen throats. 'We're not slaves,' Adams went on, gaining in confidence. 'I say he should show us his map!'

''E's right at that!' shouted one of the hands and there was a general movement forward as they rallied towards their boatswain.

'You'll dig for a year if necessary,' said Hallows, apparently unaffected by the growing atmosphere of menace.

'Aye!' said Adams quickly. 'Till every last one of us is dead wi' fever. *Then* you'll find!'

The effect of this speech upon the men was electric. I did not see how Hallows could hope to contain their pent-up violence much longer.

'Well?' cried Adams triumphantly. 'Where's your answer to that?'

Hallows smiled and threw out a hand. 'There,' said he.

A dozen heads turned.

Gaynes and two others (Jed and Leary were their names as I was soon to learn) were standing ten paces away with muskets raised. The sight of the muskets sobered up the men instantly, and though Adams continued to glare defiance at Hallows, the others hung their heads.

'Listen to me,' barked Hallows. 'I'll have obedience, by God, or this place shall be a tomb for all of you.' In a softer, more accommodating tone, he went on: 'Rebellion won't win you the treasure – discipline *will*. The stones are here. We'll touch all right, and every faithful hand shall have his share.' As he said this he looked keenly from face to face, seeking, I suppose, to judge which of the men would stand by his duty, and which would take Adams's side.

'Come,' he went on after a moment, 'we're all of us weary and plagued with heat. We'll call today a holiday – back to the stockade and double grog all round. What d'you say, men?'

Five or six of them put up a cheer – not very heartily – and the rest shuffled their feet and cast their eyes towards Adams. The boatswain was no fool. With a very creditable show of cheerfulness, he said: ''Andsomely spoke, sir! I call that 'andsome, men. Double grog it is, then!' – with a salute to Hallows – 'and we'll say no more o' the map.'

With that he shouldered his pick and spade, the others did likewise, and the whole party set off down the path that had been made by their daily marches between the plateau and the stockade.

I determined to follow at a safe distance, then wait until night should fall, and use my ears and eyes. History, it was plain, was repeating itself: the two diseases endemic to Treasure Island – fever and mutiny – were rampant, and would make us stout allies in our endeavour to defeat Hallows.

I led Abed by a circuitous route to the stockade and more than two hours passed before we came near it. It was as well that I took this precaution for we were still more than half a mile from our destination when we heard voices in the woods. Creeping nearer, we came upon four men who were cutting firewood, and one of them was boatswain Adams.

'Bide your time was your advice,' says one of the others – an Irishman – to Adams. 'Well now, it seems to me that poor ould Jack, for one, bided too long.'

His companion agreed.

'I say we're too few,' returned Adams.

'Then we'd best set about recruitin' is *my* advice,' said the Irishman, 'or they'll be buryin' us alongside o' Jack.'

''E's right,' growled one of the others.

'That's easy enough said,' replied Adams, 'but there's two, Jed and Leary, what'll stand by Gaynes and Hallows.'

'Then they can die with them,' said the Irishman. 'Now or never, Adams,' he went on. 'Strike tonight, that's my idea. Hallows won't never be expectin' it, now, for he'll be lookin' to see the crew rotten wi' rum.'

Adams pondered a moment, then nodded his head. 'Very well,' said he. 'Tonight it is.' They picked up their bundles of firewood and moved away.

We waited until they were out of earshot, then followed, and ten minutes later came to the edge of the clearing in which the stockade stood. Nothing much had changed in ten years. There was the palisade and the sandy knoll rising within it, and the log-house half-buried at the summit. A big fire was cracking outside the porch where the little stream ran down, and men were sitting about it, swilling rum, and raising their voices in a tuneless rendering of *Lillibullero*.

Night was fast falling and a chilly little wind springing up. Though it occurred to me that Vanderbrecken and the others must be growing anxious about us, I determined to wait a little longer, until complete darkness should give me the opportunity to play the spy. Adams, I was sure, would bring matters to a head within a few hours, and it would be of incalculable value to our cause to know the outcome.

Night fell.

The moon had not yet risen and a complete blackness enveloped the woods and the stockade except where the great fire sparked and glowed. Bidding Abed to stay where he was, I stole forward and crept round to the opposite side of the stockade.

I was pretty certain that no look-out would be kept, but still my heart was in my mouth as I scrambled over the palisade and dropped down into the sand upon the other side. I lay down and waited for a cry of alarm, but none came. I was about to move away when I heard a low voice growl: '*Hold!*'

I lay as still as death, but when I heard the speaker continue: 'I ain't decidin' nothing,' I cautiously raised my head. Adams and three others were standing in a huddle some ten or fifteen paces away.

'I ain't sayin' yes, nor I ain't sayin' no,' the speaker went on, 'not 'fore I's took counsel wi' me mates.'

'Decide, then,' Adams returned, 'but be quick about it, or you'll find you're too late, by Thunder.'

He walked away, leaving the others to draw closer together and confer in whispers, so that I could catch only snatches.

'We've no choice,' grunted one.

'If it's Adams or Hallows, then I says Adams,' said another.

From these and other indications I gathered that the vote was going in favour of mutiny, and after a few moments more I heard the original speaker, who seemed to have some authority over his mates, declare: 'That's decided then – and no going back.'

They moved away towards the glow of the fire on the far side of the log-house, and I scrambled to my feet. While I had been using my ears, my eyes had not been idle: I had observed candle-light streaming from one of the loopholes on the north side of the log-house, and, I know not why, nothing would satisfy me but to creep up and look inside the house itself. Crouching low, I ran swiftly up the slope, then dropped down again and covered the last few feet on my belly until I was lying directly under the open loophole.

Not a sound came from within and inch by inch I raised my head until my eyes were level with the sill. What I saw made me start so violently that I very nearly gave myself away. Hallows and Gaynes were seated at a table upon which was spread the map of Treasure Island. By the mercy of Providence both their backs were turned towards me. A partition of rough planking had been erected to close off the north-east corner of the log-house and form a private room, roughly square, for Hallows and his friend. A door, at present closed, was hung in this partition and gave, I supposed, to the log-house proper, which had been all open in my day.

Hallows wiped his brow with a handkerchief and let out his breath with a hiss of frustration.

'The key is here,' said he, tapping with a forefinger upon the map. 'It *must* be here.'

'Pity we killed 'Awkins,' said Gaynes. ''E could ha' showed us.'

'Possibly,' Hallows replied. 'But on the other hand, the sight of young Master Innkeeper tumbling off Lugger Point was quite delightful. Such pleasures are rare enough, God knows, *in hac lacrimarum valle*, and one should be grateful.'

Gaynes grunted. 'One thing's for sure,' said he, 'the crew's fast losin' what trust they 'ad in you an' this worthless scrap o' paper.'

'Perhaps,' returned Hallows. 'But will they transfer their trust to friend Adams? I doubt it.'

Gaynes shrugged and spat upon the ground. 'I'll take the air, I reckon,' said he, rising. 'See what temper the dogs is in.'

Hallows dismissed him with an indifferent wave of his hand and bent once more over the map. I crouched without in a sweat of indecision. On the one hand, there was the map, not four feet from my grasp, and Hallows, all unsuspecting, completely at my mercy; on the other hand, unless I could carry out my attack in complete silence, I risked rousing the others, and so casting away the greatest advantage we possessed – surprise. I was still attempting to make up my mind, when the decision was abruptly taken out of my hands.

Sounds of a violent scuffle came from the other side of the door – shouts, and curses, and blows. Hallows sprang to his feet and picked up a pistol. The voice of boatswain Adams rang out sharp from the other side.

'In there!' he cried. 'Hallows! Your friend Gaynes has a knife at his throat! Throw down your arms and step out here, and bring your map with you.'

For a second, Hallows hestitated. Then he picked up the map, stooped by the table, vanishing from my sight for a moment, and rose again with empty hands. Casting away his pistol, he stepped to the door and opened it. I ducked down and rose again only when I heard the slam of the door. Then I squeezed through the loophole into the room and crouched down under the table. I swiftly felt all round the underside but found no trace of the map. On a sudden inspiration I lifted up each leg in turn and found that the third had been hollowed out. There was a tubular cavity, like a musket's barrel, and inside it was the map. I had it out of its hiding-place in a trice and was about make good my escape through the loophole when I heard a man cough outside. At once I knew what had happened. Adams, fearing that *Hallows* might attempt to escape that way, had placed a guard to prevent it. I was caught in the trap designed for my enemy! Praying that the fellow would not look inside, I crawled nearer to the door, which had failed to shut completely and was open a crack, for I thought I ought to see what was toward.

Hallows was standing in the centre of the log-house, facing Adams. Beside Adams stood the Irishman, who had Gaynes in a grip – a knife at his throat. Behind them stood five or six of the mutinous hands, while the remainder, who numbered Jed and Leary among them, were being held at musket-point in a corner.

'Well, men,' Hallows was saying, his voice completely cool and unafraid, 'I see that some of you have decided to throw in your lot with boatswain Adams.'

'Aye – all but five,' returned Adams, with a smirk.

'I trust,' said Hallows, 'that when he betrays *you*, as he's now betraying me, you'll have the decency to remember that I warned you – those few of you,' he added, 'that are left alive.'

Bitterly though I hated Hallows, I could not but admire the manner in which he faced out his rebellious crew. Though his life was plainly forfeit, he showed not the slightest sign of fear, and spoke as if it was more in sorrow than in anger.

Such a display of confidence could not fail to impress the others, and even Adams looked less sure of himself.

'Enough o' that,' he growled. 'Let's have the map.'

'Don't you see his game?' said Hallows, ignoring the boatswain and appealing directly to the mutineers. 'Once *Adams* has the map . . .' and he spread his hands in a gesture more eloquent by far than any words.

That Hallows's speech had sowed the seeds of doubt in the mutineers was evident in their faces – and Adams could see it.

'The map,' he repeated swiftly. 'Hand it over, or I'll shoot you down and take it anyway.'

Hallows shrugged. 'As you desire, Mr Adams,' said he mildly, and reached into a pocket. I could not think what he was at, unless it was to gain time by the production of some other paper.

But it was no paper he drew forth. It was a miniature pistol, half the size of his hand, but lethal enough – for when it spat, Adams fell down, shot clean through the brain!

I saw Gaynes wrench free from the Irishman and then I was up and leaping for the loophole – through which the sentinel, alarmed by the gunshot, was attempting to enter. He met my fist full in his face and fell backwards – but as he toppled he fired his musket. I was not hit, but my presence was betrayed!

I dived head-first through the loophole, rolled down the slope, picked myself up, and ran full tilt for the palisade. As I reached it and jumped up, a musket spoke from behind me, I felt a searing agony in my shoulder, and fell back inside the stockade.

Abed's frightened face appeared between the stakes and I had just time enough to hiss at him: 'Get away!' before I was seized, hauled brutally to my feet, and found myself face to face with Gaynes.

I make no attempt to describe the expression on the overseer's face when he first saw who it was he had captured. He stared, and stared, and stared, and stared while Leary held me fast. At length, his tongue flicked out to moisten his lips and he croaked: 'Hawkins! Hawkins, by Satan's power!' He whipped up a pistol and pressed it to my neck; then he and Leary dragged me across the stockade to the log-house.

I remember that, in spite of the burning pain in my shoulder and the bitter mortification of knowing that I had by my own folly wrecked our enterprise, I wondered how Hallows would take it when he saw me.

As it was, when we entered the log-house there was no sign of him. Jed and the faithful hands were holding the remnant of the mutineers at bay, but with only a musket and a pistol between them. Adams lay dead where he had fallen, and beside him lay the Irishman, also dead.

Hallows was in his room: I heard a crash as he tipped over the table, and a shocking oath. A moment later he flung through the door, his face transfigured with rage at the loss of the map, which of course he had just confirmed.

At the sight of me he stopped in his tracks and uttered a strange sort of sob. For a moment he stared as Gaynes had done, then a shriek of hysterical laughter escaped from his lips, to be followed by wail upon wail of helpless mirth. Mastering himself at last, and wiping his eyes with his sleeve, he walked over to me, saying: 'My dear, dear, *dear* Mr Hawkins! This is wonderful indeed, most supernaturally wonderful that *you*' – here he felt inside my coat and brought out the map – 'you of all men should rise up from the dead to pull my irons out of the fire for me.'

Holding the map up high, he advanced towards the mutineers, who were gaping like idiots.

'Gentlemen,' says Hallows, 'here's news for you. May I present Mr Hawkins. You all know the name, I trust – ah yes! I see you do – well here's Mr Hawkins come to teach us how to read the map and lead us to the treasure!'

At this the wretched fellows looked so miserably cast down that it was almost comic to see them.

'I see you blush, gentlemen,' Hallows went on in the same elated tone. 'I see you shift your feet and avert your eyes, as well as you might, mutinous, blockheaded rabble that you are. But I'm a generous fellow – dammit, I'm the very soul of charity. Your recent lapse from duty shall be forgotten; you shall partake in my good fortune; more – I'll add his share, and his' – pointing to the two dead men – 'to your own, if you're with me.'

'I be with you, sir!' cried one of them.

'And I!' echoed the others.

'Then you may bury this vermin,' said Hallows, giving Adams's corpse a kick, 'and sharp about it.'

The men jumped to obey and while they dragged Adams and the Irishman out, Hallows turned to me.

'Well now, Mr Hawkins,' said he crisply, 'you're not alone, I imagine. How many are there in your party?'

I was silent.

Gaynes gave a twist to my wounded arm that made me cry out with pain.

'No, no, Mr Gaynes!' says Hallows. 'That won't do! We must preserve the health and comfort of our friend at all costs.'

He smiled at me mockingly. 'This is not a large island,' he continued. 'It will be no trouble to Mr Gaynes to locate your friends, I fancy – and deal with them. In the meantime, Mr Hawkins, we have much to discuss.'

Chapter XXXIII

Narrative continued by Dr Livesey:
The Dutchman's Tale

It was not more than two hours after dawn that a cry of 'Land Ho!' from the cross-trees had us running to the weather bow and scanning the horizon to the south-west. Trelawney was beside me, clapping his brand-new telescope to his eye. 'That's Treasure Island, by Heaven,' said he. 'Here, Livesey, take a squint.'

I accepted the invitation and peered through the glass. Sure enough, there was the familar outline of Spy-glass hill.

'Brings back some memories, what?' said Trelawney.

'Yes,' I agreed, 'and pretty dark ones too.'

Trelawney sniffed, cleared his throat, and looked away; I

knew that he was thinking of his three servants, old Redruth the gamekeeper, Hunter, and Joyce, who had perished upon Treasure Island, and for whose deaths he had never quite forgiven himself.

Leaving him to his thoughts, I went below to my quarters to see to the priming of my pistols. A few moments later, Smollett entered and the slight flush upon his cheek told me that he was out of temper.

'Livesey,' says he, 'will you come to the fo'c'sle – I'm hanged if *I* can talk any sense into the old fool.'

When I asked whatever he meant, he told me that Ben Gunn had gone mad!

'Shut himself up in the fo'c'sle locker and won't come out!'

I accompanied him at once to the fo'c'sle, where we found three or four of the hands standing about one of the lockers and laughing among themselves.

'Up aloft, you men!' barked Smollett, which wiped the smiles off their faces. As they scurried away, I knocked upon the door of the locker, and feeling a trifle foolish, called out to Ben.

'I ain't 'ere!' came the muffled reply from within.

'Ben,' says I, 'it's the Doctor. Whatever ails you, man?'

'I ain't a-comin' out!'

Smollett shrugged hopelessly and said, *sotto voce*: 'It's Treasure Island! He's scared half to death.'

Putting my mouth to the door, I called out: 'Ben! Ben – this is foolishness.'

'I ain't a-comin' out,' he repeated through the planking, 'and I ain't a-settin' foot on that benighted island, an' that's flat, an' that's it, an' all about it – axing your pardon, Doctor.'

'Ben,' I began, 'there's no possible—'

' "Arm can come to Ben Gunn," says you. No disrespect, sir, but Ben Gunn, 'e knows better. I's seed it all predicked in me dreams, sir – marooned again, an' livin' on goats, an' berries, an' me heart sore for a Christian diet.'

'Well now, Ben,' said I, beginning to see a way out, 'I've a bottle of rum in my cabin. Let's you and I take a tot or two together and talk like sensible men.'

There was a long silence, then: 'Rum, sir?'

'The finest Jamaica rum – and I've a Cheshire cheese in my locker.'

After a further prolonged silence the door creaked and swung open a crack. 'That there cheese you mentions, Doctor,' says Ben. 'Would you be offerin' me a morsel o' that?'

'Only step out of the confounded cupboard,' said I, 'and you shall consume it all.'

At last Ben emerged from the locker and eyed me solemnly. 'Would that be in order, then, sir,' says he, 'if I were to 'ave it *toasted*, like?'

'Any way you desire, my good fellow,' says I.

'And you won't, you won't be leavin' Ben Gunn behind in that place, sir?' he said, gripping my arm.

I was about to reassure him yet again when a cry 'Ship ahoy!' from aloft had us all tumbling up the stair on to the deck.

We ran to the rail to see a small ketch rolling scuppers in the swell not a quarter of a mile away on our larboard beam.

'She's adrift,' cried Smollett, and strode away bellowing orders to heave-to and lower a boat. The ketch indeed was wallowing helplessly, her booms swinging, her sails flapping and cracking like blankets on a line. Smollett had a boat launched in a trice, and with six strong men bending to the oars, it very soon overhauled the ketch, which the current had drifted closer to the schooner. A hail from one of the men informed us that there was a man aboard.

'Is he alive?' shouted Smollett.

'Can't rightly tell, Cap'n,' was the reply.

'Bring him aboard and we'll see,' ordered Smollett, and we watched as two of them heaved the man, with some difficulty, into the boat, while the others set the ketch to rights.

We had the devil of a business landing our catch for the fellow was a veritable giant of a man, and appeared to be lifeless. As we heaved him over the rail Ben Gunn ran forward, highly excited, and said: 'Shiver me spars! It's the Dutchy! It's the Dutchy hisself!'

We laid the Dutchman – Vanderbrecken – upon the deck and I swiftly knelt by him and felt for his pulse. To my immense relief I found that he was alive and, moreover, that his heartbeat was strong and regular. We carried him to the Great Cabin (it took four men to do it!) and settled him in Trelawney's own berth. Upon examination, I found a monstrous contusion on his cranium but no other visible wound, and forthwith administered salts. I thought I should have to bleed him, for the salts had no apparent effect, but just as I was about to send for my lancets his eyes flickered open and he let out a deep groan as his senses returned.

'Thanks he to God,' muttered Mr Morgan, who was beside me.

'Morgan, by the Thunders,' said Vanderbrecken in a very weak voice, and then: 'Ben Gunn!'

''Isself!' said Ben, pleased as punch. 'And no sperrit, says you!'

Vanderbrecken attempted to rise but I bade him lie still. 'You've taken a blow that would have killed an ox,' said I, and gave him a cordial to drink.

'This is Dr Livesey,' says Morgan, 'and Mr Trelawney, and Captain Smollett.'

'Ah,' the Dutchman sighed, drinking off the preparation, 'Jim's friends.'

'And yours too, sir,' says Trelawney heartily, 'if you'll do me the honour to shake my hand.'

'That will do for later, Trelawney,' said I.' 'Our business now, if Mr Vanderbrecken is up to it, is to hear his report.'

Vanderbrecken nodded and raised himself up with an energy that astonished me. Forthwith be began to tell his tale, the first part of which is already known to the reader. He came to the point at which Jim and Abed Jones went off to scout for Hallows and continued:

'We wait. Hour after hour, we wait – and the lady, Isabella, she grow anxious. Night comes. I decide. I say we must go out ourselves and look for them. So. We are about to go, when we hear a man running – running like the Devil. Abed Jones it is! He has run from the stockade, run so fast that the blood is coming from his ears! He tell us Jim is taken – taken by Hallows!' He paused to let the sensation die down, then went on: 'The lady says we attack the stockade at once, and I agree. But Silver' – here Trelawney started to huff and puff – 'Silver, he say the stockade is like a fortress. "Powder, that's what required, I reckons," he says, and I agree with him. So. We make a plan. Silver, Boakes, and Abed Jones will go to Hallows's ship, seize it, and get powder. I will stay with Isabella to guard our own boat.'

He shook his head grimly from side to side. 'I think perhaps,' said he, 'it was not a good plan. Silver – he does not come back—'

'Treacherous hound!' exclaimed Trelawney.

'—But with the dawn we do haff visitors: *Gaynes*—'

'Villain!' cried Trelawney.

'Hush!' I begged him.

'Gaynes,' continued Vanderbrecken, 'and six of his men.'

Again he shook his head and smote his fist into his hand. 'What could I do? There were too many of them! I kill three, maybe four, and then—'

'Isabella!' cried Morgan. 'What of Isabella?'

'I don't know,' replied the Dutchman, wringing his hands. 'I don't know. I am struck down and' – He shrugged helplessly, then turned a pleading face towards us. 'I think Jim haff need of his friends,' he said.

'And by Heaven we'll aid him!' said Trelawney. 'Every last stitch of canvas, Smollett!'

'No, no,' cried the Dutchman. 'We take the ketch.'

'That's sense,' Smollett declared.

'I'll *swim*, confound it, if it'll get me to Treasure Island faster!' roared Trelawney.

Chapter XXXIV

Narrative Resumed by Jim Hawkins: The Legacy of Darby M'Graw

Soon after dawn, Hallows mustered his men outside the log-house and divided them into two parties: the first to stay behind to guard the stockade and the stores of food and ammunition; the second to go a-treasure hunting!

I had passed quite the most wretched night of my life, tortured now by the throb of my wounded arm, now by my own imaginings. I had seen Gaynes and his gang creep up upon our party unawares and all my friends killed, and, worse, Isabella taken – all because I would play the spy. No man ever reproached himself more bitterly and I would gratefully have given up my life in order to call back time. That it would soon be over in any case seemed pretty certain – as soon as Hallows discovered that I knew no more of the secret of the map than he did himself. The only ray of hope was the fact that Gaynes and his party were nowhere to be seen. Their absence suggested that they might have had a brush with Vanderbrecken and come off worse, but the mocking, confident smile on Hallows's face belied this.

Hallows tied a rope around my neck, himself taking up the loose end, while one of the others was ordered to march behind me with a pistol to my back.

'We must not lose our friend Hawkins, must we men?' cried Hallows, and the treasure-hunters chuckled and slapped their thighs, as excited as children.

And so we set off, Hallows at the head of the file, leading me like a dancing bear, exactly as Long John had done ten years before and in pretty much the same circumstances. Skirting the anchorage, we trudged through the heavy, boggish ground below the plateau, then gained the higher slopes, where the scent of broom and the spice of nutmeg and pine mingled together upon the sweet early-morning air. All the men were armed to the gunwale and bowed down with picks and shovels and bread and pork. Hallows had the map in his hand and from time to time, when the pace faltered, he would wave it in the air like a flag to encourage the men. At last we came to the diggings and Hallows called the halt. The men laid down their various burdens then shuffled into a rough half-circle round me.

'Well then, young Hawkins,' says Hallows cheerfully, 'here is your moment of glory at last.' Holding the map before me, he went on: 'My confederates and I are most anxious to hear you tell us precisely where the treasure lies.'

My hour had come. I squared my shoulders and said: 'I know as much or as little as you do yourself.'

Some of the men growled furiously at this, but Hallows merely smiled.

'A predictable response,' said he, then called out: 'Jed! Leary!'

All heads turned towards one of the great mounds of earth from behind which stepped Jed and Leary, who – to my unspeakable horror – held Isabella between them. She looked pale and exhausted and there were bloodstains upon her clothing though I thought that she had taken no wound herself.

'I need hardly tell you,' Hallows was saying, 'that the purpose of this drama is to stimulate the faculty of memory in you, Hawkins. *Forsan et haec olim meminisse iuvabit*, as Roman Virgil has it.'

'I know nothing,' I cried desperately, as Leary put a knife to Isabella's throat. 'For the love of God don't you think I'd tell you if I did?'

'Dear me,' said Hallows. 'This is most ungallant of you – unless I have been mistaken in supposing that this lady, who has fallen so providentially into our hands, has some claim upon your heart, or at least upon your honour.'

Imagine if you can the horrible position I was in. Unless I could tell Hallows *something*, Isabella would be put to torture in front of my eyes; yet even if I lied to him, and invented some story, it would serve only to postpone her sufferings and, eventually, the deaths of us both.

'Listen to me,' I pleaded, 'there's only one man who knows the secret of the map – John Silver, who was Flint's quartermaster. He's here – he's somewhere upon the island, I swear it!'

'Is this another lie?' says Hallows.

'*That it ain't!*' came the blessed, glorious voice of Long John Silver.

He was standing alone in the shadow of the tall tree, some dozen paces away.

As the others stood in gaping silence, and even Hallows stared, Long John heaved forward, his eyes flicking round the circle of men, a faint smile upon his lips. He halted in front of Hallows, resting upon his crutch, and nodded his head.

'John Silver,' said he, 'formerly quartermaster to Captain Flint, an' privy to certain knowledge.'

Hallows raised his pistol and pointed it at Silver – but Long John only smiled more broadly.

'What Jim Hawkins says,' he went on, 'is the plain truth. There's only *me* knows the secret.'

'I see,' returned Hallows, moistening his lips, and then: 'You would appear to be alone.'

'So I be,' said Long John, 'in a manner o' speaking.'

As he said this we were all startled by the sudden boom of a cannon. It came from the anchorage below – from Hallows's own ship – and it sent every bird upon that side of the island shrieking into the air. As the echo died away: 'You hark to that, Mr Hallows?' said Long John. 'Well now, on the count o' ten, or thereabouts, you'll hear her speak again.'

Ten seconds crawled by – I could see Leary counting under his breath – and sure enough the cannon roared once more, its thunder rolling up from below and being answered furiously by the birds. Long John shifted a pace and scratched his chin. Then, in a high, clear voice, so that every man present should hear him, he addressed Hallows.

'Now I reckon that's proof enough, to the satisfaction of all you gentlemen o' fortune, that I has possession and command o' your ship – which confers, in its turn, command o' the whole bucket o' brine, as the saying is.'

If Hallows was shaken by this overturn, he did not show it. Instead, he matched Long John's smile and said coolly: 'I think I could recapture my ship with no great difficulty.'

'I ain't sayin' as you could not,' replied Long John. 'But on my side there's this to consider: without a ship there's no carryin' off the treasure; but without me, there's no treasure to carry off.'

Hallows nodded sagely. 'If that's so, then the weight of advantage would appear to be evenly balanced, seeing that *I* have the map.'

'Right you was,' says Long John. 'Even balance, equal shares: that's my proposition.'

Hallows regarded him through half-closed eyes for a long moment, then turned to Jed and Leary and the others. 'Well men,' said he, 'you know as much as I do. What do you say?'

Jed looked to Leary who nodded shortly. The others, following their lead, grunted their willingness to agree the bargain.

'You have your answer, Silver,' said Hallows. 'Equal shares for all.'

'Right then,' said Silver, brisk and businesslike. 'First, let's see Jim Hawkins here released, and his lady; then you'll oblige me wi' a sight o' the map.'

Hallows slipped the rope off my neck and I ran instantly

to Isabella's side. Long John, meanwhile, had the map in his hands and was devouring it with burning eyes. 'Aye,' he sighed after a moment, 'there it be, as plain as plain.'

Every eye was fixed hungrily upon him as he looked up from the map.

'Well, mates,' says he, 'we've a fair march ahead of us, so best be started.'

'*March?*' cried Hallows dangerously. 'The treasure lies *here* – or hereabouts.'

'Does it so?' returned Long John softly. 'You've been shiftin' dirt for days and have you struck?'

'Precisely *where* are we to march?' said Hallows.

'To Spy-glass hill, yonder,' was the reply.

Hallows snatched the map from Long John's hand and conned it. 'I see no mark,' he said harshly. 'What treachery is this?'

'Treachery?' says Silver mildly. 'Talk you of treachery with the Articles agreed not one minute before?' With a complete suddenness, he turned to one of Hallows's men and said pleasantly: 'Here, you, mate, fetch me that keg there – for a one-legged man can't spin a yarn while standin' on his pin.'

The man jumped to obey as if he had been commanded by Hallows himself, while that gentleman looked from the map to Silver and back to the map again.

Silver settled himself down on the up-turned keg and took off his hat. 'Well now,' he began – and never in this world, I should think, did a story-teller have a more attentive audience – 'Well now, it were this way. Three year ago – thereabouts – I fetched up to Tortuga; in pretty low water, too, I won't deny, though we'll say no more o' that. There I found an old shipmate' – he paused – 'Darby M'Graw.'

Leary was the only man there (other than myself) who recognized the name.

'Darby M'Graw,' he cried. ''Im what were with Flint at the end!'

'Ah,' says Long John, cocking an eye, 'I thought I knew

234

your dial. Leary, ain't it? What sailed with England.'

'Belay that!' cried Leary hoarsely. 'What o' Darby, what o' Darby M'Graw?'

'Well,' resumed Silver, 'as you says aright, Darby, he were at Flint's side at the end, and heard the last mortal words spoke above board by that blue devil. When I fetched up alongside, Darby were in the last extremity hisself – had the horrors on him for a taste o' rum. "Silver," says he, "you fetch me a bottle o' grog aft an' I'll tell you Flint's dying words. I'll tell you where he stowed his gems. I'll teach you how to read his map." '

Long John looked up, his great, pale, wide face shiny with sweat and his eyes glinting like brilliants. Hallows and the rest of them were gazing upon him, lips parted, eyes round, absolutely in his thrall.

' "On Spy-glass hill," says Darby M'Graw,' Long John continued, reliving every moment, ' "On Spy-glass hill," he says, his teeth rattling in his head, and *death* starting yellow in his eye. "*The mark of the water.*" '

Hallows, shaking all over as if afflicted with an ague, was conning the map.

'There's a stream marked,' he croaked.

'Aye,' says Long John, 'and a plash o' water where she tumbles over a rock.'

The spell was broken. The men crowded round Hallows, jostling him, desperate for a sight of the map. While they were thus occupied, Long John tipped me a prodigious wink. Stepping to his side, I had just time to whisper: '*Where's Gaynes?*' before Hallows brought his crew to order.

'Picks and shovels, men!' he roared. 'Jump to it!'

Chapter XXXV

The Mark of the Water

We started the ascent of Spy-glass five minutes later. Hallows – with the map – took the lead, setting a brisk pace. Long John, Isabella and I trailed towards the rear of the column, with Jed and Leary stationed behind us on purpose by Hallows, who naturally anticipated treachery from Silver, just as Silver was expecting it from him!

As we toiled up the thickly wooded cleft that gave to the heights of Spy-glass, Isabella told us her tale. She kept it brief, careful to reveal nothing that was not already known to Jed and Leary, who were close enough to hear every word we said.

Gaynes had attacked in force, at dawn. Though Vanderbrecken had fought like a Trojan, the odds had been overwhelming and he had been struck down and cast adrift in the ketch; but not before he had accounted for no less than four of Gaynes's men – leaving only Gaynes himself, Jed and Leary alive. They had taken Isabella to the diggings, where Gaynes left them, and there they had waited until the arrival of the treasure-party.

Long John said almost nothing during this recital, but from his black looks I could tell that some secret plan of his had been spoiled by it. Here, I think it would be best to acquaint the reader with the explanation of how Long John had taken possession of the ship, how he had made his timely entrance into the scene at the diggings, and why he was presently so cast down. I should stress, however, that at the time, I was completely ignorant of it all. Well then, the plan had been to raid the ship for powder. Silver, Boakes and Abed had been commissioned by Vanderbrecken to accomplish it. It took them some hours to reach the anchorage, but when they arrived they found their luck was in: a jolly-boat was drawn up on the sand. They launched her immediately and rowed out to the ship.

Two men had been left aboard to guard her and both of them were lying dead drunk in the scuppers. Silver and Boakes had them over the side and feeding the fish in a moment; then they broke into the armoury. By this time, dawn was coming up. They rolled three barrels of powder to the side and lowered them one by one into the jolly-boat, where they stowed them away. They were about to pull back to the beach when Silver's sharp eyes spotted movement ashore.

It was the treasure-party, of course, setting off for the diggings. Silver saw me through his telescope and instantly revised his plan. Boakes remained aboard the ship, to prime and load the cannon, and be ready to touch her off twenty minutes after he saw Silver's signal from the plateau. Abed was sent off back to the North Inlet to fetch Vanderbrecken. Silver himself followed the treasure-hunters, with the result we have seen.

Now, cunningly though Silver had laid his plans, there was one factor he had not brought into his calculations: the attack upon the North Inlet. The first evidence he had of it was, of course, the appearance of Isabella, and by then it was too late to alter the terms of the bargain he intended to strike with Hallows, even though he had been counting upon Vanderbrecken to reinforce him and so turn the tables.

We were now moving beside a stream and the excitement of the others grew intense, since it was the very 'water' marked upon the map, and it meant that we were drawing near to our destination. When Hallows stopped suddenly, therefore, the men ran forward with eager cries. We followed on, rounded a bend in the stream, and saw not the 'plash of water' we were expecting but a very different sight.

There was a stretch of level ground beside the bank of the stream. The trees stood back from it and lush grass grew there. It was a pretty spot, like an English meadow, bright with wild flowers and dappled at the edges with shade. Near to the stream, under a spreading oak, a rude hut had been built. Its roof had long since fallen in, half its timbers were rotted away, and creepers and weeds had invaded it; but the shape of its doorway could still be discerned, and a square where a window had been. Nearby were two grass-grown mounds and upon one of them was still standing a roughly fashioned wooden cross.

'By the Powers,' breathed Silver, 'I reckon that'd be old Jago and the other buried there, an' you'll find young Dick inside the 'ouse, sure as a gun.'

Hallows and a couple of the others were already peering inside the ruin and a shout confirmed that they had found something of interest. I ran forward with the rest and looked through the sagging doorframe. Lying upon the ground was the skeleton of a man, curled up, as if he had lain down to sleep. A few tatters of clothing still clung to his bones, and in his hand was clutched the remnants of a book.

'That's Dick for sure,' whispered Silver, coming up behind me. 'That'd be his Bible now, what he spoiled to make the Black Spot, remember – I said no good would come o' that. 'Twere he put up the crosses for the others, you may lay to it, for he always were a pious lubber, were Dick.'

Hallows's men were huddling together, some of them crossing themselves, and all of them, even Jed and Leary, looking very scared – your most hardened buccaneer will quail before anything that smacks of spooks and spirits and auguries.

'That's an omen, that is,' muttered one.

'It ain't good luck, fer sure,' said another.

'That's right,' agreed a third. 'Ain't never seen but evil fortune follow from a thing like this.'

Hallows spoke out quick and clear. 'Mr Hawkins,' said he, 'when you and the others quit this island ten years ago you left three of the party marooned here, did you not?'

'We did,' said I. 'We had no other choice. But we left them arms and stores and tools.'

'Well there you are, men,' said Hallows. 'That's all there is about it.'

'Aye,' said Silver, 'that's all the story; no need for any hand to be afeared. You'll find no ghosts nor sperrits howling here,' which cast half of them down again, just as he intended. 'There's but a short step to go, I reckon,' he went on, addressing Hallows, 'and since we're stopped here, in this sweet spot, I has a proposition to put.'

'*Another* proposition?' replied Hallows sneeringly.

'I proposes we disarms – all of us – 'fore we proceed.'

'That,' replied Hallows with a thin smile, 'would appear to argue a certain – lack of trust on your part, Silver.'

'I don't reckon it that way,' returned Silver coolly. 'It's common prudence, that's all.'

'Very well,' said Hallows, after a moment, and drew his pistols from his belt. He threw them down upon the ground and waited for Silver to do likewise. Silver obliged, adding a cutlass and a knife to the pile. When the others saw Silver disarmed, they started to divest themselves of their weapons, and soon there was a veritable magazine of muskets, pistols, cutlasses, and knives heaped up.

'Satisfied, Mr Silver?' said Hallows when it was done.

I was on the point of warning Silver about the miniature pistol, but spared myself the trouble; for Silver's response was to step up to Hallows and search him thoroughly. Having found nothing more deadly than a snuff-box, Silver stepped back with a nod.

'Note that I do not reciprocate,' said Hallows. 'I suggest we be about our business.'

We proceeded for a mile or more and were then forced by the increasing steepness of the ground and the thickness of the vegetation to abandon the stream and strike out eastwards. It was a stiff climb, all the same, and Long John's coat was soaked right through to a darker blue by the time we gained more level ground and turned west, back towards the stream. A few minutes later, we heard the roar of tumbling water and rushing forward – Silver slipping and cursing like a madman – we found ourselves at the summit of a considerable fall.

In fact, there were two falls. The first, at whose head we stood, was twenty feet high. It cascaded on to a spur below where a pool had been formed. Roughly in the centre of the pool, but with a shade in favour of the left-hand side, was a big, black rock, which divided the water into two separate flows. The greater of these ran past the right flank of the rock swiftly and violently enough to raise up a foam, then plunged over the lip of the pool and down, fifty feet, into the bed of the stream. The lesser flow ran to the left of the rock but did not touch it directly, for a stretch of gravel lay in between. The water there was shallow and did not plummet into the depths below but rather trickled down the face of the spur to be lost in the haze of spray at the bottom.

Now, while I was taking in these details, Silver was looking round him, his chest heaving with his recent exertions, and his eyes raking the falls and the surrounding rocks and trees – and Hallows was watching Silver.

At length: 'Well, Mr Silver,' says Hallows evenly, 'what next?'

'Fetch me that map aloft,' growled Silver, and for the first time I detected a note of uncertainty in his voice. Hallows must have sensed it too, for he gave Silver a very hard look as he handed him the map. Silver scanned it for above a minute, then once again peered about him and down into the pool. His face was very white now, and there was a sweat upon his brow that owed nothing to the climb.

'As I supposed,' said Hallows softly. 'Treachery.'

'Stow that!' roared Silver. 'I'm lookin' for Flint's mark!'

'A likely tale,' said Hallows. Turning to the others, he continued: 'First, he leads us into the wilderness. Next, he disarms us. What *now*, Silver?'

'You dog!' cried Silver, a sort of agony in his voice. 'I tell you there's a million or more lies inches from where we stands. There's Flint's mark here if we can read it.'

'Treachery, Silver,' returned Hallows, 'there's a stink of it about you.'

'The mark o' the water!' raved Silver. 'Flint left his mark!'

'If he did,' said I, 'then it's upon the map – we'll find it.'

I spoke quietly enough, but in that over-heated atmosphere it had a sobering effect. Hallows stared at me a moment, then snatched the map from Silver's hand and while he scanned it, I went on: 'The gems are hereabouts, that much we know – and they were the joy of Flint's soul. I take it he was a cautious man?' – this to Silver.

'As the Devil,' Silver replied hoarsely.

'Very well, then,' said I. 'He would have left no visible mark or sign – therefore, the clue is on the map.'

They were all hanging on my lips now, even Hallows. I turned to Silver. 'Say again what Darby M'Graw told you – his exact words.'

Silver knitted his brows, his cheek twitching, and the sweat running into his beard.

' "On Spy-glass hill, look for the mark o' the water," ' croaked Silver.

The answer to the riddle came to me in a flash, and it was so simple, so obvious, that I very nearly burst out laughing. I stepped up to Hallows and held out my hand for the map. He gave it to me without a murmur. I turned about to face the sun and held up the map in front of my eyes. The watermark showed up, blue-grey, as clear as printing against the strong light.

Black Rock, W. side, 5 paces SE.

I lowered the map and turned to Silver. 'The mark of the water,' said I. 'The watermark.'

'By gum, you've worked the trick,' he breathed, snatching the map from me and holding it up to the sun. Shivering with excitement, Hallows plucked the map from Silver and he, in his turn, held it up. Then the others rushed forward, whooping and grunting like a herd of swine, and the map was wellnigh torn to shreds as it passed from hand to hand.

Hallows was staring down at the black rock in the pool. 'Five paces south-east,' said he, tearing off his hat, 'but that would be under the water.'

'Precisely,' said I. 'Who would ever think to dig underwater?'

Chapter XXXVI

The Treasure

It proved easy enough to climb down to the pool. The rocks by the side of the fall made a natural staircase which even Silver was able to negotiate without difficulty. We came to the edge of the pool on the western side and splashed across to the gravel beach under the lee of the black rock. Silver sat down upon a ledge, and placing his crutch across his lap, he took off his hat and mopped his brow. Isabella and I placed ourselves near him while Hallows fetched a compass out of his pocket and took a bearing. Using the centre of the rock's side as his starting-point, he took five long paces forward into the water, which was not more than six inches deep and pretty sluggish.

'Lay on, men,' said he, and Jed and the others entered the stream with their shovels and started to scoop out the loose stones and mud. The shovels soon proving ineffectual, they fell to their knees and scrabbled with their fingers. Hallows stood over them, the water running round his ankles, his eyes cast down, wholly bound up in what was going forward. I happened to glance at Silver.

His eyes were fixed on Hallows and the others, but his fingers were busy about the brass ferrule of his crutch, which he was deftly turning, until it came away.

The crutch was hollow!

At last I understood where Silver had kept his money all these months – inside the crutch! But it was not gold that he slid out of it now – it was steel: a long, fine stiletto blade that in a trice he had transferred to his sleeve. He was screwing the ferrule back into place when a great shout arose from the stream.

It was Leary. He was lying face down in the water, his right arm buried up to the shoulder in mud and stones, his face squinting with emotion.

'A chest!' he cried. 'A sea-chest!'

Silver whipped his crutch back under his arm with an oath and sprang forward. Jed and the others were aiding Leary, digging with their arms like a pack of mongrels after a bone, until a second shout went up – and, between them, Jed and Leary hauled out of the water a Spanish chest with a domed top, bound all about by wrought steel. They carried it out of the stream and laid it down upon the dry gravel.

The steel was mostly rusted away but the hard teak of which the chest was built had been proof against its long immersion. Leary took up a pick and with one short blow knocked away the rotten clasp of the lock. Then he knelt down and with shaking, palsied hands he raised the lid.

I think that, for a moment, all of us were blinded as the fierce rays of the noontime sun struck the interior of the chest. It was as if a whole constellation of stars had been trapped within – diamonds and rubies and sapphires and emeralds blazed and glittered with a brilliance that seared the eyes. For a moment I felt sick and dizzy. I found that I was holding Isabella's hand and that she was gripping me as tight as a vice.

A shadow fell across the sea-chest, dimming the radiance within. Hallows had stepped forward and was gazing down at the treasure. After a moment, he raised his eyes – to meet those of Silver, who was facing him, three paces away. Silver was very pale, but otherwise betrayed no sign of emotion. 'Well now,' said he softly, 'ain't that a sight?'

'A sight indeed,' returned Hallows – and at that moment we heard the distant bellow of the ship's cannon. A slow smile spread across Hallows's face and his eyes glinted with something of the fire of Flint's gemstones as he raised his arm. In his hand was the miniature pistol.

'That's Gaynes, I fancy,' said he, 'telling me that he has repossessed the ship. He was listening all the time, you see, to our former conversation and has now duplicated your own trick.'

Silver started forward with an oath, but Hallows thrust his pistol at him. 'Have a care,' he said. ' 'Tis only a plaything, such as will tuck into a man's sleeve, but at this range it is as good as a musket.'

Silver stepped back a pace and shook his head. Then, to the utter astonishment of all, he began to chuckle.

'Well, it's rich all right,' he wheezed cheerfully. 'Very rich, I should say. A friend, has you? Well so has I, by Thunder. You poor misbegotten lubber – look aft!'

Hallows did no such thing, of course, but Isabella and I did – and so did Leary and the others – to see Abed Jones standing ten paces away, with quite half a dozen pistols in his belt, and a loaded musket aimed at Hallows. Leary let out a cry of rage and jumped to his feet. Hallows whipped his head round and Silver instantaneously swung up his crutch, catching Hallows a blow that knocked him sprawling. Leary sprang at Silver with a roar – only to reel backwards with twelve inches of stiletto blade thrust into his heart. He spun like teetotum and fell headlong into the stream, where he lay still, face down.

That was about the end of it. Abed threw a pistol to me and another to Long John, which put paid to any further resistance from Jed and the others. As for Hallows; when he picked himself up he found himself looking down the barrel of Long John's pistol.

At my orders, Jed and three of his fellows took up the treasure-chest, and with Silver guarding Hallows, and Abed and Isabella (armed with a pistol) watching the others, we began the long, weary, dangerous march back to the anchorage.

'Many a slip 'twixt cup and lip,' said Hallows mockingly as we set forth, and only a fool would have denied the truth of that statement. We had the upper hand for the moment, but there were the men left behind at the stockade to be considered, and Gaynes aboard the ship, and a hundred opportunities for Hallows himself to turn the tables along the way.

As we marched, Abed told me his story, which was simple enough. On Long John's orders he had run back to the North Inlet, there to find four corpses – two upon the beach, two floating in the water – but no sign of Vanderbrecken, Isabella, or the ketch. Since Silver had told him to bring the Dutchman directly to the diggings, Abed made straightway for the plateau and arrived just as we were beginning our ascent of Spy-glass.

And here I must pay my tribute to our friend Abed, as true a man as you'll meet in this world. Despite the fact that he was half-dead with exhaustion, having done nothing but pelt about hither and yon since he landed upon Treasure Island, he played out the game like a veteran. He had shadowed us all the way to the ruined hut without once betraying his presence, and when he saw us disarm, had the sense to bide his time and strike at the optimum moment. That we all owed our lives to his quick wit and sterling courage is incontestable, and let those who hold that the black man is essentially inferior to the white take note: no white man could have wrought better than Abed Jones, and few could have done half so well.

All the way to the anchorage I had my chin on my shoulder. All my instincts told me that the stockade party were at hand – but they never showed themselves, and we gained the beach at last without mishap. I was far from easy, however, and did not a bit like the confident smile on Hallows's face. It seemed to me that the sooner we put into operation the plan that Long John and I had agreed during the descent from Spy-glass the better it would be for us. Accordingly then, I ordered Jed and the others to set down the treasure-chest upon the sand; Abed, Isabella, and I held them at bay while Long John forced Hallows to the edge of the surf.

With Long John's pistol at his head, Hallows hailed the ship and ordered Gaynes to row ashore in the jolly-boat. To my heartfelt relief I saw the overseer obey, and out of a corner of my eye observed his progress towards the beach. I was expecting an attack by the stockade party from the woods at any moment, and could afford to pay but little attention to what was happening at the water's edge.

All went very smoothly, however. At Long John's order, Gaynes threw his weapons into the sea before he beached the jolly-boat. That done, Long John escorted him, with Hallows, back to the forest's edge. The plan now was to truss up Hallows and his confederates, load the treasure on to the jolly-boat, and see it safely aboard the ship. Long John had argued for a general massacre but I would have none of that. Humane considerations apart, I wanted to see Hallows and Gaynes standing in the dock. Abed had just begun the work of binding Jed's wrists when a fusillade of musketry belched out from the forest!

What followed next I have never to this day been able to piece together into a coherent narrative. I know that I fired all four barrels of my two pistols and I think I accounted for three, at least, of Hallows's men. I know that I was struck down by a tremendous blow from Gaynes. I know that, in all the smoke and pandemonium, Silver was dragging the treasure-chest away into the trees. I know that Jed made a lunge at Isabella and put a knife to her throat, and that I flung myself upon him and pushed him to the ground. I know that he got the better of me and stunned me almost out of my senses. The next clear picture I have is of Vanderbrecken – aye, the Dutchman himself – running Jed through with his cutlass, while Squire Trelawney, Dr

Livesey, Ben Gunn, and half a dozen jolly Jack Tars laid about them with furious energy.

I raised myself up – Isabella's arms about me – and saw Hallows and Gaynes, bearing the treasure-chest between them, making a desperate dash for the jolly-boat. Long John was in pursuit, floundering helplessly in the soft sand. Hallows and Gaynes reached the jolly-boat. They heaved the treasure-chest over her side and launched her into the surf. Scrambling aboard, they unshipped the oars and bent to them with demonic energy.

On the beach, the fight was over – the sand was strewn with the bodies of Hallows's crew, and Squire Trelawney, bellowing like a bull-calf, was leading his victorious tars down to the water's edge, where Long John, raving and cursing, was attempting to prime a pistol. I jumped to my feet and ran towards the sea. Hallows and Gaynes were making famous speed towards the ship. Mr Trelawney was drawing up his men in a regular line, military style.

'Disciplined fire, men!' he roared. 'Take your time! Aim true! Await the command!'

I caught a cry behind me. It was Abed.

'The powder!' he gasped. 'We never don' shift the powder!'

Long John heard him. His eyes bolted out of their sockets and his mouth formed into the shape of a desperate 'No!' – but his voice was drowned in the thunder of Trelawney's muskets.

A moment later, the jolly-boat exploded with a blast like Armageddon and Hallows, Gaynes, and the treasure were pulverized into dust!

Chapter XXXVII

And Last

Night had long since fallen before we had buried the dead (who included Boakes) and Mr Trelawney's schooner was riding safe at anchor half a league from Hallows's ship. It was after ten o'clock that I boarded the Squire's vessel and went below to the Great Cabin to do my best for Long John Silver.

The destruction of the treasure had at first sent Long John out of his mind. He had waded into the sea as if he expected Flint's stones to float into his hands. I had gone in after him to haul him away and found him standing waist deep, his eyes empty of all expression, tears rolling from them into his beard. I had led him back on to dry land, and he had followed me like a blind child, and had not uttered a word when the Squire ordered him to be clapped in irons. Mr Trelawney's intention, I knew, was to take him back to Jamaica to stand trial; my purpose now was to persuade him out of it.

'Confound it, no!' he was roaring, as I entered the cabin. 'I tell you I won't be budged!'

He was sitting at the table, like a Judge, and Silver, with a stout seaman on either side, was facing him. Captain Smollett was at hand, and Dr Livesey was leaning over the table, arguing with Mr Trelawney.

'Once before you swayed me,' the Squire went on, 'don't prosecute, you said, and see the result!'

'Trelawney—' the Doctor began.

'No, Doctor!' cried the Squire, thumping his fist upon the table. 'The law's the law and – dash it all! – I'm Acting Governor of Jamaica.'

'Well now, Trelawney,' said Dr Livesey, observing my entrance, 'here's Jim Hawkins. You're bound to listen to him.'

The Squire humphed and snorted as I stepped up to the table. 'Hawkins!' said he. 'I suppose you've come to plead for the monster.'

'For plain justice, sir,' said I. 'That's all. John Silver's saved our lives over and over again.'

'I don't give a ha'pence if he's saved every life from here to Kingdom Come,' returned the Squire furiously. 'How many lives has he *taken*, hah? Answer me that, sir! I'll answer for you, sir! Enough to hang an archangel twenty times over, sir!'

I was about to give an angry reply when Silver himself spoke.

'If I may humbly beg to say a word,' said he, in a low, spiritless voice.

Trelawney stared at him a moment, then, with an impatient sniff: 'Say on then, villain.'

'Well, sir,' says Silver, 'I'll not be the cause o' strife an' dissension between friends, sir, not I. You ship me back to Execution Dock and swing me if you will.'

'But Long John!' I protested.

'No, Jim,' said he, very mild but very firm; then turning back to the Squire, went on: 'I had my dream, sir, like any other man, an' it kep' me head to wind through fair weather and foul. But now it's all to dust and Davy Jones, an' I'll tell you what, sir: John Silver's lost his heart for life – and that's the truth.'

Well, there was no more to be said, and even Trelawney seemed to be moved by the dejected figure Silver cut as he was taken away to the fo'c'sle hold.

We dined very late, and what should have been a celebration of victory was more like a funeral wake. A deal of wine was drunk, however, and I was pleased to see it, for it meant that the company would sleep sound – which would suit my purpose. I was determined like iron, you see, to save Long John Silver, as he had saved me.

Accordingly, I waited up until the small hours and then crept out. There was but one man on watch and I ordered him below. Then I swiftly lowered some casks of water, and other provisions, into one of the long-boats, which was tied up alongside. Taking up a hammer and a strong chisel, to strike away Silver's irons, I crept below to the fo'c'sle hold.

Not a soul was stirring – the ship slept like the dead – but as I approached the place where Silver was confined, I heard the rasp of a file upon iron and voices whispering! Stealing forward, I heard Silver say: 'Ben Gunn, you're a true ship-mate, so you are, and no mistake.'

'Silver,' came the tremulous reply, 'I'm afeared – an' I ain't afeared to own it!'

'Well, that's manly, Ben, manly, I say,' returned Silver 'and if it be in your mind, now, that you're doing counter to your dooty, well I ain't so well placed to persuade you against your own true self, now, am I?'

I grinned to myself in the dark. Trust Silver to have set in train his own plan for escape! 'No need,' I breathed, slipping into the hold and laying a hand on Ben to steady him.

'Why, Jim—' was all Silver said.

We had him free in a few moments and bundled him up the stair on to the deck.

'There's food and water in the long-boat,' I told him, 'and here's a brace of pistols, and powder and shot.'

'As I's remarked afore, you're oak, Jim,' said Silver, taking the arms, and gripping my hand.

'Then I'm sorry to think that you were not counting on me,' I replied.

'Ah well,' says he, with that slow, cunning smile of his, 'I'll tell you straight: I wasn't sure – and that were always the way it was between you and me, I reckon.'

With those parting words he turned and lowered his crutch into the long-boat and himself after it. I cast off the painter and he bent to the oars.

It was a cloudy night and a sea-mist was rising, presaging the dawn. As the long-boat slipped swiftly across the still water towards the open sea, I put my telescope to my eye to take my last look at Long John Silver. The moon sailed out from behind a cloud as I did so and I saw him well. He had shipped his oars and taken up his crutch and was unscrewing the ferrule. He tipped up the crutch and from its hollow stem cascaded a brilliant stream of precious stones! Somehow, during the battle upon the beach, the unconquerable rascal had contrived to secrete a part of Flint's hoard!

A moment later, the mist enveloped the long-boat and Silver vanished from my sight. I lowered my telescope, and though it was, without doubt, my imagination at work, I swear I heard Silver's deep laugh roll across Captain Kidd's Anchorage and his voice strike up the old song:

'Fifteen men on the dead man's chest–
Yo-ho-ho, and a bottle of rum!
Drink and the devil had done for the rest–
Yo-ho-ho, and a bottle of rum!'

There is not much more to tell. The Squire was greatly incensed at first by Silver's escape and vowed to prosecute *me*! After a few days, however, his fury abated, and by the time we were back in Jamaica, he was speaking of it as an excellent joke.

A week after our return, Isabella and I were married by Mr Morgan. Mr Trelawney rewarded Abed Jones with his freedom and offered Vanderbrecken the management of the plantation. The Dutchman accepted the post, but on condition that the Squire freed all his other slaves!

'Give a man a just wage and he will *work*,' he declared. 'Do it, and I double your profits for you in a year!'

After the most fearful row, good Mr Trelawney capitulated and – as he had predicted – earned for himself the undying enmity of his fellow planters. Their contumely wrought the most wondrous sea-change in the Squire's ideas, and immediately upon returning to England, he bought himself a seat in Parliament and became a famous stalwart of the Abolition Movement. Vanderbrecken was as good as his word and before long there was not a more prosperous plantation in the West Indies, nor a more Christian one; for Mr Morgan fulfilled his dream and built his church.

I took back my wife to England and purchased an estate not ten miles from the Admiral Benbow and my mother and Ben Gunn came to live with us. I made over the inn, lock, stock, and barrel, to Abed Jones, for he had never forgotten Silver's words to him, and the tale of the Negress who had kept the Spy-glass tavern on Bristol quay, and he was set to be an innkeeper. Of Silver himself we heard no more; but with his portion of Flint's gems behind him, we reckon he is prospering at last.

Many is the night when we draw up our chairs to the fire – Isabella, Abed, the Squire, the Doctor, and all our good company – and while Ben Gunn takes round the wine, and my mother nods her grey head in a doze, we live past perils and adventures over again. We talk of the *Saracen* and Moxon's treachery; of Don Pedro's cheerful, deadly smile; of Hallows and Gaynes; of Garcia and slavery in the Spanish mines. But always we return to Silver: blackguard and hero, thief and provider, cheat and defender, betrayer and saviour, enemy – and friend.

THE END.

Mollie Hunter
The Stronghold £1.25

Winner of the Carnegie Medal for an outstanding book for children . . . A splendidly vivid story of the Orkneys in ancient times, when the Roman raiding ships came slicing through the cold grey seas in search of slaves. Coll and the young tribesmen build the strange stone towers that stand fast against the might of Rome.

Grant Campbell
Scottish Hauntings £1.25

A chilling collection of hauntings from a country steeped in legends and ghost stories. Grant Campbell brings to light many stories which until now have only been talked about in hushed voices. The stories are gathered from every region of Scotland – a land full of magic and mystery.

Sinéad de Valera
Irish Fairy Tales £1.25

From the land of pixies, fairies, witches and druids, twelve strange and wonderful stories of sorcery and magical spells – from the evil fairy who could take the form of any animal, to the giant who stole the king's crown . . .

Older Piccolo fiction you will enjoy

○ **A Pistol in Greenyards**	} Mollie Hunter	£1.50p
○ **The Stronghold**		£1.25p
○ **Which Witch?**	Eva Ibbotson	£1.25p
○ **Astercote**	Penelope Lively	£1.25p
○ **The Children's Book of Comic Verse**	Christopher Logue	£1.25p
○ **Gangsters, Ghosts and Dragonflies**	Brian Patten	£1.50p
○ **The Cats**	Joan Phipson	£1.25p
○ **The Yearling**	M. K. Rawlings	£1.50p
○ **The Red Pony**	John Steinbeck	£1.25p
○ **The Story Spirts**	A. Williams-Ellis	£1.00p

All these books are available at your local bookshop or newsagent, or can be ordered direct from the publisher. Indicate the number of copies required and fill in the form below   12

....

Name...
(Block letters please)

Address...

....

Send to CS Department, Pan Books Ltd,
PO Box 40, Basingstoke, Hants
Please enclose remittance to the value of the cover price plus:
35p for the first book plus 15p per copy for each additional book
ordered to a maximum charge of £1.25 to cover postage and
packing
Applicable only in the UK

While every effort is made to keep prices low, it is sometimes
necessary to increase prices at short notice. Pan Books reserve the
right to show on covers and charge new retail prices which may
differ from those advertised in the text or elsewhere